FRENCH ROAST

FRENCH ROAST

Sandra Balzo

**SEVERN
HOUSE**

First world edition published in Great Britain and the USA in 2022
by Severn House, an imprint of Canongate Books Ltd,
14 High Street, Edinburgh EH1 1TE.

Trade paperback edition first published in Great Britain and the USA in 2023
by Severn House, an imprint of Canongate Books Ltd.

severnhouse.com

British Library Cataloguing-in-Publication Data
A CIP catalogue record for this title is available from the British Library.

ISBN-13: 978-1-4483-0673-2 (cased)
ISBN-13: 978-1-4483-0678-7 (trade paper)
ISBN-13: 978-1-4483-0677-0 (e-book)

All Severn House titles are printed on acid-free paper.

Typeset by Palimpsest Book Production Ltd.,
Falkirk, Stirlingshire, Scotland.
Printed and bound in Great Britain by
TJ Books, Padstow, Cornwall.

ONE

'You have an appointment with Helen Durand?' Surprised, I glanced up from the table I had been clearing in my Brookhills, Wisconsin coffeehouse, Uncommon Grounds.

Face half obscured by the espresso machine, Amy Caprese pushed a strand of short fuchsia hair behind one multiply pierced ear. 'I shouldn't be long. It's really not—'

'The barista needs a shrink?' Sarah Kingston rounded the corner from the storeroom. My business partner had the ears of a bat. 'And here I thought *we* were shrinks.'

'Just because people dump their problems on us all day, every day, doesn't mean we don't have some of our own.' I glanced at Amy, who admittedly had her head screwed on tighter than either Sarah or I did. 'Nothing personal.'

'No offense taken,' she said, leaning through the service window to continue the conversation. 'I was just reading that some therapists set up sessions in coffeehouses rather than offices because patients feel more at ease chatting.'

'I can see that,' I said.

'We could use that in our marketing,' Amy said. 'Maybe Helen—'

'Wait.' Sarah was holding up her hands in a double stop sign. 'The shrink charges their usual fee but has no overhead. The patient is happy because they have this comfy-cozy session in a familiar setting. What about us?'

'Exposure and repeat business,' Amy said. 'I assume they order a couple of drinks at a minimum.'

'And what? Sit here for an hour taking up space?'

'That's no different from anybody else,' I pointed out.

The truth was that customers wanted to feel welcome to stay as long as they wished. For our part, we wanted to pay our rent. And that's where Amy excelled – maintaining that beautiful balance between hospitality and marketing.

And, therefore, we needed *her* to be well balanced. 'Take all the time you need,' I told her now. 'The morning trains have come and gone.'

Uncommon Grounds was situated in Brookhills' historic train station, which serviced commuter train traffic into Milwaukee fifteen miles to our east.

'If you're not back,' I continued, 'Sarah will stay to cover for lunch. Right, Sarah?'

'Right, Maggy,' my partner semi-parroted, as Amy circled from behind the counter to front-of-house. When our barista collapsed into a chair at the table I'd been clearing, though, Sarah exchanged a concerned glance with me.

'You know there's no shame in seeing somebody, Amy,' I told her, taking the chair across from her. 'Sarah and I certainly have.'

'Please?' Sarah snorted. 'Maggy likes to talk a big game, but she was strictly minor league therapy-wise. "My dentist husband cheated on me with his hygienist, wah, wah, wah." That's all she had.'

'Well, it was hurtful,' I said defensively. 'Besides, this isn't a competition.'

Sarah took the chair next to me. 'I'm just saying that you divorced him and got over it, right? I bet you didn't even take anti-depressants.'

'I tried one,' I said. 'But they made me gain weight.' Which *was* depressing.

'Wow, big whoop-dee-doo. Gained a few pounds. You should live in my shoes.'

Sarah's size nines could do without me, thank you very much. 'You're saying because you're bipolar and I'm not, I don't have a right to be unhappy?'

'No . . . well, yes. I'm saying that I have a legitimate disorder. You were just sad for a while.'

'They call it situational depression,' Amy said. 'Rather than clinical.'

'And I'm clinical.' Sarah sat back in her chair, hitching a thumb toward her chest. 'I'm about as clinical as you can get.'

'Amen,' I said under my breath.

Amy suppressed a grin. 'Well, personally, I think you're amazing, Sarah. I have no reason to complain in comparison.'

We really didn't talk much about Sarah's condition in the shop, at least not in a caring, sensitive way. It was more me asking her if she was off her meds when she was being particularly annoying. And, honestly, Sarah seemed to prefer it that way.

Now, her face reddened. 'I . . . well, thanks.'

Amy shifted in her seat. 'I'm sorry, I didn't mean to be too—'

'Nice?' I asked pleasantly, to move things along.

'I was going to say personal.' Amy smiled. 'But yes. I'm sorry I committed "niceness."'

'Forgiven,' Sarah said gruffly. 'Just don't do it again.'

I was studying Amy. 'This thing, this problem . . . you would tell us if it had to do with work, right?'

'Pfft,' Sarah sputtered, before Amy could open her mouth. 'What is there to complain about at work? You and I are absolute joys to work for, Maggy. And, besides, Amy pretty much runs the place and us, anyway.'

'It's true,' Amy said, moving her chair back a smidge, as if distancing herself from the conversation. 'And no, my' – she was searching for a word – 'my concern is not work. It's personal.'

That narrowed things down. 'What did Jacque do?'

Jacque Oui was Amy's beau and owned Brookhills' upscale market, un-eponymously named Schultz's. Jacque was considerably older than Amy, pompous and nearly comically French, his accent only thickening in his decade and a half in the US.

Jacque was also my third cousin, as I'd recently found out thanks to my son's dabbling on a DNA website. The news hadn't exactly thrilled me since I'd always thought the man arrogant. Jacque, in turn, thought that I . . . well, I'm not sure he actually gave me much thought.

'Nothing, really.' Amy's nose had turned red. 'We're just going through a rough patch.'

I fished a napkin from my apron pocket and handed it to her across the table. 'So, you're doing couples counseling with Helen. That's very sensible.'

'Actually, no. Not couples.' She blew her nose. 'Jacque can't make it.'

Or didn't want to, more likely.

'Jerk,' Sarah said.

My partner having said what I was thinking, I was free to take the high road. 'Ted wouldn't go with me either. It's not necessarily the worst thing.'

'You ended up divorced,' Sarah reminded me.

Oh, yeah.

'Don't get me wrong,' Amy said. 'Jacque is the one who suggested I see Helen in the first place.'

'He is?' Sarah glanced sideways at me. 'As in "you're crazy so go talk to someone and I'll stay here cuz I'm just fine?"'

'No, not at all,' Amy said. 'Jacque knows he's been difficult, and Helen is a friend. Her husband Denis and Jacque have known each other since university in Paris.'

'And they both ended up here?' Women might go to the bathroom together, but they usually didn't emigrate. 'That's quite a coincidence.'

'Not really. Denis and his daughter Molly had been living here for like three years when Jacque decided to move after his divorce. Denis suggested Brookhills and let Jacque stay with them until he got his own place. This was before Denis married Helen, of course.'

'You won't find it awkward confiding in a friend of Jacque's?' I asked.

'I don't think so,' Amy said. 'Denis aside, Helen's credentials are pretty spectacular. She has a PhD and her internship was spent in Chicago working with at-risk kids.'

'You're a fine person to ask that question anyway, Maggy,' Sarah said. 'Didn't you want to do your couples counseling with Father Jim at Angel of Mercy?'

'What's wrong with that?' Amy asked. 'Or isn't Ted Catholic?'

'No, he's not,' Sarah informed her. 'But neither is Maggy.'

'But Jim is an excellent counselor,' I told Amy.

'*And* a former lover,' Sarah prodded.

'Oh.' Amy sat back. 'That is kind of a conflict of interest. Certainly worse than Jacque knowing Denis.'

'Unless Jacque was doing Denis.' This was from Sarah, no surprise.

I groaned. 'I didn't "do him," as you so charmingly put it. We dated in high school, but nothing happened.'

'Sure it didn't,' Sarah said.

'It didn't. Not sexually, I mean. We didn't go—'

'If you say "all the way," I'll scream,' Amy said, covering her ears.

'It does make you sound like a dinosaur,' Sarah told me. 'An adolescent dinosaur.'

Says the adolescent dinosaur herself. I sniffed. 'I didn't bring the subject of Jim up, if you'll remember. All I was trying to say is that I think it's a shame Jacque won't go to counseling with Amy.'

'He just has so much on his plate right now,' Amy said, tracing her thumbnail on the table. 'And it's me, really, not—'

Sarah groaned.

'What?' Amy asked.

'"It's me, not him,"' Sarah parroted. '"We're going through a rough patch. Jacque has so much on his plate." Maggy isn't the only dinosaur here.'

Amy squinted at her. 'I don't know what you're talking about. I'm just—'

'You're explaining away Jacque's behavior,' I finished for her. 'With timeworn excuses, no less.'

Amy sent me a dark look even as Sarah nodded approvingly. 'All my years of shrinkage have rubbed off on you, Maggy. Congratulations.'

I cleared my throat. 'Thank you. I think.'

'It's just that we expect more from your generation,' Sarah continued to our barista. 'You know, "I am woman, hear me roar" and all that?'

Amy's face screwed up. We'd lost her again.

'Helen Reddy?' I tried.

'Ready for what?'

I didn't mean Helen Durand, of course, but Helen Reddy. Trail-blazing Australian songwriter, singer—

'Never mind,' Amy said, interrupting my thoughts. 'But Jacque can't take the time to see Helen because he is legitimately busy. In fact, he's trying to keep his business afloat, if you really care.'

Schultz's Market had been around for more than fifty years. It started as a small mom-and-pop grocery store and then, under Jacque's ownership these last fifteen years, had morphed into a high-end market, specializing in seafood.

And I did care about Jacque, but only as far as it affected Amy. 'The business is putting pressure on your relationship?'

'Along with other things,' Amy said. 'But, yes, money is tight to the point that Jacque sold his house and is using the flat above the store when he's not staying at my place.'

'Don't lend him money,' Sarah warned.

'You don't pay me enough to lend money.'

True. 'I think what Sarah is saying is that Jacque is a big boy—'

'And certainly old enough,' Sarah took over. 'If he hasn't figured out how to keep his business solvent by now, he's not going to. You can't let his cash-flow problems become yours.'

'But these cash-flow problems, as you call them, were caused by Kip Fargo,' Amy said. 'Which does make them mine, like it or not.'

Amy had dated Kip, the wealthy head of Fargo Investments, during an earlier 'rough patch' with Jacque. Kip being dead now, I probably shouldn't speak ill of him.

But I had Sarah for that.

'Kip Fargo,' she repeated. 'If that wart on the behind of Brookhills' financial community was still alive, I'd pop him.'

I frowned. 'Disgusting, but I do understand the sentiment.'

A realtor by trade, Sarah had sold Kingston Realty when she partnered with me in Uncommon Grounds. The proceeds of the sale had been invested with Fargo Investments, and when both it and Kip himself went belly up, she'd lost most of it.

Profit margins on coffee not being what they were on real estate, I often wondered if she regretted her decision to give up the business to throw in with me.

'I curse the day I sold the realty.'

No need to wonder any longer. 'I noticed Schultz's is shortening its hours,' I said to Amy. 'Is that for cost-cutting?'

'If so, it's stupid,' Sarah muttered, still smarting.

'Why is it stupid?' Amy was frowning now. 'Uncommon Grounds has limited hours on weekends.'

'That's because the trains don't run as often.' Office workers and shoppers heading downtown made for busy weekdays in the depot, but fewer trains on weekends naturally meant fewer customers.

'Which is why we shouldn't open on Sunday at all,' Sarah said. 'But Maggy doesn't have the heart to disappoint the old farts from Brookhills Manor.'

Brookhills Manor was the retirement home down the street. 'Those old farts are steady customers.'

'Until they die.' Sarah was rubbing her chin. 'But I do think it's a bad idea for Schultz's to reduce hours with Bright and Natural Foods entering the market.'

Amy sniffed. 'Bright and Natural is not competition.'

'I wouldn't discount Jamie Bright,' Sarah said. 'He's a savvy guy. Not to mention a little cutthroat.' Jamie was the founder of Bright and Natural Foods, a growing national chain of organic grocery stores.

'You know him?' I asked, surprised.

'Of course,' Sarah said. 'He grew up here.'

'Then why is Brookhills going to be his fiftieth store rather than his first?' I asked. 'I can't believe you didn't try to sell him a property when he started out.'

'Oh, she did,' Amy said. 'Schultz's.'

Oh, my. This could get interesting. 'When was this?'

'Maybe fifteen years ago,' Sarah said.

'Jacque outbid him,' Amy said, although she would have been thirteen at the time.

I glanced at her and she shrugged. 'Jacque told me.'

'It's true,' Sarah said. 'Jamie was just starting out, so Jacque had the deeper pockets then. Now, Jamie could probably buy and sell the Frenchie ten times over.'

Amy's bottom lip jutted out. 'But I bet he doesn't inspire the kind of loyalty that Jacque does from his employees.'

'Jacque?' Had I heard right?

'Sure, look at Becky Ronstadt.'

'The two-hundred-year-old cashier?' Sarah was grinning. 'I

wouldn't be surprised if Becky was the one who painted "Oui Suck" on the front window of Schultz's last week. O-U-I, not W-E, of course.'

'That's pretty funny,' I said, and then sobered in response to Amy's scowl. 'But if Jacque is cutting hours, it follows that employees are going to be upset. Especially long-term, perennially grouchy employees like Becky.'

Amy glanced out the front window and lowered her voice. 'I do know something interesting about Jamie Bright, but you can't tell anybody.'

'Who would I tell?' I asked. 'Sarah is already here, and Tien is on vacation in Iceland.' Tien Romano made all of the delicacies we sold at Uncommon Grounds and also ran a catering business out of our commercial kitchen.

'Don't tell Jacque I told you.' Amy glanced around again, as if the man was going to jump out from behind the condiment cart. 'But Jamie Bright made Jacque an offer.'

'Bright and Natural wants to buy Schultz's?' Sarah asked, just to make sure she'd heard right.

'Yup.'

I was almost afraid to ask. 'And what did Jacque say?'

'That Jamie could stick it.'

Or *steeek eeet*, I imagined. 'You didn't suggest he consider it?'

'Of course not,' Amy said, a little testy again. 'Schultz's is an icon in Brookhills. An institution.'

'I suppose that's why Jamie wants it,' I said, trying to reason through the big fish wanting to eat the little fish. Besides, of course, that it could. 'Instant credibility in the market.'

'And maybe revenge,' Sarah pointed out. 'Maybe Jamie wants payback for Jacque buying the location out from under his nose.'

'But it's going to cost him a lot more now than it would have fifteen years ago, even adjusted for inflation,' I said. 'Jacque has vastly improved the place.'

'Nice.' Amy flashed me a smile. 'Did that hurt?'

'A little,' I admitted.

'He may think it's worth it,' Sarah said, 'since Jacque is his only—'

'Helloooo.' A dark head poked in as the door opened,

sleighbells clattering against the door's plate-glass window. 'Oh, good, you're still here.'

'Helen,' Amy said, turning to check the time on the depot clocks arrayed over our order window. 'Am I late for our appointment? You didn't need to come get me.'

'No, no, I'm the one who is running late.' Helen stepped in, shoving a hand through her short dark hair. Colorful chunky earrings were Helen's trademark – today's were bright yellow – along with a slash of fuchsia lipstick. 'Molly and I have been off visiting colleges and just got back into town this morning.'

She pulled a chair away from the next table and turned it to sit. 'I absolutely refused to drive into the wee hours last night. Or, God forbid, let her do the same. She's had her license for two years and already has had three accidents.'

'And she's still driving?' I asked, a little horrified.

'She wouldn't be if it were my decision,' Helen said. 'But Denis is a marshmallow as far as his daughter is concerned. I couldn't change that even if I wanted to.'

'How old was Molly when you and Denis got married?' Sarah asked.

'Just turning four,' Helen said. 'They were living on Poplar Creek. Pretty location, but the cottage is small and even back then it wasn't safe for bringing up a child. Luckily, I had space enough for all of us.'

She checked her watch. 'I must run. Can you give me a half-hour, Amy?'

'Of course.'

'Great. Ciao, everybody.' Her fingers waggled through the opening as the door closed.

'I do like the woman,' Sarah said, coming back to the table. 'I don't say that about everybody.'

'You don't say that about *any*body,' I pointed out.

'Cruel, but true.'

Meanwhile, Amy had sunk back into her chair, seeming relieved at the temporary reprieve. 'Do you think I should go ahead with this?'

'Seeing Helen or dumping Jacque?' Sarah asked. 'I'd say thumbs-up on both, myself.'

'Seeing Helen,' Amy said, not rising to Sarah's bait. 'And

yes, I know I'm being silly. Even Becky recommended her, of all people.'

'Wait.' I held up a hand. 'You're talking about the same Becky Ronstadt? The one who works at the market?' And lives across the street from me.

'Yes, she noticed I'd been feeling down.'

If the implication was that Sarah and I were insensitive because we *hadn't* noticed, I couldn't argue with that.

'How does Becky know Helen? Is she seeing her, too?' If Current Becky was Post-Therapy Becky, I had to question the therapist.

'Helen has really helped Egbert.'

'Egbert.' Sarah cocked her head. 'Becky's sixty-four-year-old son, who still lives at home and does consulting work out of their basement?'

'And whose mother still calls him home for dinner every night?' I contributed.

Amy bit her lip so as not to smile. 'Apparently, he doesn't mind that so much now.'

I'd say, "low bar," but whatever gets you – or Egbert – through the day.

'I do wonder how they'll do next month when Becky isn't working anymore,' Amy continued.

'Jacque is canning her?' Sarah asked. 'The man is all heart, isn't he?'

'*Becky* is retiring at the end of this month,' Amy said. 'She's earned it after all these years, don't you think?'

'I don't know,' I said. 'What does Becky think?'

'She's getting a lovely retirement package,' Amy said. 'Eight weeks, fully paid.'

Sarah gave me side-eye. 'Notice that she's not answering?'

'I do,' I said, thinking Amy could spin with the best of my old colleagues in public relations. 'How long has Becky worked at Schultz's?'

'She was a cashier when Jacque bought the shop,' Amy said. 'But she told me she took her first job there bagging groceries when her husband walked out on them. Egbert was in first grade.'

'Fifty-seven years,' Sarah said, doing the math. 'And Jacque is giving her eight weeks of severance? Big of him.'

'I know,' Amy admitted, her cheeks reddening. 'But with everything else going on with Jacque, I can't . . .' She let it drift off.

Sarah and I exchanged looks.

'Is it more than just the business?' It was a guess, but our earth-mother barista usually didn't get in this kind of funk over finances. 'Do you want to talk about it?'

Silence.

I felt myself flush. 'I absolutely understand if—'

'His wife.' Amy swiveled her head my way. 'That's what's coming between Jacque and me. His wife.'

I glanced uncertainly at Sarah again before returning to Amy. 'Naomi Verdeaux is dead.' I was as certain as if I'd seen her body. Which I had.

'And he sure as hell can't be pining over her,' Sarah said. 'They were already divorced.'

'For years,' I chimed in. 'And I'm not sure he even liked her much when they were married.'

'Yes, I know Naomi Verdeaux was Jacque's ex-wife,' Amy said, exasperated. 'Though that's probably open to question now, too, come to think of it.'

I didn't get it. 'What's open to question?'

'Her ex-ness.'

Sarah went to open her mouth, but I held up a hand. 'Are you saying Jacque and Naomi weren't divorced?'

'I'm saying,' Amy said tautly, 'that they may not have been married.'

'Then what's the problem?' Sarah asked, being logical.

'Paulette,' Amy said. 'Paulette is the problem.'

'And Paulette is?' I led.

'Jacque's ex-wife in Paris,' Sarah said, finally comprehending.

'Only, it turns out, she's not,' Amy said.

'In Paris?' It seemed the lesser of the two evils.

'No.' Amy lifted her head, and a single tear traced an all-natural black mascara path down her cheek. 'Nor is she his *ex*.'

TWO

'You're saying that Paulette pre-dated Naomi, who pre-dated you.' Just so I had it straight.

'It's not unusual to be married more than once,' Amy said, a little defensive now. 'Jacque is forty-two, and with age comes baggage.'

'As you well know, Maggy,' Sarah said, tossing a grin my way. 'Being divorced and in your forties and all, yourself.'

I had just the one ex-husband, thank you very much. 'Baggage is one thing; bigamy is another. If Jacque and Paulette didn't divorce in France, Jacque committed one count when he married Naomi here in the US and it would be a second count when you got married, Amy.' After an on-again off-again courtship of three years, Jacque and Amy were engaged. Or at least they had been.

'You're making it sound worse than it is.' Amy's lips were tight. 'They were really young when they married, and while Jacque appreciates a nice glass of wine, Paulette preferred drugs – crack cocaine, I think he said. One day, she just didn't come home.'

'But they were still married,' I said.

'Yes,' Amy said a little impatiently. 'But Jacque filed for divorce, saying Paulette had abandoned the marriage. After two years, even if the person still can't be found, I guess a judge can rule that you're divorced. Which is what happened.'

According to Jacque, presumably.

'*Altération définitive du lien conjugal.*' The words had come from Sarah.

'You're versed in French divorce law?' I asked, surprised.

'I've been binging French detective shows in which the hero is divorced and smokes and drinks a lot. There are more of them than you might think.'

'You speak French?' Amy asked.

'Of course not,' Sarah said. 'They have subtitles.'

'Subtitles?' I was astounded. 'You hate subtitles. I can't get you to go to a foreign film with me.'

'Right?' Sarah seemed as surprised about it as I was. 'But it turns out that reading subtitles is no different from reading close captioning, which I do all the time.'

Amy was frowning, concerned. 'Are you having trouble with your hearing?'

'It's not my hearing; it's the programs these days,' Sarah said. 'People talk too fast.'

'Or the music or background is too loud,' I agreed. 'I turn on CC, too.'

'You do realize how ancient you two sound?' Amy asked. 'You may actually pre-date the dinosaurs.'

Sarah gave a half shrug. 'We're just a couple of years older than your Jacque, so I hope you're OK with lettering slapped across your favorite shows.'

'I like to make my captions really big,' I teased.

'And yellow type is so much more legible than white.'

'Very funny.' Amy's face had dropped. 'And here I am worrying about little things like whether I'll ever be able to marry the love of my life.'

I patted her hand. 'Let's not jump the gun. If this *lien conjugal* thing does apply, then there's no problem, right? Jacque did what he was supposed to.'

'How long ago was this?' Sarah asked.

'According to Jacque, they got married straight out of college and she took off just short of their second anniversary.'

'Then Jacque was maybe twenty-three or twenty-four when she left,' Sarah said.

'And now, suddenly, she shows up,' Amy said, standing to check the clock.

'Here in Brookhills.' Brookhills wasn't on the 'just happened to be passing by' list for long-lost spouses. 'If they haven't seen each other for years, how did she find him?'

'Excellent question.' Amy crossed to the condiment cart and retrieved a napkin to swipe at an imaginary spot on our table.

'Could have found him online,' Sarah suggested. 'I've found lots of old classmates that way.'

'You've reconnected with them?' I asked, a little surprised. 'That's nice that you stay in touch.'

'Reconnected?' Sarah repeated. 'No. And if I wanted to "stay in touch," I would have.'

'So' – I spread my hands wide – 'why search online?'

'Curiosity,' Sarah said. 'See how fat they got or if they lost their hair. Better yet, if their parents died and they're selling the house.'

Now that made sense.

'I don't know how or why,' Amy said, 'but she just showed up at the store.'

We were back to Paulette. 'When was this?'

'Yesterday afternoon. Jacque wasn't there.' Amy sat back down with the napkin, crumpling it. 'Becky called him on his cell, and when he didn't answer, she tried me. Said some woman was there for him.'

'She didn't tell you who it was?'

'Not at first,' Amy said. 'But when I pressed her, she put her hand over the phone and asked.'

'Did you recognize her name?' I asked.

'She didn't give a name. Just "*La femme de Jacque*."'

'Jacque's wife or woman,' our French scholar told us.

'Correct,' Amy said unhappily. 'Becky asked her for a translation, twice, just so I wouldn't miss it.'

'Nice of her,' I said. 'You do remember that it was Becky who ratted on you to Jacque the night Kip Fargo proposed.' Live-streamed it to Jacque from the restaurant, if memory served.

'I know.' Amy sighed. 'She pretends she's being thoughtful, but I think she gets a kick out of making trouble. I'm not sure she even tried Jacque's phone first.'

'Ya think?' Sarah asked. 'Of course the old witch noticed you were feeling down; she's the one who caused it.'

'To be fair,' Amy said, 'she first recommended Helen to me last week.'

'You were depressed last week?' We really had been oblivious.

'Only about Jacque's moods. Which are understandable, given what was going on with the business and all.' She shrugged. 'Now that seems like nothing.'

'The tip of the emotional iceberg,' Sarah said.

I blinked.

But Amy just sighed and got up to toss the napkin in the bin before turning back to us. 'OK, I'm going.'

'Good,' I said.

As she disappeared into the back to take off her apron, I groaned. 'Tip of the emotional iceberg, Sarah? Really?'

She flashed a grin and then sobered. 'Old Becky is a nasty piece of work, isn't she? She knew Amy was already down but had to make that "guess who's here" phone call to torture her.'

'I think she considers Amy collateral damage,' I said. 'It's Jacque that Becky loves to torture.'

'And now the perfect tool – the long-lost wife from Paris – has fallen into her lap.'

'Wow,' I said, studying her face. 'You *are* waxing poetic today, aren't you?'

'It's the foreign shows. There's a lot of nuance in subtitles.'

I wasn't sure what to say, so I just went with what I'd been thinking since I heard about Paulette. 'I'm dying to get a gander at this woman.'

'You should, Maggy.' Amy was slinging her purse over her shoulder as she came around the corner. 'Go to Schultz's and nose around. Make Jacque squirm. Why should Becky have all the fun?'

'You're all right with that?' Sarah asked Amy. 'Jacque's squirming, I mean.'

'Absolutely.' Amy stopped at the door and, hand on the knob, turned. 'I haven't met Paulette myself yet. Would you report back here, Maggy? I'll be done with Helen in an hour.'

I was already untying my apron.

'What about me?' Sarah protested. 'Why can't I go?'

'Because somebody has to stay.' Amy opened the door and waved me out ahead of her. 'And it's your turn, Sarah.'

'It's not, you know,' I said as the door closed behind us. 'I'm forever abandoning Sarah to go off and snoop.'

'Actually, it's me you abandon most times. But I'd prefer that you be the one to do this particular inquisition. You'll at least pretend to be nice when you meet Paulette.'

A classy woman, our Amy.

'You want me to be nice to your fiancé's wife?' I was tidying the chairs around our outside tables.

'The woman who believes she's still my fiancé's wife,' Amy clarified as she watched me. 'Truth is, I don't know who the villain is. It might be Jacque.'

'What does he say about all this?' I asked curiously, straightening from my labors. 'I assume you tracked him down after Becky's call and he went to see Paulette?'

'No. He was too chicken. Rushed over to my house to sweet-talk me instead.' She started down the steps. '*Ma chérie*, my ass.'

I wasn't sure that confronting Amy was the coward's way, in this circumstance. Then again, I hadn't met the wife.

I followed Amy down the steps to the sidewalk. 'Where will I find Paulette? Do you know where she's staying?'

I was hoping it might be the Hotel Morrison down the street, since my former partner Caron Egan owned it. And would let me loiter in the lobby until I wore her down and she gave me Paulette's room number.

'Actually, you're in luck,' Amy said, stopping short to check her phone. 'Jacque is meeting her at Schultz's at eleven. That's twenty minutes.'

I pulled up, so as not to tread on her heels. 'But he has talked to her, right? At least on the phone or text?'

'Nope. If you hurry, you'll have a front-row seat. Journeys end in lovers meeting.'

Shakespeare. And here I'd been impressed with the iceberg.

'What about you?' I called as she started away from me. 'Are you sure you don't want to be there?'

She stopped again and turned, a second mascara-tinged tear tracing its way down her cheek. 'To see or not to see if he loves her. I think I prefer not.' And kept walking.

Told you she was classy.

THREE

The site of this particular 'lovers meeting' was just six blocks east of Uncommon Grounds along Brookhill Road, the main east/west thoroughfare to downtown Milwaukee on the shores of Lake Michigan. Rather than backtrack to the parking lot to retrieve my car, I opted to walk to Schultz's Market, thereby arriving at the store's glass automatic doors at five minutes to eleven.

As I passed by the 'out' door to reach the 'in,' I was nearly nailed by an emerging shopping cart.

'Watch it!' Becky Ronstadt snapped, stopping abruptly. 'Carts have the right of way.'

'Mother.' The middle-aged man trailing behind her was trapped in the entranceway as the door went to close on him.

'Blame her,' his loving mother said, meaning me. 'Besides, the door has a sensor.'

'The door *had* a sensor,' Egbert Ronstadt retorted, slipping past her. 'But it's older than you are.'

'Are you OK?' I asked as he rubbed his shoulder where the door had caught him.

Egbert Ronstadt wasn't a bad-looking guy – in his sixties, with salt and pepper hair and a bit-too-shaggy mustache under wire-rim spectacles. From what I understood, he worked in IT from that basement office Sarah had mentioned, so the man was technologically and professionally astute. In fact, put a tweed jacket on him and he might pass for a college professor. But standing next to his mother in cargo shorts and an 'I love dirt fishing' T-shirt, he was . . . Eggy.

And then there was his charming mother. Toad-shaped, with in-your-face burgundy hair and an attitude to match. 'If my boy isn't OK, it's your doing. You're not supposed to loiter in front of these doors.'

'Loiter—' I broke off. It didn't pay to argue with Becky and, more importantly, I didn't have time. 'Is Jacque inside?'

'Yes, but if you've come for the main event, the French woman isn't here yet.' She squinted at me. 'Did Amy send you or are you out snooping on your own?'

'Yes,' I said. 'And I assume you're not working today?'

'You assume wrong,' she said. 'I'm just making sure Eggy loads these bags into the car properly and I'll be back in.'

Egbert's lips tightened, and I watched as he counted to five, flexing each of the fingers of his clenched right hand. Then he turned to me and said pleasantly, 'Did you know my mother retires next week? It's going to make my life a living hell.'

Becky beamed at him.

'I'm sorry,' I said, confused. 'I'm not quite sure what to—'

'No need to be sorry,' Egbert said, waving his mother away from the cart to push it himself. 'She's really old, so with luck she won't live that much longer. And if she does, I can always smother her with a pillow.'

Mother and son exchanged affectionate smiles.

'Oh,' I said lamely. 'I—'

'There's no need for you to reply,' Egbert said, wheeling the cart past me. 'Saying exactly what I'm thinking is merely my coping mechanism.'

'And saying it keeps you from actually doing it?' I hoped.

'So far,' he said, cheerfully directing the cart toward his Rav4.

'That's good,' I called after him.

'Can't promise about tomorrow,' he said, raising a hand. 'Or next week.'

'It's all about communication.' Becky was watching her son open the lift-back. 'Put those eggs where they can't break,' she called.

Egbert threw her the middle finger.

'That Helen Durand is a genius. She—' Becky broke off as something caught her attention beyond the Rav4. 'Inside!'

I wasn't sure who she was talking to as Egbert was already in the driver's seat. 'I think he—'

'Get inside now!' She turned to dart through the 'in' door.

Taking her direction, I accelerated to follow her just as she skidded to a halt to peer out of the plate-glass window next to the door.

'Very funny,' I said, grabbing the door before it could hit me.

'Don't whine.' She pointed one age-crooked finger toward the lot. 'Look.'

I gave her a little shove so I could get out of the doorway and followed her gaze. A dark-haired woman of maybe forty was stepping out of a black car, presumably a ride-share. As the driver unloaded a roller bag from the trunk, the woman reached into the back seat and retrieved an oversized camel handbag.

'Beautiful,' I said. 'Gucci maybe?'

'Jimmy Choo,' Becky said.

'No,' I said, happy to share my encyclopedic knowledge of designer accessories I couldn't afford. 'The shoes are not Choo's, they're Louboutin. I meant the handbag.'

'Duh,' she said, practically dissing the signature red soles. 'That's Choo's large hobo bag she's holding, and her roller bag is Choo, too.'

'How do you know that?' I asked, astonished.

She shrugged. 'Egbert bought me the roller bag for my retirement. I think it's a hint that I should take a long trip.'

I'd agree. I pressed my nose to the window for a better angle, only to realize the door was sliding back into me. 'Oww.'

'*Mon Dieu,*' the brunette said, tip-tapping her way into the store, trailing the bag. 'The door. Did it hit you?'

'I'm fine, I think.' I rubbed the side of my head and then checked my hand. 'No blood.'

'You Americans, such hearty people,' she said. 'Me, I would be lodging a complaint against the establishment.'

I kind of liked the woman. Or maybe I just liked the fact she wanted me to sue Jacque. 'I'm Maggy Thorsen.'

'And I am Paulette Oui.' A pong of cigarette smoke wafted off her as she went to shake my hand.

'Oui.' I was playing dumb. 'Are you related to Jacque?'

'I am,' she said, gesturing that we should move away from the doors and into the wine section of the store. 'And you? You are a friend of Jacque?'

'Yes,' I said, following her. 'For a number of years now – since he moved to Brookhills, really.' It was a bit of a stretch. I didn't necessarily consider Jacque a friend even now.

'Those would be the years when I do not know him, since I remain in Paris.' She was surveying my jeans and Uncommon Grounds T-shirt. Happily, I'd taken off my apron. 'You are not his type.'

Ouch, though absolutely true. 'No,' I told her with a smile. 'He prefers them younger.'

'Very true,' she said, smiling back. 'You do indeed know him.'

If they had been together in college, what 'younger women' had he gone for back then? High-schoolers?

A movement from behind a display of dark sea-salt chocolate truffles caught my attention. Becky must have ducked there to spy, but now she was peeking out, her eyes casting daggers at me. I wasn't sure if it was because I was making nice with our visitor or she just wanted in.

'Becky,' I called, curious to see the interaction between the two women. 'Have you met Paulette Oui?'

Of course, I knew that she had, from what Amy had told me.

'Oh, yes.' Becky stepped out. 'We met yesterday when Mrs Oui came to see Jacque. He wasn't here, unfortunately.'

'Mrs Oui,' I repeated, knowing full well that Becky was purposely feeding me lines. 'What relation to Jacque did you say you were?'

'I am *la femme de Jacque*.'

'*Femme*?' I was feigning uncertainly. 'But that means—'

'Woman,' she translated. 'It can mean many things in my language, but in this instance, it is wife.'

'In *this* instance,' Jacque's voice corrected as he skirted a display of Bordeaux to join us, 'it is *ex-femme*.'

'Jacque,' Paulette greeted him. '*Mon mari*.'

'*Ex-mari*.' He tweaked again.

Jacque Oui was maybe five feet nine, with black hair, just graying at the temples. He had sported a mustache when I met him, but Amy had convinced him to get rid of it.

'You shave your mustache,' Paulette said, touching her cheek to his. 'And perhaps you have shrunk a bit, too? No?'

'No.' He pulled away. 'But what are you doing here, Paulette? You disappear in Paris and now you reappear here nearly twenty years later? How? Why?'

Those were exactly the questions I wanted answered, so I stayed quiet as the sliders opened again.

'You go,' a curly-haired boy said, pushing a girl who was likely his sister into the store.

'Fine.' She shoved him back. 'Then you stay.'

Their weary father gave Jacque an apologetic smile as he steered them in. 'Stop it, you two.'

Jacque nodded and waited until they passed before he beckoned to Paulette. 'We will go into my office.'

Damn. That would make it harder to eavesdrop. Becky had seemingly evaporated when Jacque appeared, but I trailed the two as Jacque ushered Paulette through the store to the office. As he turned to close the door, he nearly caught my nose. 'Maggy?'

'Maggy Thorsen with the doors,' Paulette said, amused. 'You seem to have the problem.'

'I do today,' I said, smiling back. And then, under my breath to Jacque, 'Amy sent me.'

His eyes went buggy, as if he couldn't decide if that was a good thing or not.

So I elaborated. 'If you don't let me in to chaperone, you'll never see Amy again,' I whispered. 'Is that what you want?'

He let go of the door, and I entered. The room had a desk, a couch and a side chair. I took the side chair. Paulette was already seated on the couch.

'This Amy you whisper about' – Paulette's eyes took the measure of me – 'I take it that she is the woman who is young?'

I nodded. 'She is. And she is my friend.'

'Jacque,' she said, patting the couch for him to come and sit beside her. 'What have you done to all of us, that I must come here to keep you from hurting yet another?'

'What have I done to you?' He glanced uneasily at me even as he sat down next to her. 'Paulette, you are the one who deserted me.'

'Yet here I find you in another country, where you have already married another who is not this Amy. Did you legally divorce this Verdeaux woman?'

Apparently Paulette had done her research before hopping on a plane.

'Naomi is dead,' I told her. 'So even if not . . .' I shrugged, feeling very French in my attitude.

'That bullet, it is dodged perhaps,' Paulette said. 'But there is Amy.' She nodded my way. 'I applaud her for sending a surrogate, so she does not get her hands dirty with you, Jacque.'

'You have no right to even speak her name,' Jacque said, a vein throbbing in his temple. 'She is none of your concern. I am none of your concern. I divorced you many years ago. Legally.'

'But for this divorce to be legal, you must have searched for me. Did you search for me, Jacque?' She was leaning into him, her face not three inches from his. 'Did you search hard?'

'For two years.' He slid away from her. 'Then I petitioned for divorce.'

Paulette folded her arms. 'I did not receive notice of such.'

'Because you chose to disappear.' Jacque shrugged. 'I was required to prove that all effort had been made to notify you and the court ultimately granted the divorce.'

'You did not try. I will prove *that*.'

'You did not want to be—'

A sneeze came from just beyond the open door.

Jacque got up and slammed it closed.

'The doors here' – Paulette lifted two hands into the air – 'you use them as weapons.'

'I'm OK.' Becky's voice sounded mushed, as if she had her ear to the other side of the closed door.

I cleared my throat. 'So, Paulette, when did you get here?'

'More importantly,' Jacque said, 'when will you leave?'

'I arrive in the United States two days ago. Wednesday.' She was directing her reply to me. 'I arrive here in this shop, specifically' – she pointed to the linoleum floor of the office – 'just yesterday.'

Now she turned her attention to Jacque. 'Though my Jacque was nowhere to be found.'

'Much like "my" Paulette many years ago,' he parroted. 'But you are no longer that to me. You are not anything.'

She blinked. 'You do not need to be unkind, Jacque. I came many miles to find you.'

'Why?' It was a blunt question and none of my business,

but Jacque had already asked it once without getting an answer.

'Why do I come?' Paulette asked. 'Why, because I receive an invitation. It would have been very impolite to refuse an opportunity to come to visit my husband, no?'

'An invitation?' It would certainly explain how she knew he was here. I swiveled to Jacque. 'You knew where she was?'

'No, no,' he sputtered. 'It is not that—'

'You are surprised that I said yes, no?' Paulette stood up. 'But now, I am bored. And tired. Take me home so I can rest, Jacque. We will speak later.'

'Home?' I was confused. 'She's staying with you, Jacque?'

'But, of course,' she said, with a catbird smile. 'I am his wife, so that which is Jacque's is mine, no?'

'No,' he said. 'Paulette is not staying here. And she is not my wife.'

'Staying here?' Paulette's lip curled. 'Oh, Jacque, have you come so few miles from your youth that you live above a . . . shop?'

'There is a small suite of rooms.' He nodded to a door, obviously stung by Paulette's disdain. 'Amy and I, however, live—'

I had been shooting daggers at him and now I beckoned for him to join me at the desk and away from Paulette. 'What have you done? Invited her here to play sister-wives?'

'No, no, of course not. I . . .'

Paulette had pushed the panic bar to open the door and was sniffing the outside air. 'This is not a suite. It is a . . .' She shuddered. 'I was going to call it a courtyard, but that is too polite. It is an alleyway. Full of trash and smelling of rotted vegetables and the dead fish.'

'Yes, Paulette. As you can very well see, it is an alley.' He pushed past me to step out. 'We are a store and have deliveries.' He pointed to a pile of wooden pallets and an aging delivery truck nearby. A battered gas can and old tire completed the tableau.

'Deliveries, yes. And . . .' She was glancing around, and her gaze lighted on the trash and recycling cans a bit farther down the alley. 'The bins. They explain the *parfum de poisson*, no?' She laughed.

If I was certain that Jacque hadn't deceived Amy and maybe

Paulette – oh, and don't forget Naomi – I'd have felt sorry for him.

Not getting an answer, Paulette shrugged. 'You have lost your sense of humor, my Jacque.' She pointed to a wooden staircase that led to the upper floor of the building. 'And these? They are to your *pied-à-terre*, Jacque?'

'As I said. A modest suite of rooms – bedroom, living room and kitchenette,' Jacque said sullenly. 'But we live—'

I raised my hand, and he stopped as though I was going to hit him. 'Don't bring Amy into this,' I said to him in a low tone. 'Do not tell her where Amy lives, don't even tell her Amy's last name.' It was my fault the woman knew even her first.

'But what should I do?'

I'd never seen Jacque Oui at a loss before. 'You are going to call Amy and tell her Paulette is staying and where.'

'Could you—'

'Absolutely not.'

'I cannot—'

'You can and you will,' I snapped. 'Call Amy. Tell her how she' – I head-gestured toward Paulette's back – 'came to be in Brookhills, where she is staying and why. The truth,' I warned, as he opened his mouth to protest.

He closed it, and I continued, 'Then you sort out this situation with your wife before you make any more promises to Amy.'

He opened his mouth, but nothing came out.

'Do you understand?' My index finger was in the air.

He nodded.

'Jacque,' Paulette called from the foot of the staircase. 'My suitcase, *s'il te plaît*?'

'*Bien sûr*,' Jacque said, and then caught my look. 'One moment,' he called to her as he pulled out his phone. 'I must make a call.'

'Amy is at Helen's office, in case she doesn't answer her mobile,' I told him. 'Then she'll be back at the shop.'

I grabbed his sleeve as he turned away. 'One way or another, you get hold of her. Now.'

FOUR

'The big question now is whether Jacque reached Amy and told her that Paulette is ensconced in his flat.' I returned a filled cream pitcher to the condiment cart by the door. 'This is not news I want to break.'

Sarah, having restocked the napkins, was now bent over in front of the cabinet, fishing for sweetener packs inside. 'I don't blame you. Jacque made the mess; let him clean it up.'

'If he can.' I swiped a rag across the top of the condiment cart.

The noontime period between commuter trains was usually quiet – the province of stay-at-home moms and dads and the seniors at Brookhills Manor coming in to grab one of Tien's salads, soups or sandwiches. With Tien on holiday, though, the lull was even more pronounced. But it did give me time to fill Sarah in on Jacque's ex-wife and us time to tidy up the shop for the afternoon rush.

'You're obstructing,' Sarah said, elbowing me out of the way as she straightened with a rainbow-colored handful of various artificial sweetener packets.

'Then wipe it yourself,' I said, dropping the rag. 'And can we please make sure there's a sweetener or two that's not composed of chemicals on the cart?'

'Sure,' she said, dumping the packs into a bowl and going back into the cabinet. 'But I'm certain the sweetener manufacturers would tell you they're all derived from perfectly natural ingredients.'

'I'm sure they would,' I said. 'But please humor me.'

'Like I don't spend half my life already doing that.' Sarah resurfaced with packets of raw sugar in one hand and a sticky plastic honey bear in the other.

I took the bear and used the rag to wipe the sticky off it.

'Uh-oh,' Sarah said, and I turned to see what she had. Amy was pounding up the porch steps.

'I'd say in answer to your original question' – Sarah was

stepping back out of range – 'that signs point to yes, Jacque has told Amy his maybe not-so-ex-wife is sleeping over.'

Our barista had gotten to the door and now she yanked it open so hard it crashed against the wall outside and ricocheted back at her.

'Are you OK?' I asked as she blasted past us.

'Like you don't know.'

As she disappeared around the corner, I grimaced. 'I was hoping that Jacque telling her himself would shield me from the fallout.'

'Too big of a bomb,' Sarah said, beckoning for me to leave the cart and follow her to the back. 'I predict it will rain down on us for days unless we can contain the damage.'

Amy was slipping her Uncommon Grounds apron over her head as we entered the office. Sarah leaned against our stock shelves. 'How did it go with Helen?' she asked in a sing-song voice.

'Just ducky.' Amy was struggling to undo a knot in the apron strings.

I made a move to help, but when she glared at me, I decided to stay out of swinging range. 'Jacque told you about Paulette staying at the flat?'

'Just as I was about to leave.' She leveled her eyes at me. 'How did he know I'd be there, do you suppose?'

'You said he suggested you see Helen,' Sarah pointed out, standing on tiptoe to peer at the stock of coffee beans on the shelf behind her.

'Yes,' Amy hissed. 'But he didn't know when.'

'I told him where you were,' I admitted.

'Because Maggy was chicken to break the news to you.' Sarah was now sliding five-pound plastic bags of coffee beans forward and back on the shelves.

'Because it's Jacque's responsibility,' I said, distracted by my partner. 'Just what are you doing?'

'Checking the packaging dates and letting out any gases.' She made a bag of Libarica beans fart by releasing a one-way valve. 'See?'

And heard. 'Anyway, if Jacque didn't have the balls to tell Paulette to stay in a hotel, I was afraid that he—

'Wouldn't have the balls to tell me,' Amy said.

'Exactly. Meaning either I'd have to tell you or you would find out and want to know why I didn't.' I folded my arms. 'So I made him promise. And because I knew he would call your mobile and leave it at that if you didn't answer, I told him where you were.'

'He came to Helen's office and spilled in person?' Sarah asked, leaving the beans to their own devices. 'I guess you have to give him points for that.'

'No, you don't,' Amy said. 'He called. Both Helen and I had our cell phones silenced for the appointment, so he called the office number.'

'I hope he didn't leave a message with the receptionist,' I said.

'No,' Amy said. 'He asked to speak with me and then told me himself that his ex was staying with him.'

'While you were standing right there in your therapist's office?' Sarah settled her butt on the corner of the desk. 'That was handy.'

'It actually was,' Amy said. 'Helen let me have another twenty minutes on her couch to talk it through.'

'She has the proverbial psychiatrist's couch? I mean one that you lie on during your session?' Sarah sounded jealous. 'My guy has one in his office, but I never—'

Amy's glare cut her short. 'I was speaking figuratively.'

I cleared my throat. 'For what it's worth, I don't think Jacque is intending to stay there with her. He was talking about your house and all—'

'He can intend anything he wants,' Amy said. 'I want no part of Jacque Oui until Paulette—' She stopped. 'Does she use his name?'

'She introduced herself to me as Paulette Oui,' I admitted. 'Though it could have been for effect. You know, to needle Jacque.'

'Who in their right minds would use Oui unless it was to her advantage?' Sarah asked. 'I mean, can you imagine—'

Amy held up a hand. 'No Oui-Oui jokes, Sarah. I'm not in the mood.' Giving up on the knots, she pulled the apron over her head, balled it up and tried to throw it across the room.

I caught it. 'Listen, Amy, are we OK? You told me I should go to Schultz's and report back, which I'm doing.'

Amy's eyes dropped. 'I . . . I'm sorry, Maggy. I'm just so angry with him.'

'You have every right to be,' I said. 'Sarah and I don't have a couch, but we also don't charge by the hour. Do you want to talk?'

'I want . . . to punch something.'

'You want to punch Jacque,' Sarah said, reaching past me to push the wheeled desk chair toward Amy. 'And I highly encourage that.'

Amy sat down, and I took the guest chair. Sarah stayed perched on the desk. I was going to offer to get lattes, but Amy seemed more at double-bourbon level, and we were all out.

'So tell me about her?' Amy asked, after a second. 'Paulette.'

'Let's see.' I folded the apron neatly on my lap as I tried to decide how much to tell her.

'You can just say if she's attractive.' It was as if Amy could read my mind.

'Sorry,' I said, 'but she is. Dark-haired and petite. Designer bag and shoes.'

'Of course,' Amy said, running her hand through her cropped fuchsia hair. 'And I'm perennially in jeans and a T-shirt, smelling like old coffee. How can I possibly compete?'

'That's not the question,' I told her. 'The question is why would you want to?'

'That's right,' Sarah said. 'Why compete for Jacque, period?'

'That's not exactly what I meant,' I said. 'I meant that Amy doesn't have—'

'You can forgive me for assuming that's what you meant,' Sarah interrupted. 'You don't like the man. At all.'

'I think we've covered that,' I said, glancing toward Amy. 'But my point is that Jacque fell in love with Amy – her jeans, her often rainbow-colored hair, her multiply pierced ears, her embrace-mother-earth sensibility—'

'As he probably did for Paulette twenty years ago,' Amy said. 'When they both were young.'

'But they're not anymore,' Sarah said. 'Why are you – the younger woman – worried about the older one?'

'Because I—'

'Don't say "love him,"' I warned. 'Maybe you do, but it's not a get-out-of-jail-free card.'

'But why doesn't Jacque just produce the divorce decree?' Sarah asked. 'He must have it, right?'

'Of course he does,' Amy said, seeming to set emotions aside. 'What exactly did Paulette say about the divorce? Does she simply not recognize it, or does she claim to have some legal basis?'

'She says that Jacque didn't make an honest effort to find her, and therefore this divorce decree – what was it you called it, Sarah?'

'*Altération définitive du lien conjugal.*' The French accent wasn't getting any better.

'Yes, that,' I said. 'Paulette says that Jacque didn't fulfill the conditions, and therefore she has grounds to contest it.'

'Jacque, I assume, disagrees?' Sarah asked.

'Yes,' I said. 'Though I have to say, he wasn't able to get more than a few words in.'

'Did you like her?' Amy asked curiously.

'I . . . well, I did at first. Mostly because she was giving Jacque a hard time.'

'And we know how much you love that,' Amy said.

'Absolutely,' I said. 'But by the time I left, I almost felt sorry for him.'

'Oh, please.' Amy and I were experiencing role reversal.

'I know it's ridiculous,' I said. 'But Jacque is so kind of . . . overstuffed? Pompous? When Paulette made fun of the smell of rotting vegetables and fish in the alley, wrinkling her little French nose and referring to the flat as Jacque's *pied-à-terre*' – I sighed – 'I could almost see him shrink.'

'It was his ego deflating,' Amy said, but I could tell she understood the hurt Paulette's words would cause him.

'I don't know if I did the right thing,' I told her. 'But I warned Jacque to keep you out of conversations with Paulette. Not tell her your last name or where you lived—'

'She was aware of me, though?' Amy asked. 'I wasn't sure.'

'She seemed to know there was someone. Whether Becky

told her yesterday or not, I can't say. I'm afraid I mentioned your first name today, so that's on me.'

'That's OK. I'm not afraid of the woman.' She took a beat. 'Unless you think I should be.'

'No, no. She's very . . . civilized,' I said. 'I don't see her beating you to death with her Louboutins.'

'Of course she would have Louboutins.'

'She's from France,' Sarah said. 'It's like wearing Nikes here.' The really expensive ones.

'What kind of handbag?' Amy had to ask.

'Jimmy Choo,' I said. 'Which is British, isn't it?'

'Yes.' Amy sighed. 'And fabulous.'

'But neither brand is who you are, remember?'

She got up with a sigh. 'I know.'

'What are you going to do?' Sarah asked, abandoning her desk corner. 'Go over there and knock her block off?'

I tossed my partner a threatening look. 'Of course she's not. She's going to go home and let Jacque sort this out.'

'I am?' Amy was fetching her own non-designer vegan-leather bag.

'I hope so.' I got up to follow her out of the office through the dining area to the front door.

'I will for today,' she said. 'At least, the home part. I'm too emotional right now to make intelligent decisions.'

'That sounds like it came directly from your therapist,' Sarah said, joining us.

'It did,' Amy admitted, opening the door.

'Phone or text if you need anything,' I called as she stepped out on to the porch. 'Or come by the house.' The door closed behind her.

I stood, debating.

'What?' Sarah asked, giving my shoulder a shove.

'I didn't tell her something,' I said, chewing my lip. 'And maybe I should have.'

'Should have what?'

I turned. 'Should have told her Paulette said that she didn't just show up, as Amy thinks. She was invited.'

Sarah's eyes widened. 'But why would Jacque do that? Death wish?'

'I don't know. I don't even know if it's true.' I rubbed the back of my neck. 'But it did make me wonder if Jacque knew Paulette had resurfaced in the intervening years and they'd been in touch.' I turned to her. 'Do you think I should have told Amy?'

'About the supposed invitation?'

'Yes.'

'Maggy,' Sarah said, squeezing the same shoulder she had shoved earlier, 'for the answer to that, you'll have to turn to the wisdom of the ages.'

'And what would that wisdom be?' I was almost afraid to ask.

'Damned if you do, damned if you don't.' She punched me again.

FIVE

Having already been so helpful, a few minutes before the last commuter train from downtown was due into the station, Sarah took off her apron.

'Where are you going?' I asked, looking up from the desk where I'd been trying to get a head start on balancing the day's take.

'Home. Amy is supposed to close with you, remember?'

'Yes, but she went home.'

'Because you told her to. Plus, I covered for you both when Amy went off to see Helen and you to spy on Jacque.' She retrieved her bag from the bottom drawer of the filing cabinet. 'As for me, I have a dinner date.'

'You do?' Sarah had been forced to pull a gun on the last guy she'd dated, which kind of soured her on that scene.

'Yes. The date is today, and I'm eating dinner.'

Now she was just being ornery. But she was also right that she'd held down the fort for us today. 'Fine, go ahead. I can take care of anybody who comes in from the six-thirty train. And close.' And vacuum, wipe, run the dishwasher and finish balancing the drawer. 'But would you do me a favor?'

'No.' Sarah had her hand on the doorknob out to the boarding platform and, ultimately, down to the parking lot where her classic Firebird awaited.

'Please.' I followed her to the door.

'OK, maybe. I'll tell you for sure after I know what this favor is.'

Fair enough. 'Would you call or text Amy and remind her she's doing the farmers' market tomorrow and I'll meet her here at five?' Five a.m. Ugh.

Sarah scowled. 'Why don't you just call her yourself?'

'Because I'm serving the next slew of customers and closing the shop. And I have to be back here at the aforementioned five a.m. to grind and brew coffee for Amy to take to the market.'

'And?'

'*And* I don't want to talk to her again until I make up my mind about telling her.'

'About Jacque inviting Paulette to Brookhills, you mean.'

'I really should tell her. Or at least ask her if Jacque told her.' I brightened. 'That's exactly what I'll do in the morning.'

'Best case scenario, she'll be half asleep and not hear you,' Sarah said, cocking her head. 'Worst, you'll back into the subject – in keeping with your passive-aggressive nature – and she'll clobber you.'

'Exactly,' I said. 'It—'

I was interrupted by a train whistle.

'Oops, I'd love to hear more,' Sarah said, pushing the door open as the train rumbled up to the platform. 'But gotta go.'

'You'll text Amy?' I called after her, catching the door before it closed.

'Yeah, yeah, yeah,' she groused, taking a quick right down the steps to avoid the alighting train passengers.

'You realize you'll have to text her anyway to confirm,' I said to myself. 'Since you can't count on Sarah.'

'Ms Thorsen, are you talking to yourself?' a young voice asked from behind me. 'You might want to see my mother about that.'

I turned to see Molly Durand's tip-tilted nose. She was coming up the same stairs Sarah had descended and was with another girl. About the same age, the two were virtually indistinguishable except for the fact the other girl's long hair was blonde and Molly's dark.

Yup, I was getting old. 'Hi, Molly. Oddly enough, I did see your mother today. She said you're looking at schools.'

'Yeah, she thinks I'm going to get into Northwestern,' she said, glancing at her friend.

The two girls laughed.

'I heard that.' Molly's father materialized from the crowd getting off the train, even as Molly's friend seemed to disappear into it. 'You can't be so negative, Molly.'

I was still holding the door, so I stepped aside so they could enter.

'Thanks, Maggy.' I had been surprised to hear that Denis

and Jacque had immigrated from France around the same time, since Denis retained no trace of the heavy French accent Jacque so earnestly nurtured. Denis Durand was just a normal, pleasant man, neither of which described Jacque.

'I'm not being negative,' Molly said, preceding us into the depot. 'Helen says it herself when she thinks I can't hear. "A good trade school, at best." She was imitating Helen's voice.

'If *your mother* ever has said that, it was only to motivate you.' Denis seemed exasperated, as if they'd had this discussion before.

'*Not* my mother,' Molly grumbled under her breath, and I was sure that had been said before, as well.

Denis set his briefcase on a bench to open it. We were in the train depot's waiting area, which was really more hallway running from the back to the front of the building parallel to the platform. Across from the platform door were the two restrooms and a door to our back office, kitchen and storage area. Just past that and around the corner to the front of the building was what had been the old ticketing and baggage-check windows for the train station, now our order windows and front of house.

'You and your mother just love to push each other's buttons,' he said, searching through his case. 'It's natural, right, Maggy?'

'The mother and child bond,' I agreed.

'And to what do I owe the honor of your meeting the train, my daughter?' Denis asked, straightening with his car key. 'Need a ride home?'

'It's like four blocks, Dad,' Molly said. 'But Lindsey and I are going for pizza. Can you just tell Mom?'

'Good try,' Denis said, slinging an arm around Molly's shoulders. 'But your mother is expecting us both home for dinner.'

Molly rolled her eyes. 'Daaaaaad.'

Denis held up his hands. 'Rules, remember? You're out with your friends practically every night; the least we can do is sit down to dinner as a family. That's why I took the train home rather than driving to Chicago straight from the office.'

'Fine.' Molly shoved open the door to the platform again. 'I'll be in the car. We'll have our' – air quotes, not easy because she was wedging open the door with her shoulder – "'family dinner,'' and then you can desert me to go to your big meeting.' The door slammed behind her.

'Sorry,' Denis said to me.

'I have had a teenager, you know. I'm just impressed you sit down to eat together every night.'

'Don't tell Helen, but sometimes it seems more trouble than it's worth.' Denis swung open the door to follow Molly and then hesitated. 'Maybe I should buy a coffee for the road.'

I waved him off. 'No obligation on my account. Your trip home, as Molly points out, is four blocks long. Besides, if you feel obliged to buy, then I'd feel obliged to brew a fresh pot.'

'And where would we be then?' Denis said with a grin, stepping out on to the now-deserted platform. 'I'd have a cup of coffee I didn't have time to drink.'

'And I'd have the rest of the pot I'd have to dump.' I gave him a wave and a smile and let the door close behind him.

'I'm not sure why we bother staying open for the six-thirty train,' I said to Pavlik that night. 'It means not getting home until at least seven, and we sell almost nothing to those last commuters.'

'It sounds like a self-fulfilling prophecy,' he said, following me into the kitchen. We'd had a salad that night in an effort to add variety – and maybe even some nutrition – to our steady evening diet of pizza and Chinese food.

Still, salad could be pretty boring. Very green. I was trying my best to pick up some interesting things to toss on top. Tonight had been slightly mushy strawberries from last week's farmers' market with toasted pine nuts and feta cheese.

I set our wine glasses on the counter and took the salad bowls from Pavlik to load into the dishwasher. 'I don't dissuade most people from ordering. With Denis, though, I felt as though I could read his mind. He and Molly came into the depot, had an argument, and Molly was pissy and slammed the door. By Durand standards, that was rude and demanded compensation.'

'In the form of a purchase.' Pavlik was pouring an inch

more of red into each of our glasses. We were trying to cut back on that, too.

Even more boring.

'Exactly,' I said. 'They're like the perfect family. They eat dinner together every night, and I bet Helen limits television to an hour or two a day.'

'You wouldn't be the woman you are today if your parents had done that,' Pavlik reminded me.

'I do have an encyclopedic knowledge of shows nobody remembers,' I admitted. 'But I can't blame that all on my parents. I'm just a nerd.'

'You are,' Pavlik said, holding out my wine glass.

'They're looking at some nice schools for Molly,' I said, taking it. 'Eric would have loved to go to Northwestern.'

'What did you say Denis does?'

'He has an appraisal firm in Milwaukee,' I said. 'Mostly business valuations and high-end homes and estates.'

'And his wife is a psychologist, so that's two pretty good incomes,' Pavlik said. 'Not like a public servant and a coffee slinger.'

'I think of us more as an elected official and an entrepreneur,' I said. 'But you're right that neither calling pays a fortune.'

'Good thing we each have an ex-spouse to bear half the load of college tuition.'

'And room and board,' I said. 'I was totally unprepared for how much that adds to the tab.'

'Eric's in his last year, at least,' Pavlik said. 'Then we'll have a break before Tracey starts.' Pavlik's daughter was fifteen and living with her mother, while my son Eric was twenty-one and going to the University of Minnesota in Minneapolis, about a five-hour drive away.

'Eric's last year is lasting more than a year,' I said, leading the way back into the living room. 'But I guess that's normal. He'll be done eventually.'

I stopped in front of the couch. 'Are you two going to let us sit?' I asked, looking down.

The couch had been commandeered by the other two members of our blended family. Frank was my sheepdog, and Mocha was a one-man – that man being Pavlik – Chihuahua.

Mocha lifted her head and sniffed indifferently. Frank was snoring.

'Should we just go in the bedroom?' I asked Pavlik. 'We could put a movie on in there.'

'It's eight thirty.' Pavlik set his wine on the coffee table. 'Off!'

The two canines snapped to, Mocha leaping daintily down as Frank offloaded his body parts like a 110-pound hairy Slinky. The two went to lie in front of the unlighted fireplace.

'How do you get them to listen?'

'It's the authority in my voice,' Pavlik said, sitting down and patting the couch next to him. 'And I carry a gun.'

'Sarah says they don't listen to me because I give them options.' I settled next to him and tucked a leg up under myself.

'You mean like "Would you, the dogs, like to get off the couch so I can sit?" or "Would you, the dogs, prefer I go in the bedroom?"'

'Yeah, like that.'

'Sarah might have a point.'

'She does,' I said. 'Apparently, it works for child-rearing, too, though why Sarah thinks she's an expert—'

Frank let out a bark and stood up, dislodging Mocha who had been using his foot for a pillow.

The doorbell rang.

'Who could that be at this time of night?' I asked without moving.

'It's eight thirty-two.'

'My point.' Surrendering with a groan, I unwound and stood up.

'Want me to go?' Pavlik asked, not making the slightest effort. 'It might be an early-evening axe murderer.'

I pushed the curtain aside an inch to peer out. 'Worse.'

'Our parents?' he guessed.

'My parents are dead, as is your mother. All we have left is your father, and I like him.'

'True.' Pavlik frowned. 'Then who?'

'Jacque Oui,' I said and lowered my voice. 'What is he doing here? And how does he know where I live?'

'Amy pointed out the house to me,' Jacque's voice said

through the door. 'And be aware that I can hear every word that you say.'

'That doesn't mean I have to let you in,' I said, also through the door.

A hesitation. 'I would very much appreciate a moment with you and the sheriff. I am at my wits' end.'

Pavlik chin-gestured to let him in. Again, not moving a muscle off the couch.

I ignored him. 'Don't you have a wife or a fiancée to talk to? Oh, wait – you have both.'

'Please.'

Pavlik smiled. 'Maggy.'

I groaned and flung open the door.

'Amy has kicked me out,' Jacque said. 'I know she has the reason, but . . .' He shrugged very . . . Frenchly.

'Come in, Jacque,' Pavlik called from the couch.

Traitor.

Frank was on my side, though, still barking furiously and looking about as menacing as a giant white-and-gray puffball can look.

'He won't bite, will he?' Oui murmured, edging in.

'Don't know,' I said, closing the door. 'He's never liked you much since that blizzard when you nearly ran us off the road.'

'But I did not see him,' he protested, trying to sidestep Frank. 'He blended with the dirty snow on the side of the road.'

'And me? What did I blend with?'

Oui just shrugged again.

Pavlik stood, finally. 'Sit,' he said to Frank. 'And Jacque, please sit, too. Can we get you some wine?'

Frank and Jacque obeyed, Frank dropping his butt at Pavlik's feet, while Jacque parked his in a chair. I muffled a groan and went to fetch a glass of wine for our guest.

When I handed the glass to Jacque, he held it up to the light. 'Pinot noir, I think? Very nice.'

'Yes,' I said, sitting next to Pavlik. 'Now, what can we do for you? I have to be up early tomorrow.'

Eight thirty-nine, Pavlik mouthed.

'Yes, the farmers' market,' Jacque said, taking a sip before he set down his glass. 'Amy told me about that when she, too, suggested that I leave.'

I turned to Pavlik. 'I forgot to tell you. Jacque's first wife is here from France and doesn't believe their divorce is valid.'

'You forgot to tell me that?' He was clearly astonished.

'I know,' I said, crinkling my nose. 'First I had the salads to make and then we got on to the subject of our hours at the coffeehouse and the Durands and college and all.'

None of which was nearly as juicy. This health food was obviously messing with me.

'This wife,' Pavlik said, moving on. 'She was before Naomi?'

'Oh, yes,' I said. 'Which is bigamy, right?'

'Only if they're not legally divorced,' Pavlik said.

'Paulette – that's her name – says—' I broke off and turned to Jacque. 'Did she use Oui when you married?'

'What is it that you are asking me?'

I shouldn't have thought I had to illustrate 'Oui' in air quotes. It was his last name, after all. 'Your last name – Oui. Did Paulette take it when you were married or did she keep her maiden name?'

He blinked. 'She is Paulette Badeaux.'

Pretty. I wouldn't use 'Oui,' either. 'She introduced herself to me as Paulette Oui.'

'Pfft.' Jacque waved his hand. 'That is Paulette being Paulette. If she is using my name, it's only because she wants something of me.'

'She's never married?' I asked. 'I mean, since you.'

'No, I . . .' He was thinking. 'She has not told me, but that is a good question.'

'It is.' Pavlik seemed to be catching on. 'Because if she married, it means she believed you were divorced.'

'Or she's a bigamist, too,' I said. 'Assuming bigamy is illegal in France?'

Jacque swallowed hard and nodded. 'But I did obtain a legal divorce in France. It is merely that Paulette had disappeared and therefore could not contest it.'

'Until now,' I said.

'If I were you,' Pavlik said to Jacque, 'I would contact your divorce lawyer in France, Jacque. He or she can set your ex-wife straight.'

'While you're at it,' I said to Jacque, 'be sure to ask if Paulette is right and she owns half of everything.'

Jacque was turning pale. 'Though I married and divorced in France, it would be American property rights that pertain, no? Because this is where I am living?'

'Yes,' Pavlik said. 'Which isn't necessarily a good thing in this case. Wisconsin is a community property state, so everything one acquires during marriage belongs to both of you.'

'How long ago did you marry Paulette?' I asked Jacque.

'Almost twenty years ago,' he said, rubbing his chin. 'Paulette left after two years, but I had to wait until two years to file for divorce.'

'To prove she had abandoned the marriage, right?'

A tight nod. 'She was a junkie, you know. We all liked our wine and perhaps smoked the weed. But the crack, it took me by surprise. Two years later it had killed our love and, when Paulette disappeared,' he spread his fingers wide, 'I honestly thought it had killed her as well. Now she resurfaces acting as if I betrayed *her*? That I somehow owe *her* half of what I have worked so hard to attain?' His voice had steadily risen.

Pavlik held up a hand. 'I'm not an expert by any means, so don't panic. But you do need a lawyer and fast.'

'I will telephone my attorney here the first thing in the morning.' He drained his glass of pinot. 'Perhaps he can advise me or at least refer me to someone who can.'

'Let me get you more wine,' Pavlik said, leaning across the coffee table.

'That was the end of the bottle,' I said, hoping Jacque would have better manners than I was exhibiting and take the hint. But no.

'I'll open another,' Pavlik said, getting up with the glass.

When he left, I swiveled to Jacque. 'I didn't tell Amy that Paulette said you invited her here. Did you?'

'I did not—'

'You know,' Pavlik said, returning with a new bottle of

pinot, 'if you need somewhere to stay tonight, Jacque, we have space.'

'You do?' Jacque looked at me.

I looked at Pavlik. 'We do?'

'He can't sleep at Amy's house, and you don't want him to sleep with his ex, right?'

Right. 'We do.'

SIX

'Time to go out,' I whispered to Frank and Mocha the next morning.

It was nearly five a.m., and I needed to be at the store to help Amy grind and brew gallons of coffee so she could man our booth at the farmers' market when it opened at seven. I, in turn, would be manning Uncommon Grounds.

'I'm not going to tell you again,' I hissed to Mocha, who was pretending to be asleep in the curve of Pavlik's stomach. Both he and I were side sleepers, fetal position facing inward toward each other, our bodies forming a heart. This would be romantic if that heart wasn't filled with sheepdog and Chihuahua most nights.

But we did love our dogs.

The smaller of the two got to her feet, grumbling.

'Could you move any slower?' I asked Mocha. 'And you, Frank? Up!'

He harrumphed.

We were all in a bad mood. I can't speak for the two furry ones, but my short fuse was due to the fact that Jacque Oui was sleeping in my son's room.

Oh, sure, it had stood empty except for school holidays these past four years. But still.

Passing by the closed door of Eric's room, the dogs paused to sniff. I had half a notion to open the door and let the thundering herd in, thereby ensuring that this would be the Frenchman's one and only night under my roof.

But . . . Pavlik had invited him. And it was his house, too, now.

I sighed, and Frank glanced up at me under his sheepdog bangs as we padded to the back door.

'I know,' I told him. 'I think Pavlik is worth it, too. But inviting Jacque Oui to stay is nearly a step too far.'

Car keys in hand, I opened the back door. In the lead, Frank naturally stopped to drink from the water dish, blocking the exit. With an annoyed 'grr,' Mocha resorted to the tunnel route under Frank's belly and out.

I, on the other hand, politely waited for Frank to finish and followed him on to the porch. I was debating whether I should tell Amy that the fiancé she had kicked out of her bed had slept in mine. Well, not mine, but you know what I mean.

I'd have to tell her eventually, but didn't necessarily want to lead with that news when I got to the—

'Damn!'

Standing there with my keys, I realized that Jacque had pulled his Peugeot into the driveway last night instead of leaving it parked on the street. Not a big deal, except he blocked the garage where my Ford Escape was parked.

'Just how am I going to get my car out?' I asked out loud.

Frank cocked his head at me and then lumbered over to the Peugeot, where he proceeded to lift his leg on the right rear tire. Mocha, being a dominant female, followed and did likewise, but lower.

'You're both right,' I said. 'I'll wake him.'

Frank and Mocha were behind me as I tapped on the bedroom door. No answer.

Turning the knob, I stuck my head in the room, hoping the man didn't sleep naked.

'Damn,' I said again. Jacque must be in the bathroom, but I had no desire to hunt him down in there. Or anywhere else, for that matter. I was already late.

Instead, I eyed the keys sitting on the bedside table next to his wallet.

'Should I?' I asked my accomplices.

Taking their silence for acquiescence, I grabbed the keys and ran.

I parked the Peugeot on the street in front of the shop and behind Amy's Prius. The barista was out on Uncommon Grounds' porch before I could remove the key from the ignition.

'Oh, Maggy,' she called, stopping short. 'I thought you were Jacque. What are you doing with his car?'

'Sorry, Amy,' I said, getting out of the car.

'Don't be sorry; I'm glad it was you instead of him,' she said, coming down the steps. 'I'm not sure what I would say to him anyway. But why—'

'I was feeling ornery, essentially, but I'll explain.' I dangled the keys. 'Should I lock it, or don't we care if it's stolen?'

'Jacque never locks it,' she said, coming down the steps. 'He says Brookhills' car thieves don't bother with classics.'

'That's because they don't have parts they can rip off and sell,' I said. 'Like catalytic converters.' The town had had a spate of such thefts recently.

'Oh, speaking of thefts,' Amy said, 'the sheriff's department was at Christ Christian when I drove past.'

'Just now?' Christ Christian Church was about a half-mile north of my house on Poplar Creek Road, but since I drove south to get to Uncommon Grounds, I hadn't seen any commotion. 'Pavlik didn't get a call, or at least he hadn't by the time I left.'

'I bet it was those thieves, the ones who steal the HVAC units for the copper,' Amy said. 'They probably wouldn't wake the sheriff for that.'

'I'm not so sure,' I said. 'There have been a lot of complaints. Churches, public buildings, high-end houses.'

'Big places where they can nab multiple units when nobody is there at night.' She frowned. 'Except for the houses, of course.'

'They're usually second homes from what I've heard.' Second homes that were three times the size of anything I'd ever owned, even before my divorce. 'You know, the big ones that aren't occupied year-round.'

'Like in Brookhill Estates and on Poplar Creek.' Amy was nodding. 'I imagine they would make easy picking if they don't have alarm systems.'

My stealing Jacque's Peugeot didn't sound all that bad suddenly. 'About Jacque's car. He came over last night.'

'So you stole his car.' Amy sounded pleased, but I couldn't tell for sure in the light of dawn.

'I took his car because he had blocked the garage,' I told her. 'Pavlik invited him to stay over.'

'Oh, Maggy.' Not so pleased now.

'I know,' I said, one foot on the first porch step. 'I'm sorry.'

'Why would—' The words were drowned out by the sound of a siren revving up to full blast.

As we reflexively turned toward the sound, a fire tanker truck appeared in our field of vision, barely slowing at the intersection at the corner of Junction Road and Brookhill before continuing east on Brookhill.

Amy had her hands over her ears. 'This can't be connected to whatever happened at Christ Christian. They're headed in the opposite direction.'

A ladder truck followed.

And then a squad car.

'What *is* going on, then?' I asked, moving down Junction Road to the corner so I could see east on Brookhill. 'No ambulance, so they're not transporting somebody from Christ Christian or Brookhill Manor to the hospital. And with two fire trucks, it usually means—'

'Fire,' Amy said. A single fire truck accompanied most emergency responses in our small town, but two weren't sent out routinely.

Amy was gazing down the street, eyes screwed up. 'Did they just stop?'

Indeed, the siren seemed to die out just five or six blocks east on Brookhill. The Hotel Morrison was down that way, but probably three or four blocks farther east than where the emergency vehicle lights seemed to be flashing. My ex's dental practice was closer – on the corner of Silver Maple and Brookhill Road – but I could see the upper floors of his office building from here. It, too, was just beyond where the lights and sirens had stopped.

No, this seemed to be the building just this side of the dental practice.

'Schultz's,' Amy breathed and took off, running up the street.

I hesitated, thinking to get the car, and then decided to run after her. 'Wait up,' I called, trying to keep my breathing even. 'We don't know it's Schultz's.'

Initial burst of adrenaline depleted, Amy slowed after a few more steps so I could draw even. I tugged her to a walk. 'The emergency responders are already there. There's nothing we can do that they can't do better.'

'But if it's the market, what would have caused it?' she asked. 'There is the deep fryer and the ovens in the back of the deli, but they should be off. I suppose it could be wiring. It's an old building . . . could be anything, I suppose. Anything.' The torrent of words slowed to a trickle, and she turned to me. 'And to think I was just about to berate you for letting Jacque stay over. Now I just thank God that he was safe in bed asleep when you left.'

'Yeeess,' I said slowly, realizing that I actually couldn't swear to that. 'Or in the bathroom.'

She didn't pay attention to the last. 'I should call him.'

'Let's get closer and make certain it's Schultz's first. We don't know – it could be a false alarm.'

The building this side of Schultz's was obscuring our view of the market itself, but the placement of the fire engines, squad cars and ambulances in front seemed to indicate that's where the emergency was.

'Paulette.' Amy had her hand up to her mouth. 'I'm not happy about her showing up, but I'd never wish her any harm.'

'I'm sure she's fine.' As we started walking again, another engine and an ambulance roared by. 'Remember, the upper floor has its own entrance at the back. If a fire started downstairs, the smoke alarms would have warned her in plenty of time to get out.'

As we approached the emergency vehicles both on the street and in the store's parking lot, I started to scan for Pavlik. As county sheriff, he would have been alerted and may already be here. Maybe even with Jacque.

Head swiveling, I didn't realize Amy had pulled up. 'Oh, dear God.'

Stumbling to a stop next to her, I looked up to see the now-unobstructed view of the two-story market, its upper floor ablaze.

SEVEN

took Amy's hand, and we threaded our way through the maze of emergency vehicles.

'Sorry, ma'am,' a voice said. 'You'll have to step back across the street.'

Pavlik's deputy, Kelly Anthony, was at my elbow. 'It's me. Maggy. Is the sheriff here?'

'On his way, from what I hear,' Kelly said. 'Which makes me wonder why you're here.'

I had a reputation for always being wherever there was a disaster. A well-earned reputation. Though usually the disaster was murder.

I shivered.

Amy glanced sideways at me. 'You're cold?'

'No, no, I'm not.' At dawn on this fine June day.

'Somebody walked over your grave, my mother used to say,' Deputy Anthony said. 'But again, Maggy, what are you doing here at this time of the morning?'

That time of the morning had to be about five thirty now. 'Amy and I came in early to get things ready for our booth at the farmers' market and heard the sirens.' I was counting vehicles. 'Where's the ladder truck?'

'Around the back,' Kelly said. 'Had a hell of a time getting through the alley, given all the crap . . . er, junk. Morning, sir.'

Kelly's phone pinged a message as I turned to see Pavlik approaching us. 'Oh, good. I need to talk to you.'

'Same here,' Pavlik said. 'Have you seen Jacque? He left before I got the call. We need somebody familiar with the building's layout.'

'Sir?' Kelly again. 'Oui's car has been spotted parked in front of Uncommon Grounds.'

'Jacque wasn't driving it,' I confessed. 'When I left to go to work, his car was blocking mine.'

'So you took it?'

'I went to ask him to move it, but he wasn't in the bedroom.'
I glanced toward Amy, who was waving at two people across
the way. 'And since I didn't have time to pry him out of the
bathroom, yeah, I took it.'

'He was in the bathroom, then?' Pavlik asked. 'You're
sure?'

I ducked my head. 'I didn't look, to be honest, but I figured
it was the most likely place to find a guy in the morning.'

'True,' Anthony seconded.

Pavlik signaled for his deputy to leave us. 'Jacque wasn't
in the bathroom, and Eric's room was empty. Since I heard
Jacque's car start before I got up, I assumed he'd just awakened
early and left to avoid any awkwardness.'

I waited for Amy to cross to her friends. 'You mean
with me?'

He nodded. 'But now that I know it was you in the Peugeot,
I'm at a loss.'

'I suppose it's possible he *was* in the bathroom and saw his
car was gone.'

'He'd have heard it leave, like I did,' Pavlik said. 'But then
what? We both would have been awake. I'd have heard him
moving around, especially if he thought his car had been
stolen.'

'So where does a man go before five a.m.? Especially
without his car?'

'Excellent question,' Pavlik said. 'I assume because you're
asking it, you have a theory?'

I shrugged. 'It's a bit of a hike from our house, but since
he didn't show up at the shop looking to make up with Amy,
this seems the most likely destination, doesn't it?'

'For a quickie with the ex?' Pavlik cocked his head. 'Or
are you suggesting he started the fire?'

'I'm suggesting neither. Or both. I don't know.' I shook my
head, more to clear it than anything. 'I do think Paulette
smokes. Her clothes smelled of cigarettes.'

'She could have fallen asleep with one lighted, I guess,'
Pavlik said, lifting his head to view the raging flames. 'It's
pretty intense, but then we don't know the fire load up there.
Another reason to find Oui.'

'If he left before I did, why wouldn't he have taken his car? He didn't want to wake us up?'

'It's loud,' Pavlik said. 'As I said, it woke me up when you left.'

'I suppose it's possible Jacque couldn't sleep and went for a walk.' The crack of axes breaking through the roof made me duck. 'Have they found anybody?'

Pavlik shook his head. 'I just got here, as you know, but no. Not yet.'

'Maybe Paulette changed her mind and went to the Hotel Morris—'

'We've got a body,' a voice called from above, accompanied by a whistle.

'Apparently not,' Pavlik said, squeezing my shoulder. 'I have to check in. If you see Jacque Oui, I want to know, OK?'

'OK,' I said, pivoting to see where Amy had gone. 'Amy is over there, talking to Becky,' I told Pavlik before he could take his leave. 'She's been at Schultz's for more than fifty years. She probably knows the floor plan better than Jacque.'

'Thanks,' Pavlik said and crossed to them.

I trailed after, waiting as he peeled Becky away from Amy and Egbert.

'Of course,' Becky was saying as they moved away. 'I've been here since the very beginning you know. Back then . . .'

'Mother, narrating the Jurassic era,' Egbert was saying as I joined him and Amy. 'Good morning, Maggy.'

'Hi, Egbert,' I said. 'Were you dropping your mom off for work?'

'Yes. I couldn't believe my eyes as we pulled up.'

Amy cleared her throat. 'I was just saying that I hope Jacque will be able to salvage the building and . . .' Her voice trailed off and she started again. 'Why is the sheriff talking to Becky about the floor plan, Maggy? Where is Jacque?'

'We don't know. He wasn't at the house when Pavlik left.'

'But he was there when you left, right?' She was almost pleading.

I grimaced. 'I'm sorry. He wasn't in bed when I knocked for him to move the car. I just assumed he was in the bathroom.'

'So you're the one who drove his Peugeot?' Egbert exclaimed. 'Bold move, Maggy. I saw it at Uncommon Grounds.'

'I just relocated it,' I said. 'A mile.'

'But where could Jacque have gone?' Amy asked, ignoring the car.

'For a walk?' I suggested, as I had to Pavlik. 'Maybe Jacque couldn't sleep and wanted to clear his head. Which reminds me, did you call or text him when we got here? Did he get back to you?'

'Oh, good thought,' she said, digging her phone out. 'I sent a text for him to call me.'

The uproar around us seemed to increase in volume. Power saws were rumbling somewhere, and an extension ladder passed by us to be threaded through the sliding doors and into the market.

'No call, but here's a text from last night,' Amy said, raising her voice to be heard. 'My do-not-disturb was on, so I didn't see it when I sent mine this morning.'

'What does he say?' I asked.

She stood for a second, reading it, her lips moving.

'Amy?'

She dropped the hand holding the phone to her side, and Egbert gently took it.

'That's private,' I said. 'Don't you want—'

'Four-oh-two a.m.,' Egbert read. '"I am so very sorry, my love. Please don't think badly of me."'

The din seemed to fall away, so all I could hear was Amy sniffling.

And then another whistle. 'We have a second body.'

EIGHT

'You go home now,' Pavlik told Amy. 'But I'd like to keep your phone if that's OK.'

Amy had reached out to take the mobile from him, and now her hand froze in mid-air. 'But what if Jacque calls me? Or texts?'

Her face crumpled. 'I mean, I mean, if he's not . . .' She waved toward the store, where we could see firefighters lifting the ladder into place through a large hole in the ceiling, presumably to access the flat above.

'Let's not jump the gun,' Pavlik said. 'We don't have IDs on either of the victims yet.'

'But—'

'It might be hours before we remove the bodies from the scene and transport them to the coroner's office for autopsy and identification. There's no need for you to stay here.'

'But you can tell now . . . or should I ask, can you tell now if they're male or female?' Her voice was trembling.

I thought Pavlik might have an idea at this point, but he shook his head. 'The fire was very hot.'

It didn't reassure Amy, but then it wasn't meant to. Pavlik always tried to play it straight, even in difficult circumstances. 'If Jacque gets in touch with you,' he continued, 'call me immediately.'

'But how would I?' She held out her hand. 'You'll have my phone. And I don't have a landline.'

'Maggy has her cell phone and she'll stay with you,' Pavlik told her. 'Is that OK, Maggy?'

'Of course,' I said. 'We can go to Uncommon Grounds and get a coffee—'

Amy's hand flew to her mouth. 'The farmers' market. The shop. It must be way past time to open.'

'We're not opening today.' I nodded goodbye to Pavlik as

I led her away. 'And the farmers' market will do just fine without us for a week.'

'You'll need to call Sarah,' she said in a small voice as we made our way back to the store.

'Why? She's not scheduled to work today.'

'I know.' She managed just the trace of a smile. 'But she'll want a full recounting of what's happened.'

'That's true,' I said, as we turned on to Junction Road.

'I'd prefer to get that over with now,' Amy said, glancing at Jacque's Peugeot and quickly away.

'Then it appears that you'll get your wish.'

Sarah was sitting on our porch steps. She stood to put her arm around Amy's shoulders. 'You OK?'

'You heard about the fire, I take it,' I said.

'Small town, lots of sirens. Hard not to,' she said. 'Then I started to get calls from customers, asking why Uncommon Grounds was still dark.'

'You didn't open, I see.' I led the way up the steps. 'Good.'

'I forgot my key, to tell you the truth,' she said. 'In my haste to get here.'

And not do anything. 'I'm surprised you didn't come to Schultz's.'

'They had the entire block taped off by the time I got there,' she said. 'I waited here, knowing you'd show up eventually.'

Unlocking the door, I let the other two in before I locked it behind us, leaving the 'closed' sign in place.

'Let's leave the store lights off,' I said. 'And, Sarah, why don't you get Amy a latte? I'm just going to check something.'

Even when our shop is closed, people still need access to the restrooms and waiting hall from the train platform. That meant that in addition to locking the front door each evening, we naturally locked the door that led to the waiting hall.

This was the door I unlocked now and stuck my head in.

Nobody on the benches. Not unexpected, since it was Saturday and just one round-trip train ran on Saturday morning and that was at ten. It was just past eight thirty now.

Going down the corridor, I checked the ladies' room and

then stepped into the men's room. Urinals, of course, and two stalls. No shoes visible under the doors, but I pushed open first one stall door and then the other.

'Do you think he's standing on the toilet seat?' Amy's voice asked from behind me. 'Hiding from us?'

I turned, a little shamefaced. 'There aren't a lot of public spaces you can get into this early on a Saturday. Here and some park buildings, maybe.'

'Who's he?' Sarah asked from behind Amy. 'Do you mean Jacque? His car is out front, but he must be down at the fire.'

'He's not,' I said.

'But his car—'

'Maggy stole it,' Amy told her.

Sarah pursed her lips. 'Should I ask why?'

'Sure,' I said, leading the way back to the shop. 'He had parked me in.'

'And where was that?'

I groaned. 'You're right, Amy. This is tedious.'

'Jacque went to Maggy's last night to cry on her shoulder after I kicked him out.' Amy dumped a cup of espresso beans into our grinder and flipped the switch.

Sarah frowned. 'Maggy is the last person I would think he'd go running to.'

I took three clean latte mugs from the dishwasher and put them on the counter next to Amy. 'I think he was punishing me because I made him tell Amy the truth.'

'And did he?' Sarah asked.

'He said so.'

'Everything?' Sarah glanced at Amy's back as the barista pressed freshly ground espresso into a portafilter. 'Including you-know-what?'

'That Paulette was staying in the flat?' Amy asked without turning. 'Yes.'

'And . . .' Sarah was making weird eye movements at me.

'And?' For the life of me, I didn't know what she was getting at.

Sarah spat it out. 'And why she came to Brookhills in the first place?'

Amy turned. 'You know that, Maggy?'

Argh. I held up both hands. 'Paulette said she was invited. I tried to ask Jacque about it last night and whether he told you, but—'

'He didn't.' Her lips were tight as she turned back to us, brandishing the portafilter. 'Nor had you.'

'Thanks a lot,' I hissed to Sarah as I backed up a step. 'This is exactly what I was afraid of.'

'Being poked with a portafilter?' Sarah asked.

'I'm not going to hit you.' Amy went to twist the portafilter on to the machine. 'It would be a terrible waste of freshly ground espresso.'

'And a mess to clean up, mixing with Maggy's blood and all,' said my supportive partner. 'But I still don't understand how Jacque ended up staying with you. And where is he now?'

'The how is Pavlik,' I explained. 'He said it was the nice thing to do.'

Amy was getting the milk out of the cooler, and Sarah took the opportunity to chin-gesture toward Schultz's and raise two fingers. *Two bodies*, she mouthed.

It hadn't taken long for the news to get out. 'I know,' I whispered. 'But . . .'

'Please don't.' Amy had turned with the gallon of skim milk. 'You two aren't saying anything I haven't already thought of. Jacque disappeared sometime during the night, leaving his car behind for a reason.'

'I thought maybe he wanted to slip out without waking us,' I said. 'That car is not exactly quiet.'

'I'm surprised the dogs didn't hear him leave anyway.' Sarah took the milk from Amy and went to the espresso machine.

'True,' I said. 'Though they both hate him, so maybe they were just glad to see him go.' I held up a hand to Amy. 'Sorry.'

'Like I said, no need to dance around the facts.' She hoisted her butt on to the counter to watch Sarah continue with the drinks.

'If I were Frank and Mocha, I'd have taken the opportunity to take a chunk out of him as he left,' Sarah said, turning. 'But maybe that's just me.'

'It is,' Amy said, waving for Sarah to commence frothing. 'We don't know what time he left, but Jacque sent me a text at four-oh-two. I didn't see it because I have my do-not-disturb mode on the phone set to go off at seven a.m.'

'What time did the fire start?' Sarah asked over her shoulder.

'We heard the sirens at what, Amy? Just before five thirty?'

'Earlier,' she told me. 'You were just arriving, remember? I came out to meet you.'

'That's right, and I was running a little late because of the car thing.' Truth was I was running late even before that. 'So maybe ten after five?'

'What did the text say?' Sarah asked, pushing the button to brew the espresso shots into two small stainless-steel pitchers.

'That he was sorry.' Amy's tone was flat. 'And I shouldn't think badly of him.'

'He might mean for Paulette showing up out of the blue,' I offered a little feebly.

'Or, alternatively,' Sarah dumped the shots into mugs and started two more, 'sorry for burning down my shop with me and my French wife in it.'

Amy and I both froze.

Sarah turned. 'What? Amy said no dancing, and it's what we're all thinking, right?'

'You still didn't have to say it like that.' I nudged her out of the way and poured frothed milk into one of the mugs, handing it to Amy. 'Excuse her.'

'No, no, she's right.' Amy was shaking her head. 'It's exactly what I've been thinking. There are two bodies in that upper flat. That is a fact. We can be pretty sure one was Paulette, rest her soul. The other one has to be Jacque.'

I added milk to the other mug and took it for myself. Sarah could fend for herself. 'Pavlik isn't jumping to conclusions, so we shouldn't either. The bodies haven't even been removed from the building, much less autopsied and identified. As far as he's concerned, Jacque is a missing person.' And maybe a person of interest, depending on the cause of the fire.

'That's why the sheriff took my phone,' Amy said. 'In case Jacque contacts me.'

'Or to locate him,' Sarah said. 'Do you have each other's phones on the Find My app, Amy?'

'Oh, no,' Amy said. 'That feels like spying on the other person.'

'Or it feels like knowing where to drag the creek if, for example, that other person went missing,' was Sarah's counter-argument.

'The phone wouldn't survive the water,' I snapped.

'Then it would register where he went into the creek,' she said, eyes narrowed. 'And before you say it, the app shows the phone's last known location for twenty-four hours, if I'm not mistaken.'

Wasn't she Ms Smarty Pants? 'There's no reason to think Jacque wandered into the creek.'

'I might have been using creek as a less upsetting example than fire.' Sarah sniffed. 'And you think you're the sensitive one.'

'Anyway,' I said, turning to Amy, 'Pavlik doesn't need your phone to locate Jacque's. He has other methods.'

'Which require a warrant.' Sarah dumped both shots into a mug and picked up the now-empty frothing pitcher. 'Damn.'

'How was Jacque acting when he was at your house, Maggy?' Amy asked as Sarah poured more milk into the pitcher and started up the steam. 'He didn't seem suicidal—'

'Or homicidal?' Sarah tossed in. 'Or both?'

Amy glared at Sarah before finishing with, 'Did he?'

I lifted my shoulders in an uncertain shrug. 'He was upset, but not despondent if that's what you mean. He and Pavlik talked about his divorce in France and having a lawyer sort things out. Jacque was quite clear that everything was in order.' Assuming you could believe him. But then why the disappearing act?

'You don't think he got up during the night and decided to go to Schultz's and . . .'

'End it all?' I asked. 'No. Besides, why take Paulette and the store down with him?'

Sarah had completed her latte. 'Because Paulette would have a claim on his estate if Jacque was lying about the divorce?'

'But Amy said Jacque had the divorce decree,' I said, turning to the barista for confirmation. 'Right?'

She seemed less certain now. 'I assume it's with the other French documents in his safe deposit box. As for his estate,' she continued, 'the only thing of value that Jacque has is the store. If he burned that down—' She broke off, her eyes big. 'Not that he did that. Of course.'

'Of course,' I said reassuringly, but then added, 'There would be insurance on the store, regardless, and a beneficiary for that.'

Sarah and I looked at Amy.

'Don't look at me,' she said, turning to sprinkle cinnamon on her latte. 'I don't even know if Jacque has a will.'

Horrible planning – or lack of planning – on Jacque's part, if that was true.

'Anyway, my point is that Schultz's was' – Amy caught herself – '*is* Jacque's baby. Why would he destroy it?'

'The fire may be accidental,' I pointed out. 'Paulette was a smoker.'

'Did Pavlik tell you that?' Sarah asked.

'No, I told him. I could smell it on her clothes.'

'Idiot,' Sarah said, smirking. 'Nice shoes and bag, and she stinks them up with old tobacco smoke.'

Said the now ex-smoker of about two years. But at least Sarah had finally quit.

'But if it was an accident,' Amy said, 'where is Jacque? And who is the second body?'

'Let's concentrate on the first question,' I said. 'If Jacque was in trouble, Amy, where would he go?'

'Without a car?' Amy shrugged. 'My house, maybe? It's a half-mile north on Poplar Creek from your place, but that's an easy enough walk.'

I hadn't thought of that. 'And Jacque knew you were working early.'

'I told him that I had to get up early and couldn't deal with him anymore when I kicked him out.'

'Then he might have waited until he knew you'd left and gone there,' Sarah suggested. 'He has a key, right?'

'Of course,' Amy hopped down from the counter. 'I can't believe we didn't think of this earlier. He's probably there right now. Let's go check.'

'Let's,' I said, pulling out to-go cups for our drinks.

'You know, I bet that's exactly what happened,' Amy went

on as she transferred the drinks. 'He took a walk from your house, Maggy, and ended up at mine, let himself in and went to bed, since he probably didn't sleep well, with the fight and all.'

'Probably,' I said, though I would have thought the bottle of wine he and Pavlik consumed would have helped the sleeping part.

'We'll take my car; I'm parked out front,' Amy said, handing out the cups. 'Oh, Maggy, do you think you should drive the Peugeot to my house? Jacque might need it.'

As far as the sheriff was concerned, Jacque was missing and a suspect or victim – or both – in a mysterious fire. His car was evidence. 'Let's leave it parked here. If Jacque is at the house, you can drive him back to get it.'

'Oh, good idea.' She was getting out her keys as she turned the knob and pushed. 'What?'

'I locked it,' I told her, reaching out to turn the deadbolt.

'Oh, right,' she said, shoving the door open and nearly tripping over a large male figure on the ground.

NINE

'Oops, sorry,' the man said, getting to his feet. 'I didn't know if you were open.'

'So you were looking under the door?' I asked. Sandy-haired and freckled, he went all pink under his floppy, sun-lightened bangs. 'The mail slot. I was peeking in like they do on TV to see if anybody was there.'

'Good thing for you it's an old building,' I said, eyeing our snoop. 'I don't think they do mail slots anymore. Not secure. Obviously.'

'Jamie?' Sarah asked, peering at him. 'Jamie Bright?'

'Sarah Kingston,' he said, shaking her hand. 'It's been a while. I heard you opened this place.'

'I did.'

I dug my elbow into her ribs.

'Along with my partner Maggy Thorsen here,' Sarah added smoothly.

'Good to meet you, Maggy,' he said, taking my hand. 'Sarah helped me look at retail property in Brookhills. Of course, that was back a few years now. She was still in real estate and I was yet to open my first store.'

'I understand you're from Brookhills,' I said.

'I am.' He was one of those people who looked you in the eye when he spoke. It was unnerving and vaguely seductive at the same time. 'And here we are, finally getting ready to do a Bright and Natural grand opening in my hometown.'

'Good for you,' Amy said dryly.

'Thank you.' He cocked his head. 'You're Amy Caprese, aren't you?'

'Yes.' Amy seemed surprised. 'Now, if you'll excuse us?'

'Yes, of course. I'm very sorry about the fire. Would you tell Jacque that? I know we're competitors of sorts, but . . .' He seemed to lose himself in his thoughts. 'Well, it's just the worst thing imaginable.'

'It is. Now . . .'

'Yes, of course,' he said again, moving aside. 'I'll let you go.'

'We'll be open tomorrow if you want to come back,' I told him as I passed.

'Great,' he said with a smile and those eyes again. 'I'll be here.'

'Hugh Grant,' I said under my breath as we descended the porch steps. Jamie had remained where he was.

'What?' Amy was marching us down the sidewalk to the Prius.

'A red-haired Hugh Grant,' Sarah said. 'I thought the same thing when I met him.'

'That boyish charm.'

'It won't age well,' Amy snapped.

I exchanged looks with Sarah as we got into the hybrid. 'Has with Hugh.'

'Can you believe the nerve?' Amy sputtered as she slid into the driver's seat and turned. 'What are you both doing in the back seat?'

'I . . . well, I don't know,' I said. 'I can move up if—'

'Don't bother.' She started the car and shoved it into reverse to pull out of the parking space. '"Tell Jacque I'm so sorry." Boo-hoo-hoo. I wouldn't be surprised if he set the fire. He's probably hanging around Uncommon Grounds to do the same.'

I punched Sarah in the arm as we accelerated out of the parking lot. 'Why didn't we think of that sooner?'

'Oww.' She rubbed her arm. 'Because reputable business people don't commit serial arson? And what good would it do for him to burn down the depot?'

'Forget that part,' I said. 'I just mean Schultz's fire. Maybe Jamie Bright is not the golden boy everybody says. His company grew awfully fast.'

'Probably mobbed up,' Amy said from the front. 'Just because you think he's charming, Sarah, doesn't mean Jamie hasn't done bad things to get ahead.'

'Maggy thinks he's charming, too,' Sarah muttered.

'Charming can be a great asset for a criminal. He looks you directly in the eyes and lies, lies, lies.'

'We don't even know the Schultz's fire was arson,' Sarah pointed out.

'And yet minutes ago, you were willing to believe Jacque burned the place down to kill his ex-wife and commit suicide.' Amy took a hairpin right turn on to Poplar Creek Road a little too fast.

Sarah slid sideways practically on to my lap.

I shoved her off me. 'Put your seatbelt on.'

'It's on. I just pull it out really far, so it doesn't restrict me.'

'Restriction being the very point of a seatbelt,' I said. 'But back to Jamie. He might have a financial motive for burning down Schultz's – to rid himself of a competitor.' And I do love me a good financial motive.

'While Jacque has both personal and financial motives,' Sarah said. 'Paulette and insurance.'

'True,' I said as we passed my house.

'Oldest trick in the book,' Sarah said. 'Jacque is in financial trouble and can't pay his bills or payroll. Suddenly, his store burns down.'

'He gets an insurance settlement and can start over,' I said.

'With the added benefit of getting rid of the French wife, in this case,' Sarah said.

'The long-lost wife,' I said, liking this more and more, 'who is threatening to claim half of everything he has accumulated.'

'What are you talking about?' Amy slammed on the brake as a white van pulled out of Christ Christian's parking lot, cutting her off and then proceeding to putt-putt along in front of her.

I leaned forward. 'I hate to say it, but what if Jacque is lying and there is no divorce decree in that safe deposit box? Or Jacque messed up and Paulette genuinely has a basis for contesting their divorce?'

'Right,' Sarah said. 'Even if she agreed to a divorce now, she might be entitled to half of everything he owns.'

'Wait,' Amy said. 'Half of everything he's earned since they got married like twenty years ago?'

'Yes, but cheer up,' Sarah said. 'He would get half of hers, too.'

Amy wasn't cheering up. 'That's crazy.'

'And probably not relevant now,' Sarah said, 'since we're pretty sure she's dead. Lucky for Jacque. Assuming he's still alive.'

'He and Pavlik were discussing community property laws when I gave up and went to bed last night,' I told them.

'Pavlik.'

'Yes. He—'

'Is here,' Amy said.

We had arrived at Amy's white Cape Cod-style house. In front of it was parked Pavlik's car, along with two other squads, lights flashing. Pavlik and a deputy were on the front porch.

Amy hopped out and ran up to the sheriff.

Sarah and I exchanged looks in the back seat.

'Did she turn off the car?' Sarah asked.

I leaned over the seat to see the display. 'It says the key is not in the car, but I think it's still running.'

'How can you tell, damn electric things?' Sarah grumbled.

'It's hybrid,' I said, straining to hit the power button.

'All I'm saying is that I sure as hell know when my Firebird is running.'

'As does everybody else, including the environmental protection people,' I said. 'Though at least you don't have to worry about catalytic converter thieves. You don't have one to steal.'

'Au contraire, 1975 was the first year they were required,' Sarah said. 'Are we safe to get out now?'

'I think so.' We climbed out of our respective sides and joined Amy and Pavlik.

Amy turned as we approached. 'Jacque's not here.'

'At least, he's not answering the door,' Pavlik said. 'But now that you're here, Amy, can you let us in to be sure?'

'Of course,' Amy said, unlocking the door.

'It would be best if you waited here, ma'am,' the deputy said politely.

'Why?' Amy asked.

'Just protocol,' Pavlik told her. 'Jacque is missing and we can't be sure he wants to be found.'

'Come on, Amy,' Sarah said, with a significant glance at Pavlik. 'We'll wait here on the porch.'

As they moved away to a wrought-iron bench, I beckoned Pavlik off the porch and on to the grass to one side. 'You couldn't get into the house, so why are you all still here?'

'Waiting for a warrant,' he said, joining me under a silver maple tree. 'But this is a lot easier.'

'You could have called my cell. We would have come over.'

'Honestly, I didn't know how Amy would react to that. And I didn't want to raise her hopes that he would be here.'

'Or give her a chance to warn him in case she already knew where he was.'

'Exactly.'

'If he is inside and not answering the door, there are only two logical reasons. He's killed himself—'

'Or is hiding.'

'Because he set the fire.'

Pavlik nodded.

'And, presumably, didn't die in it himself.' I was watching the sheriff's face. 'Anything new on the bodies?'

'They've just been moved to the morgue with a few personal items that survived. A passport for a Paulette Badeaux, for one.'

That answered one question. 'Badeaux is her maiden name.'

'I assumed as much, but we're confirming that. The body closest to the door was almost certainly female given the size and thickness of the bones and the width of the pelvis.'

'And the other?'

'Almost certainly male.'

'But no ID?'

'None that survived the fire. We only have the passport because it was in the kitchenette, away from the source of the fire.'

'Which was where? If Paulette was smoking—'

'The front door. Somebody poured an accelerant through the mail slot and lit it.'

That startled me. 'Another Jamie Bright.'

'What?'

'Who,' I corrected. 'Jamie Bright, the owner of Bright and Natural Market? He was trying to buy Jacque out. We just caught him peeking through the mail slot at Uncommon Grounds.'

'Did he have a can of gasoline in his hand?'

'No.'

'Then maybe not as pertinent as it might seem.'

'Maybe not.' I frowned. 'But it is a weird coincidence.' I shook myself. 'Anyway, you say the woman's body was close to the source of the fire?'

'Yes, like she had attempted to put it out or maybe was trying to escape that way. The wooden stairs were completely burned out, though, so even if she had gotten through the flames, she would have had to jump down. Just the one flight, though, so she probably could have survived it.'

'Do you think it was on purpose?' I asked thoughtfully.

'The fire? Of course it was. I just told you how—'

'I meant the stairs burning. Was it just a natural result of the fire being started there, or do you think somebody purposely eliminated the stairs as an escape route?' Somehow that compounded the ugliness.

'Whoever set the fire had to use the stairs to get back down,' he said. 'Unless—'

'Unless they stayed in the apartment,' I said. 'What about Paulette herself?'

'Some crazy vendetta against Jacque? Seems like she had more to gain by staying alive and keeping Jacque's main asset intact.'

'So the man, then,' I said. 'He poured the accelerant in front of the door, lighted it and went . . . where was he found?'

'In the bedroom,' he said. 'On the bed.'

I blinked. 'That's odd, don't you think?'

He gave a half-hearted shrug. 'There are more things in heaven and earth, Horatio.'

Shakespeare again. 'He was lying on the bed like he was sleeping? Was there just the one bed in the flat?'

'Yes, to the first question. And also yes – one bedroom with one bed in it. Plus a couch in the living room.'

'Jacque started the fire and then went to sleep?'

'We don't know it was Jacque, but it's possible. He could have taken something before he laid down so—'

'So he wouldn't be conscious when he was burned alive?' An ant was crawling up my shoe. I started to flick it away but decided to leave it be. 'Too bad he wasn't as considerate of Paulette.'

'I'm not saying that's what happened, but it might explain why this person laid down on the bed. Conversely, he could have been drugged by Paulette.'

'Who then set the fire but was overcome before she could get out. That works better, doesn't it?' I frowned. 'She might expect to inherit with Jacque dead, but, as you say, the store was an asset. Why burn it down?'

'We'll know more after the autopsies. There was also . . .'

'What?' I prompted as he trailed off.

'There was something else.' Pavlik leaned down and let the ant that was exploring my sneaker laces crawl on to his finger. 'A plastic-wrapped packet of white powder taped to the toilet tank.'

Cliché, but effective in surviving the fire. 'Cocaine?'

'Apparently.' Pavlik raised his hand to let the ant crawl off his finger and on to the silvery-white side of a maple leaf. 'It's Jacque's flat, so normally we'd assume the cocaine belonged to him, but given what he told us about Paulette's drug use . . .' He shrugged.

'And powdered cocaine is ever so much more elegant than a zipper bag of crack rocks.' I was imagining the woman kneeling on the toilet lid in her Louboutins hiding her stash. 'But where would she have gotten it?'

'She couldn't have flown in from Paris on Wednesday with a bag of cocaine,' Pavlik said. 'But it's possible she found a connection in the interim.'

'Or maybe somebody else at Schultz's was using the flat to hide their stash?' I suggested. 'Jacque has been staying with Amy since he sold his house so the flat was empty. Until last night, of course.'

'That's pretty risky. One overflowing toilet or stuck water valve and they'd be found out.'

'Amy?' a voice called.

I turned to see Helen Durand climbing out of the driver's seat of a Cadillac Escalade. Molly was in the passenger seat.

'Oh, my dear,' Helen said, hurrying past us to the porch where Amy and Sarah were now standing, speaking to a sheriff's deputy. 'I heard about the fire and stopped by Uncommon Grounds. When it wasn't open, I was afraid you or Jacque had been hurt.'

'No. I mean, I wasn't there and Jacque, well, Jacque . . .' Amy dissolved into tears.

Helen pulled her toward her and addressed us over the younger woman's shoulder. 'Jacque is . . .?'

The deputy had disappeared, and I glanced at Pavlik, not sure how much he wanted to say.

'Missing,' Pavlik filled in. 'And you are?'

'This is Helen Durand,' I said. 'I don't know if you've met her and her husband, Denis.'

'And our daughter, Molly,' Helen said, nodding toward the girl coming up the walk. 'I'm a psychologist and my husband Denis runs a valuation firm. And you are—'

Pavlik was in black jeans and a navy dress shirt rolled up at the sleeves. My favorite leather jacket had been relegated to the closet for the summer.

'This is Sheriff Jake Pavlik,' I said, as Pavlik pulled out his badge.

'Oh, Sheriff,' Helen said. 'I'm so sorry. I'm just a little discombobulated. '

'I overslept,' Molly said, shoving a lock of dark hair behind one ear. 'And Dad is in Chicago, so she had to take me to work.' The 'she' apparently being Helen.

'Yes, I was going to drop her at the floral shop, but when we saw the fire and couldn't find Amy at Uncommon Grounds, we came right here.'

'You're working at Clare's Antiques and Florals?' I asked Molly. Clare's was just a block from Uncommon Grounds.

'Just for the summer,' Molly said, as her mother occupied herself with Amy. 'What happened, Maggy? I heard somebody died.'

Pavlik had moved away, too, so it was up to me to answer. Vaguely. 'They haven't identified them yet.'

'Them?' she asked, eyes big. 'Was it two people? How did it start?'

Damn. 'I said "them" because we don't know if it was a man or woman.' I was lying, but, as usual, I knew more than

Pavlik probably wanted me to say. Especially to a curious teenager.

Helen must have heard because she glanced our way. The psychologist would be aware of Paulette's visit from Jacque's call to Amy yesterday.

'Text Clare,' she instructed her daughter, 'and let her know you'll be there in a few minutes.'

Molly frowned. 'Clare is chill.'

'Well, I'm not,' Helen said firmly. 'Go to the car and text her. I'll be right there.'

As Molly sullenly obeyed, Amy stepped back, sniffling. 'I'm so sorry to fall apart like this.'

Sarah, who had been relegated to the sidelines, pulled a napkin from her jeans pocket. 'Here.'

'Thanks.'

'What exactly is going on here at your place now, Amy?' Helen asked, still frowning. 'The police, I mean.'

'They're looking for Jacque,' Amy said.

'Then he spent the night here,' Helen said, looking relieved. 'I was afraid maybe he was in his flat when . . .'

'He wasn't here last night,' Amy said. 'He was at Maggy's.'

Helen cocked her head to look at me. 'I didn't know you and Jacque were close. In fact, I had the impression you didn't like each other.'

'And you were right,' I said. 'But he's my cousin.'

'And blood is thicker, as they say,' she said.

'Isn't it?' Sarah affirmed.

'So Jacque is safe at any rate. That's a relief.' Helen was searching her jacket pockets, presumably for her car keys, and stopped. 'But then why isn't the sheriff's department at your house, Maggy?'

'Because the sheriff already lives at Maggy's house,' Sarah told her.

'Jake Pavlik is my fiancé,' I told Helen.

'Well, that's very handy.'

'Isn't it?' Sarah said again. 'But Jacque took off during the night.'

'Whatever for?' Helen asked, and then her face changed.

'They can't believe he had anything to do with the fire, can they?'

'We don't know,' Amy said. 'The deputy just asked for a toothbrush or something that belongs to Jacque for DNA.'

Helen laid her hand on Amy's arm. 'Don't you think Jacque should be the one who decides to provide his DNA?'

'But he's missing,' Sarah pointed out. 'And everything in his own flat has gone up in smoke, literally.'

'But is this a criminal investigation?' Helen asked Amy. 'Jacque owns the building. Of course they're going to find his DNA and fingerprints all over it.'

I thought the reason for the DNA request was to try to identify the second corpse, but I wasn't going to say that to Amy now. Especially in front of Helen.

'What's the harm in giving them his toothbrush?' Amy asked, puzzled.

'It's just that Jacque – especially if he might be accused of something – has rights. If the police are investigating the fire as arson, his DNA could be used in the prosecution.'

'Or it could exonerate him.' Short of beckoning Pavlik over – and he was nowhere in sight – I thought I should be the voice of reason. 'There might be other people with a grudge against Jacque and Schultz's. Bright and Natural has been trying to buy him out, he's laying off people—'

'You think a disgruntled employee set the place on fire?' Amy asked.

'Personally, I'd lay my money on Egbert Ronstadt,' Sarah said. 'The prospect of Becky being home non-stop could drive anybody over the edge. And he seems to sail pretty close to it anyway – right, Helen?'

'No, not right,' Helen said indignantly. 'Egbert is coping . . .' She let the rest of the sentence go, belatedly realizing Sarah was trying to draw her into chit-chat about a patient.

'Jamie Bright,' I offered up. 'Amy and I caught him peeking through our mail slot.'

'Whose mail slot?' Sarah asked.

'Ours, at the shop.'

'And what does that have to do with setting a fire at Schultz's?' Helen asked, forehead puckered.

'There's a mail slot in the flat's door,' Amy said, tipping to it. 'Is that how the fire was started?'

I'd said too much. 'I heard it burned the wooden steps, so I figured it was a possibility.'

'Sure you did.' Sarah knew I knew more than I could say. But sometimes said it anyway.

'Helen?' Molly called from the car. 'If I must go to work, can we go?'

Helen gave her daughter an exasperated look and turned to Amy. 'Anyway, I'm just saying that Jacque has rights, and I'm not sure you want to be the person who lets the police circumvent them.'

'The man is missing.' I was exasperated, too.

'I know, I know,' Helen said, holding up a hand. 'I just want Amy to have the benefit of both sides of the argument.'

'What two sides do you think she is talking about?' Sarah asked as we watched Helen and Molly drive off. 'Alive and dead?'

'Or good and evil.'

TEN

I checked the time. 'It's not even eleven o'clock yet.' We were sitting on the porch steps as the deputies wrapped up their search.

'Maybe we should open the shop,' Amy suggested.

Sarah groaned. 'Do we have to? It's Saturday, so it'll be quiet anyway.'

'Look at it this way,' I said. 'We have nothing else to do but wait for information, worry and theorize,' I told her. 'We might as well do that in Uncommon Grounds.'

'We could do that here at Amy's house, too,' Sarah pointed out. 'The deputies are leaving, and nobody will bother us.'

'What are you going to do about the sheriff's request for DNA?' I asked Amy as I stood to brush garden soil off the seat of my jeans.

'I'm going to wait,' she said, getting up, too. 'I understand what both he and Helen are saying, but I just can't make a decision right now.'

'That's fine,' I assured her, even as Sarah rolled her eyes. 'Jacque will probably turn up any minute. And, if not, you can decide then.'

Sarah made a rude noise but managed to disguise it with a cough. 'Anyway, Uncommon Grounds or not?'

'Uncommon Grounds,' Amy voted, waving for us to follow her back to her car. 'You don't have to come if you don't want to, Sarah. It's your day off, after all.'

'I'm sure anybody who stops in will mostly want to talk about the fire, anyway,' I told Amy. 'We probably won't be serving much coffee.'

'I'll come,' Sarah said. 'But don't think you're going to maneuver me into closing, too. That honor belongs to you, Maggy.'

Again.

* * *

I was right about the local gossips coming by. Between when we turned on the interior lights and I went to the door and flipped the 'closed' sign, a crowd had gathered. And by crowd, I mean a threesome of seniors – Gloria Goddard, Sophie Daystrom and Henry Wested – from Brookhills Manor.

'It's Saturday; you're a day early,' I told them as they took seats around a table. Amy and Sarah were already working on their drinks. 'Goddard's Gang meets tomorrow.'

Gloria Goddard's Pharmacy had been a tenant in the strip mall that housed Uncommon Grounds' original location. When the mall was destroyed by a monumental spring snowstorm, Uncommon Grounds moved to the depot and the group of seniors that previously met at the pharmacy lunch counter for coffee moved to Uncommon Grounds.

As for Gloria Goddard, she had retired and moved to Brookhills Manor. She raised her hand now. 'Wherever Gloria Goddard goes, the Goddard Gang forms!'

'Dang right, Gloria,' Sophie Daystrom seconded. 'Now, where are our frickin' drinks? It's not like you don't know what the heck we're going to order.'

Sophie looked like a fluffy old lady, but she had the mouth of a sailor who had found euphemisms.

Sophie's partner, on the other hand, couldn't be more of a gentleman. 'Now, you pipe down, Sophie,' Henry Wested said, setting his signature fedora on the table next to them. 'It's kind of Amy to be making our drinks at all under the circumstances.'

'Amy knows I'm grateful,' Sophie said and then lowered her voice, presumably so the two behind the counter couldn't hear. 'We heard rumors that the wife Jacque abandoned in Paris showed up and Jacque killed her and set the store on fire.'

'Accidentally – or not – getting caught in the fire himself,' Gloria supplemented, watching my face expectantly. 'True or false?'

'Ummm, false?' I think.

'Now, girls,' Henry said. 'From what I understand from Jacque, this situation with the French wife is not what it appears.'

'Then why did he kill her?' Sophie demanded, drumming her burgundy fingernails on the tabletop.

'We don't know that he did,' I said, going to fetch Sophie's cappuccino. 'Jacque is missing.'

'Then he's not the man in the flat?' Gloria asked. And as an aside, 'I had a flat like that above the pharmacy and, believe me, I'd never have entertained a male caller there.'

'Of course you wouldn't,' Sophie said. 'Besides, it's practically your workplace, and as my mother always said, "Sophie, don't get your meat where you get your bread."'

'Your mother told you that?' I asked.

'Yes,' she said. 'It means don't have sex with people at work.'

'I got that,' I said. 'But your mother—'

'A remarkable woman, ahead of her time,' Sophie said. 'Ran a butcher shop, which made the meat-and-bread thing a little confusing. Took me years to figure out what she was talking about.'

I snuck a glance at Henry as I set down Sophie's drink, but he was busy fiddling with his cell phone.

'Luckily for you, Gloria,' Sophie continued, 'you had your Hank for nearly fifty years.'

Gloria smiled, remembering fondly. 'Until he was mistaken for a deer one autumn and shot.'

'Ah, deer-hunting season in Wisconsin,' Sophie said. 'At least the man went happy.'

'Personally, I've never understood the allure,' Henry said, putting down the phone.

'Well, to be fair, dear,' Sophie said, patting his hand, 'you got to shoot things in the war.'

'It's ice fishing that baffles me,' Gloria said. 'Pitching a tent on a frozen lake, so you can cut a hole in the ice to fish?'

'I think copious alcohol helps,' Sarah said, placing a latte in front of Gloria and a cappuccino before Henry.

He nodded his thanks.

'Henry,' I said, pulling over a chair to sit. 'You said the situation with Jacque's wife is not what it appears?'

'Oh, just something Jacque told me over a cognac,' he said, taking an appreciative sip of cappuccino.

'They talk food,' Sophie said, patting her husband's hand. 'He knows that Henry is something of a gourmet.'

Henry blushed. 'It's true that Jacque is kind enough to bring the occasional prime cut of meat or a particularly good piece of fish to apply my modest talents to. And we do talk of food, as Sophie says, but also of France. I believe Jacque misses it and I spent some time there after the war.'

This was a side of Jacque I hadn't seen. Kind.

'. . . visited as often as I could manage,' Henry was saying. 'Jacque tells stories of growing up in Paris with Denis and his brother, Gabriel.'

'Was it Denis or Jacque who has a brother?' I asked, surprised.

'Denis. Gabriel died very young of an overdose.' He shook his head. 'There was a terrible crack problem in the Stalingrad neighborhood of Paris – I guess you could say the dark underbelly of the City of Light.'

'Stalingrad,' I repeated. 'But that's—'

'Northeast part of Paris,' he told me. 'After his wife died, Denis decided to bring Molly here and start afresh. And after Jacque's divorce, he followed. '*And*,' Henry said pointedly, turning to his wife, 'it was Paulette who abandoned Jacque, not the other way around.'

Sophie leaned in. 'And suddenly, she shows up here?'

'I'm thinking gold-digger,' Gloria said, joining in. 'Jacque is worth something now. He wasn't when they were young.'

'See? See?' Sophie's voice went up. 'What did I tell you, Henry? It's always about money or sex.'

'Usually money, at our age,' Gloria said.

'That's not always true,' Sophie objected. 'Henry and I still enjoy a romp, don't we, dear?'

'We certainly do,' Henry said, picking up his cell phone again.

'We widows wouldn't know about that.' Gloria sniffed.

'I was widowed once, too, Gloria,' Sophie said, as Amy brought a latte for herself and handed one to me. 'You just gotta get back up on the horse.'

'It was a good idea coming back here,' Amy whispered in my ear. 'I feel more . . . normal.'

'We'll take care of you, dear.' Gloria's hearing certainly hadn't suffered with age. 'Now, where do you think that Jacque of yours could have gone?'

'If he's not dead, of course,' Sophie added.

And this conversation comforted Amy somehow? It was like dealing with a pack of wrinkly Sarahs.

'I honestly don't know,' Amy said, pulling up another chair for herself. 'He spent the night at Maggy's.'

All eyes swiveled my way. 'Why was that?' Henry asked.

'Amy kicked him out.' I could be honest, too.

'And Maggy is family,' Gloria reminded everybody. 'It's touching, really. Your long-lost cousin needed you.'

'But what happened?' Sophie asked. 'How did you lose him?'

'He was sleeping in Eric's room, but when I got up to go to work at five, he was gone.'

Henry frowned. 'But his car is right out front here.'

'I took it.'

Henry cocked his head, more disappointed than disapproving.

'It was blocking my car.'

I got a nod of understanding from him. 'Quite inconsiderate, given you were putting him up.'

'Exactly my thought,' I said.

'It begs the question, though, of where he went,' Henry continued. 'And on foot, apparently.'

'We don't know that.' Sophie was swirling her cappuccino. 'He could have requested an Uber or called a taxi.'

That hadn't occurred to me for some reason. Jacque certainly could have punched in a request from his room and tiptoed out to wait for the car. I pulled out my phone.

'Going to text Pavlik?' Sarah asked, coming up behind me.

I dipped my head. 'It's possible they didn't think of it either.'

'Doubtful,' Sophie said.

'Or they've already checked,' I continued.

'It's so nice that he doesn't mind you meddling in his business, dear,' Gloria said. 'Some men would, you know.'

'I know,' I said. 'I'm a lucky woman.'

'Did you think of something, Henry?' Amy asked.

The elderly gentleman was staring off into space. 'Oh, I'm sorry. No, I was picturing Maggy's house and possible routes he could have taken from there on foot.'

'Schultz's, of course,' Sophie said. 'To set the fire.'

'We thought of that,' Sarah said. 'But then where is he now?'

'Dead,' Sophie said.

Henry was exasperated. 'I'm trying to find alternatives, Soph. If he didn't start the fire – or even if he did, but didn't die in it – where would he be holding out now?'

'We checked my house,' Amy said before they could ask. 'He hasn't gone back there.'

'And with the police and fire presence,' I said, 'he certainly wouldn't go to the store.'

'Friends?' Henry asked.

'Denis and Helen, of course, but Denis isn't in town,' Amy said. 'And Helen says he hasn't been to their place.'

'What about the woods?' Henry suggested. 'Could he be hiding there?'

'The woods along Poplar Creek?'

The creek and its woods ran behind the properties on the west side of Poplar Creek Road, one of which was Brookhills Manor. My house was on the opposite side of the road. 'Why? Have you seen something?'

Henry frowned. 'No, I can't say I have. But I was awakened by dogs barking in the early hours this morning, which is what made me think about it.'

I picked up my phone again.

'What now?' Sarah inquired over my shoulder. 'You want Pavlik to drag the creek?'

I glanced at Amy's face and put the phone back down. 'Of course not.'

I'd tell him tonight.

ELEVEN

'I invited Amy to stay tonight,' I told Pavlik as he settled on to the couch that night. 'But she preferred to stay at her house in case Jacque showed up.'

'We could have told her if he did,' he said, rolling his head around as if his neck was bothering him. 'We're watching the place.'

'I figured you would be,' I said, giving his shoulder a rub. 'Did you get my text about whether Jacque might have called a taxi when he left? Or used an Uber?'

'I did, and we had checked it out, but it was a no-go. No pick-ups anywhere near our address, especially in the wee hours.'

'Speaking of wee hours, Henry said barking dogs woke him up early morning, as though somebody was in the woods behind the manor.'

'Then they're better watchdogs than our two,' Pavlik said, as Frank settled his big ol' head in the sheriff's lap. 'I can't believe they didn't wake up when Jacque left.'

'They hate him,' I said. 'Both of them peed on his tire. No small feat for Mocha.'

'That's my girl,' the sheriff said, as the chihuahua hopped up on the other side of him.

He patted my hands in thanks for the massage. 'I suppose Jacque could have crossed the road and disappeared into the woods. But why?'

'Don't know,' I said, shaking my head. 'None of this makes sense unless he did torch the shop. Which doesn't make sense either. He's not my favorite person, but I can't believe he laid there in Eric's room last night and decided to kill Paulette by burning down his own store.'

'I sure didn't see it coming,' Pavlik said. 'He was upset, depressed even, but I suggested consulting a lawyer because it would set his mind at ease. From what he said, the divorce is legal and there's nothing for him to stress about.'

'Assuming he told us the truth,' I said. 'But Paulette was only part of the problem.'

'The other being . . .'

'Schultz's money problems,' I said. 'Especially with Bright and Natural's entry into the market and Jamie Bright's attempted acquisition. For my money, I still prefer Jamie for this.'

'You can't choose who you want to be a killer and then hang the evidence on them. It doesn't work that way.'

'Unfortunately.' I sighed. 'Truthfully, I kind of like Jamie. And he is beyond good-looking. But he does have a motive.'

'Simply putting Jacque out of business? From what I hear, Bright will have no trouble doing that without burning down Schultz's.'

'You're probably right,' I said, plopping down next to Mocha. 'How about an inside job? Jacque is laying off staff and he only has a dozen employees to begin with.'

'A disgruntled worker, you're thinking? They usually show up with guns, not gas cans—' Pavlik broke off, shaking his head. 'I can't believe I just said that. "Usually" – like this kind of crap has become routine.'

'I know.' I chewed my lip. 'This feels more personal, doesn't it?'

'We're looking into Paulette Oui, née Badeaux,' Pavlik said. 'She flew into Milwaukee Wednesday afternoon.'

'And showed up at Schultz's Market on Thursday afternoon, which is when Becky called Amy, looking for Jacque.'

'And on Friday,' Pavlik said, rubbing Frank's ear, 'Jacque and Paulette see each other for the first time in years.'

I waggled my finger. 'Or so Jacque says.'

'From what you've reported, he was anything but happy to see her.'

'Yes.' Mocha batted my hand to scratch her belly, so I obliged. 'Yet Paulette had her suitcase with her and was obviously expecting to be put up for the night, if not necessarily above the grocery store.'

'You didn't get the impression that Jacque had planned for that.'

'Not at all.' I stopped scratching and got another bat from

the Chihuahua's tiny paw. 'He had a deer-in-the-headlights look.'

'I wonder if that was for your benefit,' Pavlik mused. 'He didn't expect you to be there when he saw Paulette.'

'That's true,' I said, sliding Mocha to him so he could take over scratching. 'Plus, I told him that Amy had sent me, which put him on the spot.' I hesitated. 'But even if he somehow had this Machiavellian plan to put Paulette in the flat and torch it, he couldn't be sure she would actually agree to stay there. In fact, my money would have been on her calling a cab and going to the Ritz.'

'We don't have a Ritz,' he said, 'but I get your point. Let's say Paulette being there is coincidence, and this is simple arson. Why start the fire in the flat?'

'Exactly,' I said, sitting forward. 'You'd set it in the store itself, where it could be blamed on a stove or overheated wiring or something. Why be so blatant?'

'Your guess is as good as mine.' He was rubbing a dog to each side of him now. 'Maybe better, because you know these people.'

'All I know right now is that I'm confused and tired,' I said, rubbing my own head. 'Want to go to bed?'

'It's eight thirty.'

'Good,' I said, standing up. 'Let's go before Jacque shows up.'

Jacque didn't appear in the night, of course. Nor had he shown up at Amy's by the looks of her on Sunday morning.

'Did you get any sleep at all?' I asked her as the bells on the front door jangled.

'Not much,' she said, as a man wearing a red baseball cap, red sneakers, cargo shorts and braces on both knees approached the counter. 'Good morning, Egbert. Are you off detecting?'

I hadn't recognized Becky's son in this particular get-up. 'Detecting for what?'

'Coins or whatever,' Egbert said. 'It keeps me busy and out of the house.'

'Was this a Helen suggestion?' I guessed.

'Absolutely.' He nodded to Amy, who was holding up a pot

of freshly brewed coffee, to pour him a to-go cup. 'If I work it right, I'm up and out before the she-monster awakes.'

'You're certainly embracing therapy with both hands,' I said.

He grinned. 'You bet I am. Haven't felt this good in' – he stopped to think – 'well, my whole life, actually.'

'That's . . . kind of sad,' I said, taking the cup Amy had filled and sliding it across the counter to him.

'Tragic, actually,' he said, getting out a cloth handkerchief to blow his nose. 'Damn spring allergies.'

'So where do you do this metal-detecting thing – what do you call it?'

'Dirt fishing,' he supplied. Hence his T-shirt of yesterday. 'And right now I'm searching along Poplar Creek.'

'That runs behind your house,' I said, as if he didn't already know it. 'Wouldn't you prefer being farther away from—'

'The evil one? Of course.' He took a sip to lower the level of the coffee and then crossed the room to the condiment cart by the door. 'But I'm trying to be methodical. Working my way upstream from Brookhills Manor, past our house to Christ Christian and beyond.'

'Brookhills Manor,' I repeated thoughtfully. 'You didn't happen to be in the woods behind the manor early yesterday morning, did you?'

'How early?'

I wrinkled my nose, thinking. 'I'm not sure. Henry Wested heard dogs barking in the early hours, but he didn't say when exactly.'

'That could have been me, I suppose,' Egbert says. 'I was out that way before dawn.'

'Before I saw you and your mom at the fire.'

'Yup. I went out early because I knew I had to take the old bat to work at Schultz's. Or at least I thought I did.'

'What does the fire mean for your mom's retirement?' I asked.

'I don't know,' he said, tipping cream into his cup. 'I might need to get a second hobby. Who knows how long it'll take to get Schultz's up and running again.'

'If ever.' A voice and then footsteps sounded from around the corner before Jamie Bright's freckled face appeared. 'The smoke damage alone will be significant, even if the flames didn't penetrate to the lower floors.'

He smiled at Amy. 'May I have a cappuccino, please? Dry.'

While Amy busied herself with Jamie's drink, I moved out from behind the service area to where Egbert was trying to fit the lid on his coffee.

'This metal detector,' I said, taking the cup and lid from him. 'What exactly can it find?'

'Metal.' His expression said *duh*, and then he relented. 'Coins, like I said, and cans, mostly. They say it can find gold, too, but I haven't seen any.'

'Here you go,' I said, handing him back his drink, lid properly seated. 'Find anything good ever?'

'You mean like hidden treasure?' he said, grinning. 'Nah.' His face changed. 'But I did come across some scraps of copper tubing and a catalytic converter in the woods behind the manor.'

'You've heard about the thefts?' I asked. 'Christ Christian had a robbery sometime Friday night – HVAC units.'

'This was Friday morning. By yesterday morning, it was gone. Maybe that's what the dogs Henry heard were barking at – somebody picking it up.'

'Did you report your find to anyone?'

'No.' He pulled his cap off and then repositioned it on his head. 'I was a little scared, to be honest. The last thing I want to do is run afoul of a gang of thieves in the woods.'

Afoul. Who knew Egbert had a flair for the dramatic? 'You think they're hiding their loot there?'

'Maybe, but I haven't found any other signs so far.' He shrugged. 'And to be honest, behind the manor is the last place I'd stash something. Those old folks don't miss a thing.' He gazed off dreamily. 'I'm going to put my mother in the manor someday. And she'll never, ever come out.'

'Good for you.' It probably wasn't the thing to say, but then what was?

'Maggy!' Amy beckoned me back to where I'd left her to serve her archenemy, Jamie Bright.

'Well, good dirt fishing,' I called to Egbert as he went to

the door, knee braces creaking. 'And give the sheriff a call about that catalytic converter, OK?'

I got a wave as the door closed behind him.

When I returned to the counter, Jamie and Amy were still waiting. 'I'm sorry to have abandoned you, Amy.'

'You have to hear what Jamie just told me. Tell her.'

I turned to the adorable, but perhaps evil, Jamie. 'Tell me.'

'Paulette came to see him,' Amy said before Jamie could open his mouth.

'She did? When?'

This time Jamie answered. 'Thursday morning.'

'Which was before she appeared at Schultz's,' Amy said, 'looking for Jacque.'

'Paulette flew into Mitchell International in Milwaukee on Wednesday afternoon,' I said. 'We don't know where she spent Wednesday night, but she came to see you first thing Thursday, Jamie? Why?'

Jamie ran a hand through his hair. 'She said she was Paulette Oui, Jacque's wife, and had heard that we'd made her husband an offer to buy Schultz's.'

'Sophie was right. She's a gold-digger,' Amy said, sliding Jamie's cappuccino to him before pulling down a latte mug, presumably for her own drink.

'But how could Paulette have heard about the offer?' I asked, watching Jamie.

He just shrugged. 'No idea. It's not like we made a secret of it, though.'

'But she was in Paris,' I said. 'Do you even have stores in France?'

'Not yet.' He hooked his thumbs in his jean pockets and rolled forward on the balls of his feet. 'But we are scouting locations, so it's entirely possible there was an article in one of the business publications.'

'See?' Amy asked, sliding the stainless-steel pitcher back under the frothing wand. 'That's why Paulette showed up here out of the blue. She probably heard about Bright and Natural because of their possible expansion to France. When she realized they were also moving into this area, she must have thought, "Hey! Isn't that where Jacque is?"'

'And where he owns a grocery store?' I frowned. 'Seems a bit of a stretch.'

'She could have been keeping tabs on him all this time.' About to pour steamed milk into her mug, she hesitated. 'I should ask Helen if they kept in touch.'

'That's right,' I said. 'Denis knew Paulette, too.'

Jamie was regarding us with disbelief. 'You people amaze me. There is something called the internet these days, and research companies. It's not hard to track somebody down if you have some basic information. Like a name as unusual as Jacque Oui, for example.'

I eyed him. Paulette said she'd been 'invited.' Had I jumped to a conclusion when I assumed it was Jacque who did the inviting? 'Jamie, did you track Paulette down and suggest she come here?'

Jamie, who had put some bills on the counter and picked up his cup, paused. 'Why in the world would I do that?'

'To apply pressure to Jacque,' I said. 'The first thing Paulette did upon arriving in town was come to see you. Was that just a coincidence?'

'As far as I know,' Jamie said.

But Amy was staring at me. 'So Paulette was invited, but maybe not by Jacque.'

'Maybe not.' I dipped my head, shamefaced.

She turned on Jamie. 'Because why would anyone want the woman here except to cause trouble for Jacque.'

Jamie just shrugged.

The man was being unnecessarily cagey for my taste, but maybe he succeeded in business by never showing his cards. 'What did Paulette say to you? Did she just show up in your office or did she make an appointment?'

He thought about that. 'She did have an appointment, though I don't know when she made it. You'd have to ask my secretary. I only know that I saw "Oui" on my calendar and wondered what it was about.'

'Were you disappointed when you saw it wasn't Jacque?' I asked.

'Disappointed?' He flip-flopped his head, making his tousled hair even more adorably tousled. 'More . . . intrigued, I think.'

'Snake.' Surprisingly, this came from Amy.

Jamie held up his hands. 'Jacque had already turned me down, and here comes this woman who says she's his wife and owns half the store. Can you blame me for being . . .'

'Intrigued?' I repeated. 'Did she offer to sell you her half?'

He set his cup back down on the counter and nodded. 'She did – if we could come to terms on price. I got the impression there was more to her than a pretty face and designer clothes.'

I'd gotten that impression myself. 'Did she mention the divorce?'

'Oddly enough, no,' he said, his eyes narrowing. 'Was there a divorce?'

'Yes,' Amy said, before I could. 'In Paris, years ago. She has no claim on Jacque's property.'

'Huh.' Jamie ran his finger up the to-go cup and waited a count before continuing. 'She seemed to think she did.'

Amy lifted her chin. 'She's wrong.'

'Maybe we should ask the husband, ex or not.' Jamie cocked his head curiously. 'Where is Jacque, anyway?'

'Out of town,' Amy said.

'I'm not sure I believe you.' Jamie Bright was studying Amy – not just the boyish charmer any more than Paulette was just a pretty face.

He turned to me. 'Does the sheriff know how the fire started and who the deceased are?'

'You tell me,' I said. 'You seem very well informed.'

'Because I know that you and the sheriff are engaged?' he asked. 'Or that two bodies were found?'

'Both, actually.'

'And both are common knowledge in Brookhills. But I admit I do my homework.'

'Information is power?' I asked.

'It is.' He reclaimed his dry cappuccino. 'And my information says odds are that Oui started the fire and died in it.'

He nodded toward Amy. 'If he and Paulette Oui were legally divorced, then Oui's assets will follow the intent of his will or state law. If they weren't divorced, both his and Paulette's wills will enter in.'

'Don't tell me you know what the "intent" of their wills are,' I said.

'I don't, but I do know who Schultz's corporate officers are.' He smiled, a big, boyish, trust-me grin. 'Not that it matters anymore. Schultz's Market, for all intents and purposes, is no more.'

'That makes you happy.' I felt sick to my stomach.

'Oh, I wouldn't say that. But I do love to save money.'

And Jamie Bright was gone.

TWELVE

'**B**astard,' Amy muttered. We were at the window, watching Jamie Bright stride toward Brookhill Road, where he hooked a left in the direction of Schultz's.

'Did he come here just to crow?' Amy continued. 'Tell me the love of my life was dead, an arsonist and a loser?'

I thought 'love of my life' was vastly overused, but whatever. 'I think he was fishing for information. Jamie doesn't know what happened any more than we do.'

'Unless he did it.' Amy turned. 'Why else is he heading toward Schultz's? He's returning to the scene of the crime.'

'We don't know he's even going there,' I protested. 'He could be going to the library; that's just across the street.'

'Mr Internet using the library?' She disappeared into the back, reappearing with my purse. 'You have to follow him.'

'I do?'

'Yes,' she said, pushing me toward the door. 'You'll be able to poke around at Schultz's much more easily than I can. You're the sheriff's woman.'

'Amy,' I said, wrinkling my nose. 'I like to think I'm my own woman.'

'I know that, but the deputies don't.' One last shove and I was out on to the porch. 'Or the fire investigators. Now go see what Jamie is up to.'

Tucking my purse under my arm, I jogged the half a block on Junction to Brookhill and turned left. Jamie was a full block ahead of me, still heading in the direction of Schultz's.

It was good of Amy to spring me loose to go to the crime scene, now that the hot spots had been extinguished and I might be able to nose around, as she said. I hoped Pavlik or somebody I knew would be there.

Jamie was crossing the intersection of Brookhill and

Pinecrest Roads. Schultz's was about half a block up Brookhill on that same side of the road, so I kicked up my speed a bit so I could see if Jamie met somebody at the site. To my surprise, he walked right past the fire-damaged store and the squad car and fire inspection vehicles parked in front of it, and kept going.

'Where are you headed, Jamie?' I said under my breath.

I had my answer less than half a block later. 'The 501 Building. Of course.'

The 501 was the only true office tower in town, its ten stories tying it for highest building in Brookhills with the Hotel Morrison a few blocks further east on Brookhill Road. My ex-husband Ted kept his dental practice, Thorsen Dental, on the tenth floor of the 501, but I had lost track of what else was in the building now.

Slowing as I approached, I crept up to the glass door and watched as Jamie Bright stepped into an elevator. I couldn't see the floor numbers from where I was, so when the elevator closed, I gave the door a tug, hoping to get inside in time to see where the elevator car stopped.

'Damn.' It was Sunday. Of course, the building would be locked. But just in case, I gave the door another, harder pull. And a jiggle.

'Breaking and entering again?' a voice behind me asked.

I whirled around to see Ted, his office key in his hand. 'Open, quick.'

He just looked at me.

'Please.'

'Good to see you, too.' Ted had the same sandy hair that Jamie Bright did, but Ted truly was a good guy. Despite the cheating and all.

Once inside, I dashed to the bank of elevators to watch the numbers flash above the car Jamie had taken. Luckily, it was a high-ish one.

'Ninth floor.' I turned to Ted. 'I'm sorry. I just wanted to see where Jamie Bright was going.'

'Ninth floor.'

'Yes.' I nodded to the lighted numbers, now starting to move back down. 'As we both saw.'

Ted pointed to the second line of the lobby's building directory: *Bright Industries 9th Floor.*

'Guess I should just have asked you.'

'Wouldn't have been half the fun, though,' Ted said, with a grin.

'Yes, well, thanks.' I punched his shoulder. 'How are you doing? And why are you here on a Sunday?'

'Mia left her Flopsy in my office yesterday. Last night was a nightmare.'

'You know a girl can't sleep without her stuffed rabbit.' Mia was Ted's two-year-old daughter with his new ex-wife. Rachel was serving twenty to life in the county jail. (I said Ted was a good guy, just not necessarily a good picker. Except for me, of course.)

'I do,' Ted said. 'And she's with her Uncle Stephen, before you ask. And, yes, I'll be sure to bring her by sometime.'

'Thank you and thank you,' I said. 'How long has Bright Industries been in the building?'

'Enough with the pleasantries, huh?'

I smiled. 'You ran through all my small talk with Uncle Stephen and you're bringing her by. Oh, wait. There's also "Have you talked to your son lately?"'

'Yesterday,' Ted said. 'And Jamie Bright has had an office here since Bright and Natural was just an eponymous glint in his eye.'

'Really?' I said, frowning. 'I don't remember that.'

'It was tiny – not much more than a closet door with a brass plate on it. Then last year Bright and Natural took over the ninth floor.'

'I assume he has a secretary?' Jamie thought Paulette had made an appointment with his secretary. Or so he said.

'Wanda,' Ted confirmed, pushing the elevator button. 'Nice woman.'

'I don't suppose you saw a chic brunette with Louboutin pumps and a camel handbag come through the lobby on Thursday morning.'

'Must have missed her,' Ted said, with an amused grin. 'I was probably wrist-deep in gum disease.'

'Pity,' I said, shaking my head. 'You are single again.'

'And going to stay that way,' Ted assured me. 'Once bitten, twice shy.'

'I hope that you're counting Rachel as the one bite, not me.'

'Yup,' Ted said, punching the button again. 'Our marriage was pretty damned good before I screwed it up.'

'You're right about that,' I said, patting his cheek. 'But look on the bright side.'

'You mean Mia?' he asked. 'Or was that your segue to another Jamie Bright question?'

'I did mean Mia,' I said. 'But since you brought him up, what is your take on Jamie?'

Ted rubbed his chin. 'Pleasant enough, but maybe a little ambitious for my taste. I wouldn't be surprised if he comes after my tenth-floor suite next year when our leases are up for renewal.'

'But you've rented that office for almost twenty years,' I said, as the elevator reached the lobby. 'The 501 owners wouldn't do that to you, would they?'

'If Bright applied enough pressure, maybe.' Ted shrugged. 'But as for me, I have more important things to worry about than relocating my entire business.'

'Finding Flopsy?' I guessed.

'You got it.' He stepped into the elevator car and pressed ten.

I was smiling as I walked back toward Schultz's, feeling lucky to have an ex like Ted, as betrayed as I was when he cheated on me. As it turned out, Rachel was a master manipulator and Ted had been masterfully manipulated. No excuse, of course, but in my view, he had been punished enough.

I just hoped Mia took after Ted and not her mother or else the Flopsy debacle was going to look like small potatoes compared to her teen years.

'What are you smiling about?' Pavlik was standing outside Schultz's sliders.

'Just hoping nurture and stuffed bunnies can overcome nature,' I said.

Pavlik considered. 'Should I understand what that means?'

'Probably not,' I said. 'I was just coming back from Ted's office and saw you here. Thought I'd stop by.'

'Good try, but I saw you going in the opposite direction stalking Jamie Bright like you were Wile E. Coyote.'

I grimaced. 'I was trying for casual surveillance.'

'Then don't run next time,' he advised.

'Noted.' I rocked on to my toes to kiss his cheek. 'I honestly thought Jamie was coming here.'

'Returning to the scene of the crime. You still think he set the fire?'

'I would love that to be true.' I was trying to see through the glass door panels, but the ash from the blaze had coated them. 'Was the fire contained to the upper floor or—?'

'Are you asking to look inside?'

'If it's permitted,' I said.

'I'll permit it,' Pavlik said, sliding the door open manually for me. 'If the fire investigator says anything, you're a detective.'

'Got it.' I glanced sideways at him as he joined me inside. 'Gloria Goddard said it's nice that you don't mind me meddling in your business. You don't, do you?'

'Nope.' Then he thought about it. 'That's not strictly true. There was a time when—'

'Your deputies were teasing you.' I was looking off toward the back of the store where I could make out the gaping hole in the ceiling.

'I'm not sure I'd use the word "teasing." I am the boss, and all.' Pavlik waved for me to precede him. 'But, yeah. I let it get to me.'

'And you don't now?' I hoped.

'Nope.' He pointed toward the hole where I'd seen the firefighter raise the ladder. 'That corresponds to the area just inside the door to the flat.'

'Where the accelerant was poured.' And the fire had burned completely through the floorboards at some point, making it impossible to get to the door. 'Why not?'

'Why not, what?' He was picking his way through fallen ceiling tiles and fluorescent light panels to the area beneath the hole.

'Why doesn't it bother you now?'

He turned to face me. 'Because you're smart. As smart –

smarter – than any of the people who were hazing me. And you also know this town and the people in it. You understand human nature. And now that you understand the rules I have to operate under, you're careful.'

'Thank you. I—' Luxuriating in the praise, I walked straight into the extension ladder resting on its side, knocking it over.

'Careful,' Pavlik said, steadying me.

'Thanks.' I pointed at the ladder. 'Is this the only way up?'

'The firefighters were using the ladder truck to access the flat from the alley,' Pavlik said. 'But with the floor burned through now, this is it.'

'Can we—' I was tugging at the ladder.

'We cannot,' he said. 'It's not safe. The beams and floor-boards have been burned through or weakened by the water, so unless you know where to step . . .' He shrugged.

'You end up right back down here,' I said. 'The bodies are in the morgue, I assume?'

'They are.'

'Was Paulette's found just short of this area?' I asked, peering up into the hole. There were other holes, these in the roof, allowing outside light in from above.

'Yes. She may have heard something and run toward the door. But the accelerant covered the floor and was already in flames, so she would have been forced back.'

How horrible. 'The flat is just one floor up, though the ceiling of the store is quite high, isn't it?' I was eyeing the distance. 'Would you say twelve feet?'

'More like fifteen.'

'Even so, why didn't Paulette – or they – jump out of a window? If you dangled from the windowsill and then dropped, you might land with nothing worse than a sprained ankle or broken leg.'

'That's an excellent question, though I think it sounds easier than it would be under these circumstances. As for why they didn't try, an autopsy should show whether they died from smoke inhalation, burns or something else altogether.'

'You're saying that one or both of them could have been dead or incapacitated somehow before the fire started?'

'It's possible,' Pavlik said. 'The other variable, as far as the windows are concerned, is that it's an old building. The windows on the main floor here have been eliminated or just boarded over to allow shelving on all the walls.'

'They couldn't eliminate the windows upstairs,' I said. 'Building code requires an egress window in any bedroom.'

'That doesn't mean they weren't painted shut or just plain stuck.'

'Then you break the glass.'

'Then *you* would break the glass,' Pavlik said. 'I'm just saying that sometimes buildings aren't properly maintained. And people panic in the moment or are too timid, afraid of getting cut by the glass.'

And so die in a fire instead. 'I don't see Paulette as too timid.'

'Tell me about her,' Pavlik said, waving me over to the pharmacy area of the shop where chairs remained set up as a waiting area for prescription orders.

'Paulette was very pretty and stylish,' I said, taking a molded plastic seat. 'But she was also clever. I'd say wily, even.'

'Wily.' Pavlik grinned and took the chair next to me. 'Do tell.'

I warmed to my subject. 'When Jamie Bright stopped by the shop this morning, he told us that Paulette came to see him on Thursday morning, before she arrived here looking for Jacque.'

'Why would she do that?'

'She had heard that Bright offered to buy Jacque out.'

Pavlik got it in one. 'And, being his wife, she wanted part of the action?'

'Exactly. If Jacque lied – or simply messed up – and he and Paulette are still married—'

'She would likely be entitled to half of everything he owns, including Schultz's.'

'I don't know how she knew about the deal – or potential deal,' I said, 'but she told me she was invited to come here.'

'And now you think it was by Jamie Bright?'

'It's possible, right? Jamie took great delight in telling Amy and me about Paulette's visit. He also talked about Jacque's will and said there were corporate officers he could deal with, presumably in lieu of Jacque.'

'He's saying all this in front of Amy?' Pavlik asked. 'That's pretty cold.'

'He said outright that he thinks Jacque is dead. And that Schultz's is unsalvageable.' I shook my head. 'It's like he's playing all angles.'

'So how do Paulette's death and the fire figure into his plan?'

'For one thing, now there's no need for Jamie to buy Schultz's out at all. The building is damaged, meaning Schultz's is closed at a really vulnerable time – when Bright and Natural is moving into the market. Bright and Natural will have gotten a real foothold in the community, even if Jacque can eventually reopen.'

'That's assuming he's still alive.'

'Still no sign of him?' I asked. 'Or has the body been—'

Pavlik shook his head. 'No. We haven't found Jacque alive, nor can we confirm the body is his yet.'

'Did I tell you last night that Henry—'

'Thought somebody was in the woods early Saturday morning? You did, and we've expanded our search, but there's no reason to believe it was Jacque.'

'It might be something else altogether,' I said eagerly. 'Egbert—'

'Egbert?'

'You know Becky, the cashier from Schultz's. Egbert is her son. They live across the street from us. He's taken up metal detecting or what he calls dirt fishing . . . What?'

'Nothing. I'm listening. Intently.'

Hmm. 'Anyway, he told me he found a catalytic converter in the woods along Poplar Creek behind Brookhills Manor on Friday morning. Some scraps of copper tubing, too.'

'Catalytic converters have some copper, like the HVAC units, but also other more precious metals like rhodium, palladium and platinum. They're selling for a couple of hundred dollars on up – over a thousand, for ones stolen off hybrid vehicles.'

'Sounds easier than stealing air-conditioning equipment to me. Or copper pipes and gutters.'

'It is, which is why we're seeing more of it,' Pavlik said. 'You say this was behind the manor?'

'Yes, but it was all gone yesterday morning. I told him he should have reported it, but he said he was scared.'

Pavlik lifted one eyebrow. 'I hope he's not doing this "metal detecting" at night.'

'He straps on his knee braces and heads out in the wee hours of the morning, from the sounds of it. He's using it as an excuse to get away from his mother.'

'Understandable. Becky Ronstadt was here earlier, haranguing us about when the store can open. She wanted to know if she's being paid for the time it's closed.'

'She's retiring at the end of June, so just another three weeks or so.'

'She also asked about unemployment,' Pavlik said dryly. 'I referred her to the state.'

'That will teach her.' I got up and brushed off my jeans. 'There's a lot of water and smoke damage down here, isn't there?'

He nodded. 'The weight of the water from fighting the fire is probably going to take down a good portion of the ceiling, and the rest will have to be torn out.'

'I suppose Jacque can salvage a lot of the equipment,' I said, looking at the aisle of freezers and refrigeration units. 'The food?'

'The electricity was shut off, so anything perishable has already—'

'Perished?'

'Exactly,' Pavlik said, following me.

'And anything that's not perishable will be damp or' – I picked up a box of pasta and sniffed – 'smell of smoke.'

'You said Amy is working at the shop today?'

'She is, and I probably should get back.' I glanced at the back door. 'Can we take a peek at the alley first?'

'Sure.' Pavlik gave the panic bar a shove and the door swung open.'

'Eeeeewwwwwt!'

THIRTEEN

'Molly?'

Molly Durand had her hand to her heart. 'Oh my God. You two scared me to death.'

'You scared *us* to death,' I said. 'I thought we'd killed a screech owl. What are you doing back here?'

Pavlik was frowning. 'This is a crime scene.'

A uniformed deputy came running up behind Molly. 'Sorry, sir, I just stepped away for a minute to use the facilities.' He was bright red. 'She said she would stay where she was.'

'Which was chatting with you.'

The deputy turned even redder.

'You remember Molly?' I asked Pavlik, knowing full well he did.

'I do,' he said. 'I just don't remember why she would be mucking around in a dangerous area where she has no business.'

'I . . . I was working at Clare's and got bored.'

'Good one,' I said. 'But Clare's isn't open on Sunday.'

She sighed. 'OK, so I'm bored. This fire is the most exciting thing to happen here in like years.'

She pointed up toward the burned-out gap where the door used to be. 'Were there stairs leading up there?'

'There were,' I said. 'Wooden, so they burned quickly, I'm sure.'

'Was that where the fire started, then?' Her eyes were big. 'The door?'

'The mail slot,' I said. 'Somebody poured an accelerant—'

I turned to Pavlik. 'Do we know what it was?'

'Remember what I said about understanding the rules?' he asked pleasantly. 'I take it all back. Will you escort Molly out now? Please.'

Uh-oh.

'Sorry,' I whispered as I passed him. 'It's just that I like to nurture youthful inquisitiveness.'

'No, you don't,' Pavlik whispered back. 'You see a Mini-You in her.'

Ouch. Playing off Mini-Me in the Austin Powers movies. And maybe true.

'Sorry,' I said again as Pavlik's phone buzzed and he turned to answer it. 'Come on, Molly. Let's go out this way.'

We passed by Schultz's delivery truck, and the odor of burned rubber from the old tire next to it made me wrinkle my nose. A pile of water-soaked ashy remnants marked where the wooden pallets had been. Molly was subdued, but when we reached Pinecrest Avenue, she stopped and looked back. 'It must have been horrible, dying like that.'

'They may have died of smoke inhalation before the fire ever reached them, but . . . yeah.' I was being careful not to mention the other possibility Pavlik had cited – that the two had been hurt or even killed before the fire was set.

'I knew there were two bodies, you know,' she said. 'It was in the news today that it was a man and a woman, but I already deduced it was two people yesterday when you misspoke. You denied it.' Her tone was accusatory.

'I neither confirmed nor denied.'

'Because I'm a kid.'

'Because the sheriff hadn't released the information yet,' I told her. 'It wasn't up to me to tell you.'

'Fine,' she said. 'But just so you know, you can tell me all the gory details. I'm not squeamish or anything.'

I wondered how her mother would feel about that. Not that I had anything I could or would tell her. 'I don't think it pays to think too much about this stuff.'

'What stuff?' she asked.

'Like imagining how they died, and all,' I said uncomfortably. 'This isn't a movie or game.'

'I know.' She shuddered. 'But dying in a fire has to be just about the worst way to go, right?'

I hooked an arm around her shoulders and tugged her in the direction of Brookhill Road. 'Have you ever heard that the man who fears death dies a thousand deaths?'

'That's Shakespeare – Julius Caesar – and it's quoted wrong a lot,' she countered.

She really was like me. Annoying.

'The real quote,' she continued, 'is "A coward dies a thousand times before his death, but the valiant taste of death but once."'

'Very good. I like quotations.'

'I do, too,' she said and flashed a grin. 'When they're quoted correctly.'

I smiled back at her. 'I think of that, in some form, when I worry about things that haven't happened yet.'

'Or,' she said, giving a little skip to her step, 'things that are going to happen one way or the other anyway.'

'Like death?'

'I'm not thinking about my dying,' she said. 'Just what it would feel like to be trapped in a fire. What I would do. Wouldn't you jump?' We had turned on to Brookhill and were passing by the front of the store and its parking lot. 'It's not that high up.'

'I asked the same thing,' I admitted, eyeing the two upstairs windows that faced the street. The glass in both had been broken out, presumably to vent the fire. 'But they don't know at this point. The autopsy might show that they died from the smoke, like I said, and didn't have a chance to get out. The man might even have died in his sleep.'

'Mr Oui,' she said.

'We don't know that either,' I said, a little sharply.

She glanced sideways at me. 'But it has to be him, doesn't it? I heard Amy and my mom talking about how this Paulette was his wife. Who else would be up there with her?'

'I don't know,' I admitted.

'I called my dad last night,' she said. 'To tell him about the fire. We didn't talk long because he wanted to call Mr Oui.'

His friend's store had burned down. Of course, Denis would want to call him. 'Do you know if your dad got hold of Jacque?'

'No,' she said, studying the sidewalk as we went. 'Maybe Mom knows. If he didn't, by now he's probably heard there's a second body and is worried sick.'

'Don't get ahead of what we know,' I said.

'But why aren't they at least identifying the woman yet?' she asked, looking up. 'It's got to be the wife, right?'

'Ex-wife,' I said. 'But the body is badly burned. They'll need to do the autopsy and make a formal identification.'

'Plus notify family, right?'

'Right. Your dad knew Paulette back when she and Jacque were married, I think. Do you know if they were still in touch?'

We were just approaching the corner of Brookhill and Junction Road. Molly stopped and swung around to face me. 'I don't know. Why?'

Because I still wasn't sure how Paulette knew Jacque was living in Brookhills. I just shrugged. 'He might know her family in France. As you said, the sheriff will have to notify them.'

'Oh, good thought,' she said.

'When's your dad coming home?'

'Tonight, I think,' she said. 'Or maybe it's tomorrow, I'm not sure.'

'Let me know if he's heard from Jacque. And if he knows anything about Paulette's family, for that matter.'

Molly smiled. 'Should he just call the sheriff?'

Brat. 'I can pass it on to him.'

'Sure.' Molly was still smiling as she pulled her car key out of her pocket. 'I'll tell him.'

'Is this you?' I pointed to the battered white Volvo parked on the street.

'Yeah. My mom and dad say it's a safe car. Kind of stodgy, though.' She pushed the unlock on her key fob and the car tweeted.

'Safe is good,' I said. 'The first few months are the most dangerous for a new driver.'

'Don't I know it,' she said, going around to get into the driver's seat. 'It's like I'm an accident magnet the last two years.' She was already getting out her cell phone as she closed the car door.

'No text—' I broke off as my phone rang.

Probably grateful to escape a lecture, Molly started the car and was off with a wave before I hit the slide to accept the call.

'Hi, Pavlik.'

'Still with Molly?'

'She just left,' I told him. 'What's up?'

'Can you meet me in the parking lot behind Brookhills Manor?'

'Sure.' I was frowning at the phone. 'But why?'

Pavlik hesitated on the other end. 'I'd like to confirm something with you before I get anybody else involved.'

'But—'

'Are you at Uncommon Grounds?'

'No. I'm standing on Brookhill Road, just about to turn the corner to the shop. Amy's manning the counter alone.'

'Hopefully she can for another few minutes,' Pavlik said. 'Come directly here, OK? Don't say anything to Amy or anybody else.'

My mind was going a hundred miles an hour. Had Jacque been found? 'Sure. Is it—'

'Maggy!' Pavlik cut me off. 'Just come. I'm here with your metal detector.'

'Egbert,' I said, relieved. 'I know he's a little nerdy, but I did tell him to call you about the catalytic converter. Did he find something—?' I was thinking body, of course. I always thought body. 'I'm sorry,' I interrupted myself before Pavlik replied. 'I'll be right there.'

'Thanks.'

As I made my way past Brookhills Manor's mechanical equipment and into the back employee parking lot, an ambulance passed me, coming in without lights and siren. Pavlik's squad car was parked at the far corner of the lot next to industrial-sized garbage and recycle bins. He must have been called out as soon as he left Molly and me to have gotten here so fast. A crime scene van and fire truck were already parked next to the squad and the ambulance joined them.

This was not the turnout for a stolen catalytic converter. Or a stolen anything.

Pavlik was standing by the squad and waved me over. Just beyond the bins was the woods, and I could see yellow-and-black crime scene tape tied to the trees, blocking access. As

I joined the sheriff, I felt eyes on me and turned to see Sophie and Gloria at the back door of the manor with binoculars. They waved.

'Hard to keep anything quiet here,' I said to Pavlik.

'Don't I know it,' he said, lifting the crime scene tape. 'It's more the who, rather than the what, I'd like to keep under wraps until we're sure.'

'Jacque?' I asked, following him through the trees toward a cluster of people by the creek. 'Did Egbert find him? But then who—' I stopped.

On the ground was a red baseball cap turned upside down with a pair of glasses carefully placed in it.

And beyond, Egbert Ronstadt lay on his back, a trickle of blood down his chin and a dark red halo surrounding his head.

FOURTEEN

'There's no way he would shoot himself,' I told Pavlik a second time.

'But can you confirm this is Egbert Ronstadt?' Pavlik asked.

'Yes,' I said, rocking up on to my toes to get a better look over the backs of the forensics people crouched around the deceased. 'But I just saw him at Uncommon Grounds. He was happy. Talking about putting his mother in an old folks' home.'

Pavlik didn't address that directly. 'You mentioned the knee braces this morning, so I was fairly certain it was Ronstadt. I wanted to be sure before we informed his mother.'

'Becky will have a heart attack.' And wouldn't that be cruel irony after all these years? Egbert dies and his mother follows him right over to the promised land, calling his name.

'I think she's made of pretty stern stuff,' Pavlik said. 'But nobody wants to bury a child. No matter how old he is.'

I was looking around. A backpack and the remains of a campfire were nearby, and a young crime scene tech was examining what looked like a rifle. 'Does that rifle have a satellite dish and a touchscreen?' I asked.

'It's a metal detector.' The tech straightened. 'A really good one – maybe a grand or two.'

'Seems like overkill for the kind of junk you'd find here,' another white-suited man offered as he passed by. 'Those are made to find gold, not quarters and beer cans.'

But I'd moved on from the metal detector. 'He was shot, right? So where is the gun?'

'Here.' Pavlik held up an evidence bag. 'Nine-millimeter ghost gun.'

A ghost gun is an unregistered pistol that could be bought anonymously on the internet and assembled at home.

'He didn't have either of these with him this morning in the shop.' I pointed at the metal detector and the backpack.

'He must have left them outside on the porch or maybe in his car.'

'Take a quick look in the backpack,' Pavlik instructed the young tech. 'Then bag it and we'll go through it in detail back in the lab.'

'Who found him?' I asked.

'A maintenance worker at the manor was taking out the trash. He smelled smoke and called the fire department.'

'This fire was burning when they arrived?' I asked, wandering over to nudge a thick charred branch with the toe of my sneaker.

'Yes. Easy enough to put out. And then they found Egbert.'

I turned back to him, confused. 'Why would he have started a fire? It's June.'

'I wondered the same thing. He wasn't cooking anything on it, apparently. Or heating water for coffee.'

'No, Egbert bought coffee at Uncommon Grounds earlier. Did you find an empty to-go cup?'

Pavlik looked to the lab tech, who had returned to us. 'No, unless he burned it in the fire,' he said.

I wrinkled my nose. 'Cardboard cup, but with a plastic top. You'd have found that melted.'

'No sign of that. But hang on a second.' He jogged off.

'Maybe he finished the coffee before he got here,' Pavlik said. 'Or left it in the car.'

The tech was back holding a crushed to-go cup. 'It was in the backpack. He must have stashed it there to throw away later.'

'And then shot himself before he had a chance.' I shook my head. 'Does that make sense?'

The tech shrugged. 'He knew somebody would throw it away.'

'I suppose.' It might be logical that a man who had placed his hat and glasses so carefully wouldn't just toss trash in the woods.

'From what he told me, this is where – or at least near where – he found the catalytic converter and copper,' I told Pavlik as the lab tech moved away. 'Maybe he came back to take another look after we spoke and stumbled on the thieves.'

'And they shot him and left the murder weapon?'

'Why not? They were hoping we'd believe it was suicide.'

'We're not sure it isn't,' Pavlik said. 'But maybe there was more to Egbert than was apparent.'

'There'd almost have to be,' I said. 'He lived a pretty miserable existence.'

Pavlik sucked in a deep breath and then let it out. 'OK. I need to inform Becky.'

'Want me to come along?' I offered, following him toward the squad car.

'I would, but I think it's best kept official,' he said. 'Besides, she intimidates me, and I don't want you to witness that.'

'Understood,' I said. 'Just know that she's going to blame you, him and the universe. But underneath it all, she'll be devastated.'

'I know.' He stopped at his car and turned. 'You never get used to this.'

'I know.' I tippy-toed kissed him. 'Because you're a good man.'

'Thanks,' he said, opening the car door.

I'd started away and now I turned back to him. 'Will you do me a favor?'

'What's that?' He paused with his hand on the steering wheel.

I blushed. 'It's possible you already do this, as a matter of routine, but—'

'What?'

'Test the wood in the fire – what's left of it, I mean – for blood. There were some good-sized pieces. I don't think it burned for long.'

'That fire is bothering you, isn't it?' He swung back out of the car to return to the woods. 'Me, too.'

Instead of retracing my steps through the manor's parking lot to the street, I walked north along the edge of the woods to the railroad tracks and followed the rail bed to the depot. The route had the added advantage of avoiding Sophie and Gloria.

I was all for milking *them* for information, but in this case, I'd be the cow.

'My God,' Amy said when I stepped in. 'Where exactly did you follow Jamie to? Michigan?'

'I'm sorry,' I said, collapsing into a chair. 'But you wouldn't believe what's going on.'

'No, I wouldn't,' she said, her tone clipped. 'Because I've been here. By myself. Covering for you.'

'You're sounding like Sarah,' I told her.

'I'd take that as a compliment,' Sarah said, coming from around the corner.

'I do,' Amy said, folding her arms. 'Because Sarah, at least, came and helped me out.'

'Did you call her?' I asked.

'I stopped in to get the news of the world,' Sarah said.

'Good. I have news, so everybody will be happy,' I said.

Amy glanced up at the clocks. 'Two o'clock. We close at three on Sunday, so we have one hour and then I'm going home and you're closing. Deal?'

'Deal.' I was closing alone so often lately I was getting good at it. 'Now I really need a latte.'

'You know where the espresso machine is,' Amy said, sitting down with one she'd apparently just made for herself.

Sarah was behind the bakery case. 'We have two sticky buns left.'

'One for me and one for you, Sarah,' Amy said. 'You've earned it.'

Guess I was being schooled.

'Fine,' I said, getting up. 'I'll make my latte and then I'll tell you who Pavlik just found dead.'

A gasp, and I turned to see Amy's face go pale.

'Oh, I'm so sorry, Amy,' I said, returning to the table. 'It's not Jacque. He's fine – well, I don't know he's fine. But he's not the body.'

Sarah was standing with a sticky bun in each hand, eyeing me. 'You're making a mess of this.'

'You think?' I held up both of my hands. 'Please let me make a coffee. And then I'll tell all.'

And I did.

*   *   *

When I finished, Amy was as bewildered as I had felt. 'I don't get it. Why would Egbert kill himself?'

'We don't know that he did,' Sarah said. 'Seems more likely these thieves knew he saw them and waited for him to come back.'

'But why would he go back?' I asked. 'He said everything was gone by yesterday morning.'

'But there was another robbery,' Amy said. 'The one at Christ Christian. Maybe he thought the robbers would return to stash the HVAC units there and went to see.'

'It would be the perfect spot,' Sarah said, taking a piece of sticky bun. 'That parking lot is used mainly by employees. The thieves could have driven their truck or whatever back there and unloaded the loot practically into the woods.'

'But why and when?' I asked. 'The Christ Christian robbery was sometime Friday night into Saturday morning, because the police were there when Amy came in at five. The thieves would have to have dumped the stuff after the robbery and also after Egbert was there.' I was stirring my latte vigorously. 'But the real question is why? You already presumably have the units on a truck. Why would you take them off and hide them in the woods where you'd have to get another truck and move them again? Why not just take them to your buyer?'

'Because they were going to strip the copper in the woods?' Sarah guessed.

'Possible,' I said, 'but—'

'You're missing the point, Maggy,' Amy said impatiently. 'It's not about what the thieves actually did, but what Egbert thought they might do.'

I took a beat to digest that. 'Oh, of course. All we really care about is why Egbert was there. The rest is supposition.'

'Except we're supposing that the thieves were also there and killed him,' Sarah reminded us with her mouth full.

'He did say he was scared.'

'Yet he went back into the woods,' Amy said. 'Why?'

'Spend time with Becky. Bust criminal gang,' Sarah said. 'Which would you rather do?'

'You think Egbert was getting a thrill out of playing detective? I can see that.' I pointed at her plate. 'You going to eat it?'

Sarah popped the last piece of sticky bun in her mouth.
'Yup.'

'You can have mine, Maggy,' Amy said, shoving her plate
over to me.

I tore off a chunk. 'Thanks.'

'What bothers you about the campfire?' Amy asked. 'Besides
the fact it's a warm day.'

I waited until I swallowed to reply. 'It just seems that one
of those branches would make a good weapon. And they didn't
burn long enough to destroy evidence.'

'But what about the gun?' Amy asked, surprised. 'I thought
he was shot, and the gun was found there.'

'He was and it was,' I said. 'But . . . that fire. Why?'

'Easy,' Sarah said. 'They were burning something else in
it. Papers or whatever.'

'And Egbert came upon them?' I was rubbing my forehead.
'Not a bad thought.'

'It's a great thought,' Sarah said. 'And as for your burned
tree branch as a murder weapon – are you sure you're not
being misled because you think that's cool? Like the icicle.
Or the leg of lamb.'

'The absolute best,' I said, and then in answer to Amy's quiz-
zical look, 'You stab somebody with an icicle and then it melts.'

'Or bash in somebody's head with a frozen leg of lamb,'
Sarah continued. 'And cook it for dinner.'

'Eaten by the police, as I recall.'

'These are stories?' Amy asked.

'The lamb one is a short story by Roald Dahl,' I told her.
'You know, he wrote *Charlie and the Chocolate Factory* and
James and the Giant Peach. I don't know where the icicle one
is from.'

'Me neither,' Sarah said. 'It is genius, though.'

'It really is,' Amy echoed, for once not seeming bothered
by our meanderings.

But now I sighed. 'However Egbert died, it doesn't get
us any closer to finding Jacque.' I put my hand on Amy's.
'There's no connection I can see.'

'Everybody thinks he's dead,' she said quietly. 'That he's
the man in the fire.'

'Look on the bright side,' Sarah said. 'If Jacque died in the fire, he's not hiding in the woods killing people.'

Amy rubbed her eyes. 'I can't shake the feeling that none of this is real. First Kip Fargo is killed and now Jacque.'

She did have bad luck with fiancés. 'We don't know that Jacque is dead.'

A tap on the door.

'Hello?' Helen Durand stuck her head in.

'Oh, Helen,' Amy exclaimed and jumped up.

She collapsed into her therapist's arms, sobbing.

FIFTEEN

'I guess it just sank in,' Sarah said to me. 'I thought we were doing pretty well.'

'When you told her it would be good if Jacque was dead so he couldn't kill more people?'

'I believe I said to look on the bright side. If.' She resettled herself in the chair. 'And don't tell me you haven't thought about what Jacque faces if he *isn't* dead.'

Prison for arson and murder, most likely. 'I have,' I admitted. 'But I don't say it—' I held up a hand as she opened her mouth. 'Or if I do, I couch it better.'

'Couch, smouch,' my partner said. 'Amy's not stupid. She can take the truth.'

'And Helen is her therapist.'

'For like half a second.'

'You're jealous.' I glanced at Amy and Helen, who'd taken a table. 'I wish we had wine here.'

'Top shelf of the storeroom by the cups.'

The red wine looked a little muddy, but beggars can't be choosers. At least I'd poured it into nice glass latte mugs, instead of to-go cups.

Helen's hand was resting on Amy's. 'Molly was telling me about this second body in the fire. That it's a man.' She glanced at Amy.

'We don't know who it is,' I said. 'But Jacque is still missing.'

Helen frowned. 'But he must have come here certainly. His Peugeot is parked in front.'

I really had to move that damn car. 'He didn't. I took the Peugeot to work because it was blocking mine in the garage.'

'Has Denis heard from him?' Amy asked her. 'Or you?'

'No,' Helen said, shaking her head. 'I've tried him a couple of times, but the calls went immediately to voicemail.'

'As if he turned the phone off,' I said.

'Or was dead,' was Sarah's contribution. 'What?' she said when we all looked at her. 'I meant the battery.'

'Believe me,' Amy said, 'Jacque being dead is all I think about. Or his not being dead. I'm not sure which will be worse for him.'

Sarah and I exchanged looks.

'What's the theory, then?' Helen asked, as her phone buzzed. She checked it and turned it over, muting the bell. 'Jacque got up during the night and went to see Paulette? It's not so unimaginable, I suppose. But why would he leave his car?'

'It's just a twenty-minute walk,' I said. 'We theorized he didn't want to wake us up.'

'More likely he didn't want anybody to know where he was.' Amy's arms were folded against her. 'With her.'

'It's not like that, I don't think,' Helen told her. 'From everything that either Jacque or Denis have told me, Paulette nearly destroyed Jacque. He would never take her back.'

Amy sniffled. 'She nearly destroyed him how?'

'They were very young – just out of university,' Helen said. 'But there was more to it than just growing apart. Paulette apparently always drank too much.'

I had lifted my glass of wine and now set it back down.

A trace of a smile from Helen. 'I know. And fresh out of college, they all liked a drink back then. Paulette, Jacque, Denis, his first wife and his younger brother, too. But the story was that Paulette got Gabriel into harder stuff – crack cocaine.' She shifted her shoulders.

I'd heard some of this, at least, from Henry. 'I understand Denis's first wife died?'

'Yes, in childbirth,' Helen says. 'Denis doesn't want Molly to think it's her fault, so we don't talk about it. I think that's a little silly, but . . .' She shrugged.

'Jacque said Gabriel died of a drug overdose,' Amy said.

'Yes, whoever started whom on crack, it was Gabriel who ended up dead.'

And Paulette who ended up coming here. 'Is it possible that Paulette left Jacque for Gabriel?'

Helen dipped her head. 'I doubt it was a real relationship. It's more likely they simply enjoyed doing drugs together.'

'Enabling each other,' Sarah said.

The psychologist nodded approvingly. 'But I think it's significant that Paulette didn't try to return to Jacque after Gabriel died. Not that he would have taken her, as I said.'

'Jacque won't even take aspirin,' Amy said.

'Probably as a result of what happened,' Helen said, reaching for her hand again. 'Even if Paulette cleaned herself up and Jacque went there on Friday night, I can't believe it was to reconcile. He wouldn't forgive that easily.'

The cocaine Pavlik's people found in the bathroom meant Paulette hadn't 'cleaned herself up.' 'What do you think about the fire, Helen?'

'What about it?' Helen said. 'Are you asking if Jacque hated Paulette enough to set it?'

'No. I'm wondering if Paulette had reason to hate Jacque and might be vindictive enough to set it.'

'With herself in it?' Amy asked.

'And Jacque, perhaps,' I said.

'Murder-suicide?' Helen shook her head. 'I never met Paulette, so I can't judge her state of mind. But if she invited him to come back that night and he rejected her, I suppose she could have lashed out in anger. But to die in the fire with him seems . . . overkill?'

'Maybe she thought she would make it out,' I said. 'The fire was started by the door. They believe an accelerant was poured through the mail slot and lighted. But what if Paulette staged it to look that way, planning to go out the window?'

Sarah, at least, was considering it. 'And was overcome by the smoke?'

I nodded.

'But where was Jacque when she was pouring gas or whatever it was into the hallway?' Amy asked.

I bit my lip. 'The man's body was found in the bedroom.'

Amy's head dropped.

'That doesn't mean anything,' Sarah said. 'He could have been using the bathroom. It's off the bedroom.'

'How do you know that?' I asked.

'I showed the property to Jamie Bright years ago, remember?'

'Before Jacque bought it. That's right.' Sarah never forgot a fact about a property.

'Anyway,' she continued, 'in my experience, men stay on the toilet plenty long enough for someone to set fire to the place. Or Paulette could have drugged him and then started the fire.'

I frowned. 'That's probably pushing it.'

'And your entire theory isn't?' Sarah demanded. 'Woman in her designer jammies and Louboutins pouring gasoline on the floorboards and lighting it?'

I took a sip of wine. 'This is terrible.'

'It's pretty old,' Sarah said. 'It was going to be either really good or really bad.'

'Bad,' I said, setting down the mug and picking up a bottle to read the label. 'Pinot noir from 1987? I don't think so.'

'Aren't we the wine connoisseur?' Sarah said.

'She doesn't have to know much to know that,' Helen said, getting up. 'I should be going.'

'Let me know if Denis has heard from Jacque,' Amy said. 'Is he home yet?'

'No. He's had to stay another night.' Helen's composed mask slipped a bit, but she lifted her chin. 'It happens quite a bit, you know, with these conferences.'

I did know, since Ted and his hygienist-cum-wife had 'attended' a number of dental conferences together before he had broken the news that he was leaving me for her. 'Things come up.'

'Yes.' Helen said, studying me with just a hint of a grim smile playing at the corners of her mouth. 'They do.'

Amy stood. 'Thank you, Helen.'

'Come by tomorrow,' the psychologist said. 'I have a full slate of appointments, but I'll see you anytime.'

As Amy walked Helen to the door, I stood up, too.

'Snag the trash,' Sarah said, gesturing. 'By your foot.'

The burgundy foil from the wine bottle was on the floor.

'You're the one who dropped it,' I told her, snagging the foil and going to crumple it. 'Ouch.'

'Cut yourself? Serves you right.'

'It's so damn thick,' I said, examining it. 'Probably set off a metal detector—' I stopped. 'Damn.'

'Damn what?'

'I should have asked Helen about Egbert. You know, whether she thought he was suicidal.'

'You think she would say? She was his psychologist. Besides, are you supposed to be blabbing about his death yet?'

'No, you're right,' I said. 'Certainly not until the family knows, and Pavlik was just on his way to see Becky when I came here.' I tick-tocked my head. 'You know, I was wrong when I said there was no connection between Egbert and the fire. Becky is a connection.'

'Son burns down store for mother and then kills himself in remorse?' Sarah tried. 'Or mother burns down store and kills son who threatens to rat?'

I could always count on Sarah to boil things down to the simplest, most ridiculous terms.

'Get the bottle?' I gathered the mugs. 'But you're right. And as we've said, if this was simple arson, the fire would have been started downstairs in the empty store.'

I put the mugs in the dishwasher and closed the door.

Sarah, who'd followed me back, set the bottle on the sink. 'Unless the arsonist wanted to throw suspicion in a different direction, of course. Make it seem like this was about Paulette and implicate Jacque.'

'But to kill two people in the process?' I mused, turning to dump the wine down the sink. 'It's overkill, like Helen said.'

I put the bottle in the recycling and picked up a rag to go back and wipe the table. 'Or maybe it was just an accident. Not the fire, of course, but the deaths.'

I glanced around the kitchen. 'Sarah?'

And the dining room. 'Amy?'

I – and my theories – had been abandoned.

SIXTEEN

We close the store at three on Sunday afternoon, so even without Sarah or Amy's help, it was only just past four when I got home. I hadn't expected either woman to stay, really, but they could at least have said goodbye.

Given the discovery of Egbert's body, Pavlik wasn't home yet, but I heard Frank and Mocha scuffling as I unlocked the door. The moment it was open, Frank went racing around the yard looking for the perfect spot to relieve himself.

Mocha didn't race, merely stood and waited patiently for Frank to choose a bush; then, when the sheepdog was finished, she padded over to pee on the ground beneath to underline who was boss around here.

I took the opportunity to sit on the porch steps and catch the late-afternoon sun as I thought. Sarah and I had floated the possibility of Becky's involvement with the fire and Egbert's death, but I didn't really believe it. And I had a hunch Sarah was just using it to distract me so she could disappear. The fact was, for all her faults, Becky loved her son.

'I wonder how she took it,' I said aloud as my phone rang. 'Hi, Amy.'

'Oh, Maggy, I feel so badly.'

'Because you took off on me at the shop?'

'What? Oh, no,' she said, and I could imagine her hand waving in a tish-tosh way. 'I'm fine with that. It's just that all the time we were talking, poor Becky was trying to get hold of Helen.'

After Pavlik broke the news. 'That must have been the call Helen muted.'

'Yes. And a number of them after that. Becky can be a pain, so Helen didn't want to interrupt our conversation to take the calls.'

'Not realizing that Becky was in an even more immediate crisis.'

'Exactly. Helen wanted to let me know about Egbert in case I hadn't heard. I pretended I didn't know, but I hated lying to her.'

'Becky herself had just found out,' I said. 'It wouldn't have been right to tell Helen.'

'Maybe she could have gone with Pavlik when Becky was informed.'

'That's not how it works, I'm afraid. Did Helen tell you exactly what Becky told her? How Pavlik told her Egbert died?'

'That they believe he died of a head injury,' she said. 'Oops, somebody is at the door. Talk to you later.'

'Head injury,' I repeated, setting down the phone to scratch Frank's butt. 'Not suicide, obviously, since it hasn't been ruled one yet. But not a gunshot wound, either.'

Mocha had come to sit square in front of me and now she whined. 'Fine,' I said. 'Bring your little butt over here.'

I was scratching both dogs' butts – one high, one low – when Pavlik pulled in. At the sound of the car door opening, of course, both abandoned me.

After much unbridled joy, slobber and dog hair, the sheriff came to sit down next to me on the steps.

'Hi.' He gave me a kiss. 'What a day.'

'I know,' I said, kneading the back of his neck. 'How did Becky take it?'

'I thought amazingly well, until I realized she didn't believe it. She honestly thought that, somehow, we had it wrong. When she realized not, she just shut down.'

'She did reach out to Helen,' I told him. 'Unfortunately, Helen was at the shop with Sarah and Amy and me and didn't know why Becky was calling.'

'You didn't tell her?'

'No, I knew that I couldn't do that,' I said, a little regretfully. 'But if I'd realized that the call Helen muted was from Becky, I'd have urged her to take it.'

'Without telling her why,' Pavlik said, nodding. 'Did they finally connect?'

'Yes. Which is good. We don't need another suicide. If that's what Egbert's death turns out to be.'

'It's not,' Pavlik said. 'Ronstadt was dead when the gun was put in his mouth and the trigger pulled.'

My hand flew involuntarily to my own mouth. 'That's awful.'

'But better than if he were alive,' Pavlik said.

'All that blood at the back of his head was from the exit wound?' I asked, confused. 'I thought that if somebody was dead, they didn't bleed much.' Because the heart wasn't pumping.

'It wasn't an exit wound.' He held up his hands. 'Well, that's not true. Ronstadt already had been hit on the back of the head with a blunt object, killing him. Presumably, there was bleeding inside the skull and, when he was shot, the exit wound—'

I winced. 'Drained it?'

'Probably. The full autopsy will be done tomorrow.' He slipped his arm around my shoulders.

I leaned back into him. 'I was right.'

'Yes.'

'That's an uncharacteristically quick admission,' I said, turning to regard him.

'You also were right about the charred branch,' he said. 'There was blood on it, and I'm assuming it will prove to be Egbert's.'

'Careless of them not to burn that branch completely.'

'More bad luck, I think,' he said. 'The maintenance man just happened to be back there and noticed the smoke. Plus, on a Sunday, the fire department's response time was quicker than normal.'

I was mulling that over. 'I guess they wouldn't want to start the fire before they'd shot him in case somebody saw it. But they also had to worry about the sound of the shot drawing attention. If I were doing it, I'd have the fire all ready to go and light it after I shot him.'

'Good to know your preference should the situation arise,' Pavlik said a little wryly. 'But they also had to position the body for a suicide.'

'Yes, he would have fallen on his face when he was hit from behind, right?'

'Most likely, meaning he had to be turned over. The kick

of the gun, if he had shot himself, would have sent him backwards.'

'What about the glasses in his hat? Was that staged?' I asked. 'I've heard that people who commit suicide remove their glasses.'

'I've heard that, too,' Pavlik said. 'But anecdotally.'

'It's not true?' I'd seen it on television. It had to be true.

'In any case, his glasses probably would have flown off when he was hit. Maybe the hat flew, too, and the killer set them neatly nearby so any blood would be explained by gunshot splatter.'

'Smart,' I said. 'But parts of it are dumb, too.'

'Not an experienced killer,' Pavlik agreed.

'Or killers?' I asked.

'Yes.' He tapped me on the top of the head. 'You haven't asked me about the backpack.'

I'd relaxed against him again and now turned back to face him. 'Tell me. What was in it besides our empty to-go cup?'

'Oh, the usual – bottled water, power bars, energy gels.'

Sounded more like a marathon runner or serious hiker than Egbert Ronstadt in his knee braces. But maybe I hadn't given the man enough credit. 'Guess he wanted to stay out as long as he could.'

'Until his mother called him home for dinner.' Pavlik, too, had heard the sound of the maternal Ronstadt calling her young. 'But Egbert also had a fair wad of money.'

That got my attention. 'Like how much?'

'Fourteen hundred dollars.'

'In cash?' I said. 'I know he does tech work from home, but that seems a lot to be carrying around these days.'

'Unless you're in a cash-only business.'

I studied his face. 'You think he's part of this gang of copper thieves?'

'I think it's entirely possible,' Pavlik said. 'We also found business cards from a dozen places that buy scrap metal.'

'But . . .' I was trying to imagine the Egbert I knew as a master criminal. 'He runs around finding metal with his metal detector. Isn't it possible those cards are just the people he sells it to?'

'But fourteen hundred dollars is a lot of finding, along Poplar Creek. The woods run about six miles north to south, and from the sounds of it, Egbert was pretty much confining himself to that stretch.'

'He said he was going to expand to other places once his mom retired.' I rubbed my forehead. 'If he's a thief, why would he tell me about the copper and catalytic converter he supposedly found on Friday morning?'

'Covering himself,' Pavlik said. 'Notice it was conveniently gone yesterday.'

'Or so he said, but Sarah, Amy and I were talking about that earlier,' I said. 'Egbert had to have been out very early. Before he showed up at the fire with his mom.'

'I believe he was out very early most mornings.'

'When he could take delivery of what his colleagues stole overnight,' I said, tripping to it. 'Then he would have all day—'

'Until dinner time,' Pavlik amended. 'To sell or move the stuff.'

'What happened this morning, do you think? One of the gang members got nervous? Or greedy?'

'It's possible,' Pavlik said. 'There's more, though. Egbert had something else interesting in his backpack.'

'What was that?'

'Cell phones. He had a zippered plastic bag of six of them, presumably that he found with his metal detector.' Frank had come up with a slimy tennis ball, and Pavlik leaned over to palm it.

Apparently, Egbert wasn't spending all of his time hatching evil genius plans. This sounded pretty mundane. 'I suppose people do lose them when they're hiking or maybe fishing. But what good are they to Egbert? I assume they're locked.'

'Probably. Though depending on the phone, the right people could get in – maybe wipe them to sell or change IDs to access personal information.' He waved Frank off for a long one.

'Well, as I said, Egbert was in tech of some kind. He was always pretty vague about it.' And to be fair, I'd always been pretty uninterested.

'Thing is,' Pavlik said, launching the ball, 'one of the phones is Jacque Oui's.'

SEVENTEEN

So . . . Egbert found Jacque's cell in the woods by Poplar Creek?

It seemed the logical assumption, but that meant Jacque had gone into the woods after he left our house Saturday morning. But why? And . . .

'How did you identify it so quickly?' I asked Pavlik, as I tried to get my head around the discovery.

'Most smart phones these days are assigned an IMEI number – that stands for International Mobile Equipment Identity. It makes it possible to track every phone back to its owner without it being on or having a SIM card.'

'Assuming that phone is physically found.' I absently took Frank's ball myself and tossed it, ending up with a handful of sheepdog slime. 'What do you do? Just contact the company?'

'Exactly,' Pavlik said. 'But in this case, it wasn't really even necessary. When we turned on the phone, Amy's photo was the wallpaper.'

'Oh, that is so unutterably sad,' I whispered. 'Jacque must be dead.'

'Because he lost his phone?'

'And is missing.' I wiped my hand on my jeans. 'Though I guess if he set the fire, he could have tossed the phone so he couldn't be tracked. But why in the woods? It's not on the way to or from Schultz's from our house. It's the opposite direction.'

'You're assuming Egbert found the phone in the woods?'

'I am,' I admitted. 'But now that you say it, I suppose he could just as easily have found it near Schultz's during the fire yesterday morning. He and Becky showed up quite early.'

'For her shift, they said. But the store doesn't open until ten and I'm told they were there around seven.'

'Being nosy maybe?'

'Entirely possible,' Pavlik said.

'We only have Egbert's word that he was in Poplar Woods on Saturday morning discovering that the scrap metal and catalytic converter were gone,' I pointed out. 'It could all be a lie. But even if he was in the woods, he could have heard the sirens—'

Pavlik smacked himself in the forehead with an open palm. 'Becky heard the sirens. She was calling for Egbert as I was leaving to go to the fire. I should have put it together, since it was so early.'

Eeeeggbeeerrrtt . . .

'She made him drive her to the store then, rather than waiting for her shift,' I said. 'Maybe Egbert found Jacque's phone there, but why? Jacque dropped it when he set the fire?'

'Somebody else dropped it after they killed Jacque and set the fire?' Pavlik offered as an alternative.

Argh. 'Were you able to unlock Jacque's phone? Amy probably knows his passcode.' I was pulling out my own to call Amy and then stopped. 'I forgot. You have Amy's cell.'

'As it happens,' Pavlik said, 'I dropped her mobile at her house on the way home and also told her about finding Jacque's phone.'

'Was she glad?'

Pavlik considered. 'I think her reaction was similar to yours. She was relieved that there was some sign of him but couldn't quite imagine a scenario – or at least a good scenario – where he would willingly part with it. And you're right. She knew the passcode.'

Of course. But I had a thought. 'Did the passcode work?'

'Yes, why wouldn't it?'

I tipped my head sideways. 'He would change the passcode if he was hiding secrets, wouldn't he?'

'You're talking about Paulette?'

I started to reach for Frank's ball and then thought better of it. 'Yes, for a start.'

'Here's a thought,' Pavlik said, tossing the ball himself. 'What if Jacque is telling the truth? What if he had no idea Paulette was going to show up? And what if they're legally divorced and' – he held up a slimy finger to stop me from interrupting – 'she's just trying to cause trouble?'

'But why? And why now?' I staved off the slime Pavlik was waving at me. 'You're a child, you know that?'

'Me?' He tucked his other arm around my waist, bringing me closer so the finger could hover just off my nose.

'Yes, you.' I covered my face with my hands.

'You're not exactly looking like an adult here,' he whispered in my ear. 'Just because you can't see it, doesn't mean it can't touch you.'

I turned away, burying my face in his shirt. 'You haven't answered my question,' I mumbled into his pocket.

'Why now, you mean?' Pavlik asked. 'Maybe she only recently found out where he is and thinks there's something to gain monetarily. Or she wants revenge for some perceived wrong.'

'I suppose there's nothing to stop her from filing a lawsuit here or in France, even if it is entirely bogus and eventually gets thrown out. It would make Jacque's life miserable in the interim. And be expensive.' I sat up. 'If Jamie Bright isn't involved, the timing is curious, isn't it?'

'The timing of Paulette's visit, you mean?'

'Yes. Jacque has been doing well for years, but now he's in real financial trouble. First, he lost money with Fargo Investments and now an aggressive competitor is entering the market.'

'Sounds like the most *in*opportune time for Paulette to show up with her hand out,' Pavlik admitted.

'But the most opportune time for Bright. He would have done his homework on a potential acquisition. A simple background check would have turned up Jacque's marriage to Paulette.' I stood. 'I assume your people are going over his cell phone?'

'With the proverbial fine-tooth comb.' Pavlik groaned. 'Hand up, please?'

'Sure.' I grabbed the proffered hand only to get a helping of Frank slime.

'Got you.' Laughing, Pavlik stood up under his own power and turned to go into the house.

I wiped my hand on the seat of his jeans.

*   *   *

'Still no identification or cause of death on the bodies?' Sarah asked me the next morning. It was overcast and the gloom had carried over into the coffeehouse.

'No formal identification, but it seems pretty obvious the woman is Paulette,' I told her. 'The preliminary cause of death for both is smoke inhalation and carbon dioxide poisoning.' The findings had come through last night. 'You realize it's just been a little over forty-eight hours since the fire and even less since the bodies were removed from the scene and taken to the morgue?'

'Longest weekend ever,' Sarah said, yawning.

I nodded. 'I'm glad Amy has the day off, even if I fully expected her to be here anyway when I arrived to open.'

'Me, too,' Sarah said. 'Though I hoped for the courtesy of a phone call last night, so I didn't have to get up in the first place.'

'She'll still probably come by today.' Truth was I missed her and wanted to make sure she was OK.

Sarah tossed a wet rag past my head and landed it in the sink with a splat. 'Score,' she said, holding up both arms like goal posts. 'She won't want to be home alone.'

'I know.' I retrieved the rag and squeezed the excess water out, hanging it over the edge of the sink.

'About Jacque's phone,' Sarah said. 'Wouldn't Becky know if Egbert found it at the store that morning?'

'She might,' I said, brightening. 'If not, Pavlik will be able to tell its approximate movements and when it was turned off, anyway.'

'The wonders of technology,' Sarah said, bemused. 'I was just thinking we should invite Becky over for a cup of coffee. You know, her being bereaved and all.'

'If you want,' I said. 'I'd also like to talk to Denis Durand if he's back from Chicago. Since you're issuing invitations, can you arrange that as well?'

'Maybe he'll be on the ten a.m. train.' Unlike the short-run commuter trains between Milwaukee and Brookhills, the ten a.m. was a once-a-day train that ran between Chicago and Minneapolis, with Milwaukee and Brookhills as stops in between. 'You can catch him.'

'I could have if he was on a train,' I told her. 'But Denis drove down to Chicago.'

'But I thought you said you talked to him here on Friday night.' She took the rag I'd hung up and swiped at the refrigerator with it.

'You're streaking that,' I told her. 'He took the train home from his office Friday night, so they could have dinner as a family.'

'And then drove back to downtown Chicago?' Sarah said, tossing the rag back into the sink. 'Helen rules with an iron fist.'

'I think family meals are a great idea.' I squeezed out the rag again. 'I just never could get the hang of them.'

'I hear it helps if you actually cook.'

'I suppose.' I was punching up numbers on my phone. 'I could text Molly, I guess. See if her dad's home.'

'You girls are so cute,' Sarah said. 'Did you exchange friendship bracelets along with phone numbers?'

'Yes, and I have one for you if you're feeling left out,' I said, sending off the text before I put my phone down. 'She reminds me of me when I was young. Except smarter. And ballsier.'

'So not like you at all, huh?' Sarah went to snag the rag again, and I slapped her hand. 'The daughter you never had.'

'I'm very happy with my son, thank you,' I said, getting out the stainless-steel cleaner and a soft towel to give to Sarah. I pointed at the refrigerator and continued. 'It's just that Molly has made a couple of comments about not being smart enough. Maybe Helen is setting too high of a bar.'

'You're worried the psychologist isn't raising her kid right?' Sarah was spraying the cleaner on the refrigerator.

'Maybe,' I said. 'You know you can also spray that stuff on the cloth and—'

My phone buzzed and, since Sarah was ignoring me anyway, I checked it. 'Molly says she sent Denis a text asking when he's getting in today and she'll let me know.'

'Unless he's disappeared, too.' She was buffing at a scratch that I knew wasn't coming out because I'd made it.

'Molly talked to her father on Saturday after the fire, so

Denis can't be the body. Helen has been in touch with him, too.'

'I wasn't thinking Denis was dead,' Sarah said, giving up. 'Maybe he and Jacque ran away together. Secret lovers all this time.'

I smiled at the thought. 'I don't think that's what Amy meant when she said they shared a place when Jacque came from France.'

'There's no romance in your soul.'

I was frowning. 'Didn't Helen say it was a cottage on Poplar Creek? And that it is – present tense – small?'

'Why does that make you scowl?'

'I'm not scowling, I'm thinking,' I said, retrieving the cleaner and towel. 'I'm thinking that if Denis still owns it, maybe he let Jacque flop there again.'

'Oooh,' Sarah said, cocking her head. 'I like it. But then who's dead?'

'I don't know,' I said, a little shriller than I intended. 'But if Jacque did go there on Saturday morning, it would explain Egbert finding the phone in the woods.'

'If he did find it there,' Sarah reminded me. 'Which we will ask Becky, who I will invite here.'

Geez, the woman contemplates doing one nice thing . . . 'Jacque could still be there.'

'He could,' Sarah said. 'But we still have that pesky extra body.'

'Whose body?' Amy's voice asked.

'We don't know,' Sarah said. 'We're trying to figure out how Jacque could be in the woods with his phone and also dead in the market.'

'Let's assume for now, just for me, that Jacque is not "dead in the market."' Amy was sounding a little gloomy, too.

Sarah folded her arms. 'OK.'

I didn't bother asking why Amy was there because I knew the answer. She couldn't think of anything else to do.

So I gave her something. 'Amy, Jacque lived with Denis when he first came here, right?'

'Yes,' she said, shifting her shoulder bag so she could lean her butt against the dishwasher.

'Helen said it was a small cottage on Poplar Creek. Do you know if Denis still owns it?'

She straightened up. 'No. But is that where you think Jacque might be?'

'I don't know,' I said. 'But it is someplace that he could hide and where we haven't looked. And if he walked through the woods along the bank's creek to get there and back, it would explain Egbert finding his mobile.'

'Let's go look, then,' Amy said.

I wasn't sure that was such a great idea. 'Let me see what I can find out first. We can't just go wandering through the woods. In the meantime, could you two talk to Becky?'

'I will,' Amy said, repositioning her purse strap over her shoulder as if for action. 'I need to offer my condolences anyway.' She shook her head. 'I know she is devastated. Egbert was her whole life.'

'When she wasn't making the rest of us miserable,' Sarah said. 'I was going to invite Becky here—'

Amy held up a hand. 'I'll go to her, if you don't mind.'

'You don't want us there?' Sarah asked.

'I don't want *you* there.' She was already at the door.

'Don't be hurt,' I told Sarah as Amy's footsteps reverberated down the porch steps.

'What would make you think I'm hurt?' She was standing stock-still.

'Because you didn't have a comeback,' I said. 'Thing is, Amy's a little raw right now and she's probably assuming Becky is, too.'

'And?' I wasn't sure her lips moved.

'And sometimes you can be a bit abrupt.'

'I'm honest.'

'And there are times when that honesty hurts.' I tugged her arm, so she would look at me. 'It's us, not you.'

'You sure?'

'Absolutely. You're perfect.'

She rubbed at the refrigerator. 'This is a scratch.'

'I know,' I said, taking off my apron. 'I'm glad Amy is preoccupied with Becky, so I can talk to Helen about this cottage.'

'You're leaving me here to cover?'

'Absolutely. If Jamie Bright comes in, see what more you can find out about Paulette's visit to him and how that came about? I think with you both being successful business people, he might open up to you.'

'You're pandering to me,' she said, turning to watch me hang up my apron. 'I like it.'

I checked the time. 'Just going on nine thirty. If Helen hasn't started office hours, she may be at home. Do you know where the Durands live?'

Silly question. Sarah knew where everything was located in Brookhills and who owned it. 'Oak Street. It's the bungalow that backs up to her office on Elm.'

Elm was the street that ran east and west of our shop to the north, and Oak the one just north of that.

'Great,' I said, picking up my purse. 'I'll stop at home and let Frank and Mocha out on the way.'

EIGHTEEN

Frank was the size of an elephant with the bladder of a mouse, while Mocha was just the opposite. I worried about the health of her urinary tract.

'It's not good to hold it for so long,' I told her. She had stepped on the porch and stayed there, waiting for Frank to finish watering every tree and pole in the yard.

When he came back up the steps, I sighed. 'OK, Mocha. Your turn.'

If she could have sighed back at me, she would have. Instead, she grudgingly descended the steps and squatted near Frank's last effort.

Then she climbed back up and followed him in.

'I'll see you tonight,' I called to them, as I closed the door. They took no notice.

Continuing up Poplar Creek Road from my house, I turned on to Oak. I figured I'd try the house first. Even if Helen was already at the office, Molly might prove some help.

The Durands lived in a Milwaukee bungalow, a craftsman-style house so dubbed because most of the houses built in Milwaukee during the 1920s were bungalows.

This one was constructed of brick, one and a half-story high, with bay windows lined with leaded glass. The peaked-roof entranceway was up a set of concrete steps, which I mounted and rang the bell.

Nothing. I rang it again and then got out my cell. Punching up Molly's number, I called.

No answer. Not surprising; Eric didn't answer phone calls, either. Nor most emails. So, I skipped that step and went right to text. *I'm at the door. Are you home?* Send.

After a minute or two, I heard footsteps and then the door opened. 'Maggy?'

Molly's tousled head poked out.

'I'm sorry,' I said, slipping my phone into my pocket. 'Were you sleeping?'

She gave the question the non-answer it deserved. 'Want to come in?'

'Sure,' I said, stepping into the front hallway. 'Is your mom home or is she already at the office?'

Molly didn't seem any surer than I was. 'No clue. What time is it?'

'Nine forty,' I said.

'Office,' she said, leading me into the kitchen. 'First appointment is at nine thirty. Like clockwork.' This last was spoken with an edge.

She seemed to realize it and shook her head. 'Don't mind me. It's just sometimes I feel like she's there for everybody else but me.'

'Cobblers' children,' I said.

'What's that?' She swung open the refrigerator door.

'It's an old saying. The cobbler's children have no shoes.'

She turned with a quart of milk in her hand and a puzzled look on her face. 'But what's a cobbler?'

Some days I felt old, and other days I felt really old. 'Shoemakers. The saying means—'

'Oh, I get it,' she said. 'Like "doctor, heal thyself."' She held up the milk. 'Do you want a latte or is that' – she grinned – 'a busman's holiday for you?'

This kid was growing on me. I nodded affirmatively to the latte. 'You're very smart. Why do you think you won't get into any of the schools you looked at?'

'Oh, I know lots of random stuff,' she said. 'But that doesn't mean I'm smart. At least, not the kind of smart my mother wants me to be. I think she thinks I'm weird – like deficient or something.'

'We mothers think we know our kids.' I shrugged. 'Then all of a sudden you throw us a curveball—'

'Like your son Eric being gay?' she asked, pouring the milk into an air frother.

'Oh, no,' I said. 'I think I knew that all along when I look back. No, it was when he told me he wanted to follow in my footsteps and go into marketing.' I shook my head. 'I didn't even think he noticed what I did for a living before I opened Uncommon Grounds.'

'You have a problem with marketing?'

'Not at all. But if he was going to follow in anybody's footsteps, becoming a dentist like his dad pays a whole lot better.'

'Ugh,' Molly said, wrinkling her nose. 'Why would you want to spend all day messing in a stranger's mouth? Besides, everybody hates you.'

'That's pretty much what Eric says, though he doesn't tell his dad. It's just that you want your kids to be financially solvent.' So don't open a coffeehouse.

'You want them to be happy, too, right?' She brewed a shot into a mug and added the frothed milk.

'More than anything.' I took the latte. 'What makes you happy?'

She lifted her shoulders and then dropped them as she sat down. 'Don't know. I like figuring out things. Solving puzzles.'

'But not figuring out people, like your mom does? Or businesses and homes like your dad?'

'Way to make their occupations sound appealing,' Molly said. 'But no. Helen isn't my mom, you know.'

'I know.' Silence for a second. 'Has your dad talked to you about your birth mom and what she did?'

'Not really,' she said. 'She died when I was born. That was back in the olden days.'

'Eighteen years ago?'

'Exactly. The dark days of medicine, apparently.'

I didn't know what to say to that. 'Aren't you going to have a coffee, too?'

'Don't like the stuff.' She grinned. 'What did you want to see Helen about?'

'I have a question for your mom or your dad. You might even know the answer.'

'I might.' She had that get-on-with-it expression Eric sometimes painted on.

'I heard your dad had a place "back in the olden days." Your mom called it a cottage—'

'The cabin?' Molly's nose was wrinkled again. 'The one up past the church?'

'Maybe,' I said. 'If you mean Christ Christian. This place was supposed to be by the creek somewhere.'

'Yeah, it is,' Molly said. 'Though it's been years and years since I've been inside. We should go look.'

'We don't have to actually go,' I said, but Molly had already jumped to her feet. 'You can just tell me where it is.'

But Molly was digging through a drawer. 'I can't, you'll need . . . a key.' She held up a skeleton key.

'Thanks,' I said, going to take it.

She stuck it behind her back. 'Not without me. You're going to look for a clue to the fire. Or maybe even Mr Oui.'

'Molly, I don't know what we'll find. If anything.'

'You said "we" – that's you and me.'

Damn. 'We could just give the key to the sheriff and let him send his people.'

She frowned. 'You wouldn't do that. And besides, the sheriff can't search it without permission. I'm not going to give it, and my mom is very big on privacy and rights and all.' She shrugged. 'And my dad isn't back yet.'

'They can call him,' I threatened.

'Bad cell reception driving up from Chicago,' she countered, and then her face changed. 'Come on. You know you want to go. I do, too, and if you don't go with me, I'll just do it on my own anyway. You don't want that, do you?'

'No.' I was being outsmarted by a teenager. Not for the first time, but it still stung.

Since we were already fairly far north, and Molly wasn't sure exactly where the cabin was, we didn't bother going back to Uncommon Grounds to get my car. Instead, we hiked due west into the woods to Poplar Creek and hooked a right to follow it north.

'It isn't much of a creek here, is it?' Molly said. 'It's barely five feet across, and I bet it's really shallow.' As she spoke, she was veering closer to the stream.

'You'd be surprised,' I said, tugging her back. 'Eric and his friends used to play back here. They were building a bridge, and poor Mikey fell off a log into the creek. They lost him.'

'He drowned?' Molly was horrified.

And I was ashamed. 'No, he washed up two blocks down. But he was missing for about twenty minutes.' OK, almost ashamed.

'Very funny,' she said, giving me a playful sideways nudge.

'I should call Pavlik,' I said, getting out my phone.

'But what if he gets there before we do?'

'He won't, which is why I waited until now to call. Besides, you have the key.' I glanced at her. 'Right?'

'Right.' She held it up.

'Good. Oh . . . voicemail,' I said, and waited for the beep. 'Hey, you. I remembered that Amy and Helen both mentioned Jacque staying at Denis's cabin when he first moved to Brookhills. I asked Molly, and her dad does have a cabin on Poplar Creek, somewhere north of Christ Christian. She's not exactly sure where, so we're hiking up there now. Thought you'd want to know.'

'Nice,' Molly said as I rang off. 'You didn't quite invite him, but he'll know where to find our bodies if we disappear.'

'Exactly,' I said, slipping my phone into my pocket. 'It's a fine balance.'

'Oh,' Molly said, putting her hand on my arm. 'Did you hear that one of Mom's patients was killed in these woods? At first, they thought it was suicide, and Mom nearly went bonkers.'

She was talking about Egbert, of course. 'I guess having a patient commit suicide feels like a failure for a psychologist.'

'And God forbid Helen should fail at anything,' Molly mumbled.

I guessed every family has its dramas. Especially the ones that looked perfect from the outside like the Durands. But it was none of my business, and I sure wasn't going to encourage Molly to dump on her mother to me.

'Now it turns out,' she continued, 'that somebody hit him over the head, and somehow that makes her feel better. That's pretty messed-up, don't you think?'

Don't get involved, Maggy. Don't get involved.

'The man was Egbert Ronstadt,' I said. 'Did you ever meet him?'

'Not really, but he's been seeing my mom for ages. Don't

see how it helped him, though.' She shrugged. 'He was weird, but why would somebody kill him?'

'I don't know,' I said truthfully. 'I doubt it was robbery. From what I'm told, he had some expensive equipment.' I wasn't about to mention the cash.

'What kind of equipment?' she asked, squinting.

'Metal detecting.' I pointed. 'Don't trip on that branch.'

'Thanks,' she said, stepping over it. 'I don't know about that, but his sneakers cost a bunch.'

'Don't they all? I practically fall over when I see the price on whichever ones Eric wants for Christmas or whatever.'

'No,' Molly said, serious now. 'I'm talking *really* expensive. Like thousands of dollars, not hundreds.'

'Really?' I stopped.

'Those red Nikes? They're like seven grand. I think Kanye had a pair.'

Kanye and Egbert. It didn't compute. Even the cash in his bag wasn't going to buy him shoes like that, unless the $1400 was a daily take. 'Where would he get money like that? I know he does something with computers from home, but—'

'Maybe cryptocurrency or something? Or gambling. You can do that online, too.' Her mouth dropped open. 'I saw him talking to a sketchy guy on Brookhill Road outside of Schultz's. Maybe it was his contact.'

Or maybe Egbert was passing time while he waited for his mother after work. 'Had you seen this man before?'

Molly had started walking again, so I scurried to catch up.

'No, but he wasn't young. Maybe thirty or forty and kind of skinny. Not big like the guys in suits you see beating people up on TV. So maybe this wasn't a cybercriminal.'

But it could have been a copper thief. 'You need to tell the sheriff.'

She turned, her eyes wide. 'And be killed? Or have to go into witness protection?'

I'd say she was being overly dramatic, but Egbert had been beaten to death in the very woods in which we were walking.

Still. 'Neither of those things is going to happen. But I'm not sure many people paid much attention to Egbert, so the sheriff might not have many leads.'

'I do notice things,' she said proudly, starting back up again. 'People. There.' She was pointing.

I followed the direction of her finger upstream another fifty yards or so to where I could see the peak of a low roof. 'That's the cabin?'

'I think so.' She was pushing through the brush.

As we got close, I put my hand on her arm, dragging her behind a tree.

'Who's being dramatic now?' she asked, rubbing her arm.

'I didn't say you were being dramatic.' Just thought it. And she had read my mind. 'Let's just take a second to observe before we burst in.'

I craned my neck, squinting to see into the windows.

'We're going to have to be closer if you want to see in,' she said, and she took off running to the next stand of trees. Once there, she signaled me to join her.

'You really watch too much TV.' I was trying to catch my breath.

'And movies. Though with streaming, it's all practically the same now.'

I made the next move, dodging to the side of the weather-beaten . . . well, 'shack' was more appropriate than 'cottage.' Once I reached the wall, Molly came, keeping low.

'Stay down,' I said. 'I'll just see—'

My phone rang.

'Shhhhh,' from Molly.

'Shit. Sorry,' from me. Then, in a whisper. 'Pavlik?'

'Tell me you're not at the door of this cabin, about to take it down.'

'The window,' I said, raising my eyes to a level where I could see above the window ledge. 'Looks to be deserted.'

Hearing that, Molly crab-walked to the corner.

'I've got to go,' I told Pavlik. 'Molly's about to breach the perimeter.'

'Why did you take a kid with you?'

'She had the key,' I told him, following Molly. 'She also says Egbert wore seven-thousand-dollar sneakers and met with a shady guy, but I'll have her tell you about that when we get back. Molly!' I hissed.

'That's not good,' Pavlik said. 'I need you to—'

'We will,' I said, joining Molly at the door as she slipped the key into the lock. 'Soon as we can.'

Molly glanced back at me. 'It's oiled or something,' she whispered. 'Went in easy.'

'Jacque's phone last pinged a tower near Poplar Creek,' Pavlik was saying. 'Meaning close to where you are. And that's not the only thing. We found blood on it.'

'That's not surprising, is it?' I asked as Molly went to turn the knob. 'There was a lot of Egbert's blood around.'

'Not in the Ziploc in the backpack there wasn't,' he said. 'And it's not—'

Molly swung the door open.

'—Egbert's blood.' I was staring at the floor in front of us.

'Oh, God.' Molly had her hand over her mouth.

I pulled her back. 'Don't look.'

'Maggy?'

'Pavlik?' I was feeling sick. 'You'd better get up here. We've found Jacque.'

NINETEEN

'Is he dead?' Molly peeked out from behind my shoulder. 'Oh, yes.' I shook myself. 'Though I probably should check to be sure.'

'Check how?' Molly sniffled, covering her nose and mouth as I approached Jacque's body.

Jacque Oui was lying face up, eyes open, a black-edged hole in his left temple. A gun that looked to be a twin to the one found with Egbert was on the floor next to him.

I glanced back to see that Molly had backtracked to the door, her stomach getting the better of her curiosity. As I knelt by Jacque's body to check for his carotid pulse, my hand brushed his cheek. One touch was all I needed. He was cold, very cold.

'Is there a pulse?'

I jumped. Molly had rallied and was at my elbow. The girl was made of sterner stuff than I had been at her age. 'I can't feel one. He's cold.'

'Can I feel?'

Sheesh. 'No. Bad enough that I already have.'

'You mean for preserving the crime scene, right?' She was glancing around. 'There's not much here, is there?'

I stood up. Against one wall were two chairs with wooden arms, the seats and backs upholstered in red-and-blue plaid material. A square table between the two held a tall tool – maybe a detail saw or drill with a plastic cover over it. The couch across from the chairs was upholstered in the same plaid fabric but missing its seat cushions. A dark wood coffee table with thick legs was snugged a little closer to one of the chairs than the couch. 'Is this the way you remember it?'

'I was only here once or twice since I was a baby, and that was years ago.' The furniture didn't interest her; she was staring at the gun. 'You think he shot himself?'

I turned my attention back to Jacque. 'The autopsy will tell us. Appearances can be deceptive.'

Taking out my phone, I used the flashlight to get a better look at his eyes. 'Corneas are cloudy. No petechial hemorrhaging.'

'So not suffocated before he was shot, right?'

I didn't answer.

'Has rigor mortis set in?'

'Ghoulish much?' I snapped.

'Sorry.' She backed away, palms of her hands out defensively. 'But I'm not the one looking into the dead guy's eyeballs. And he's a friend of yours, no less.'

'Relative, actually,' I said softly.

'Oh, I'm sorry,' Molly said. 'I didn't know.'

'I didn't either, until recently,' I told her. 'But my concern right now is for Amy.'

'Oh,' Molly said, crestfallen. 'I like her.'

'Me, too.' We all love Amy. Including Jacque, which is why I should have tried to love him. 'The sheriff's department should be here soon,' I said, getting out my phone again. 'Meanwhile, don't touch—'

'Look! I found his phone.' Molly was holding up a small cell phone.

I cringed. 'I told you not to touch anything.'

'Actually, you didn't tell me that,' she said, holding the thing out between two fingers now as if it was going to bite her. 'At least not until after I picked it up.' She glanced around uneasily. 'And I may have touched a couple of other things, too.'

'Never mind,' I said, as I punched up Sarah's cell. 'They'll take our prints for elimination. Sarah,' I said into the phone. 'Is Amy back yet?'

I listened as she groused about the fact that neither Amy nor I had returned. When she finished, I said. 'We found Jacque and he's dead. Don't tell Amy, don't tell anybody. But when Amy gets back, keep her there, OK?'

I listened for a second. 'I know. Me, too. Thanks.' I rang off.

Molly was in the kitchenette. 'What are you doing?' I said as she went to pull open a drawer.

'Investigating,' she said over her shoulder.

'No.' I pulled her away. 'You're *touching.*'

'But you said they'd eliminate our prints anyway.' She pushed a dark hank of hair out of her eyes, looking as though she was going to cry.

'That doesn't mean you're free to leave more of them around,' I told her, unswayed by the tears. 'Now, where's that phone you found?'

'Here.' She picked the mobile up from the counter.

'Put . . . it . . . down,' I said stiffly.

She swallowed and followed my direction. 'Fine.'

Fine. The small black phone looked to be just that – a phone. Nothing smart about it.

'Burner, don't you think?' Molly said in my ear.

I jumped and moved away a smidge. Kid was crowding me. 'Probably. Question is whose is it? Jacque's was' – I hesitated – 'already found.'

I knew I wouldn't get away with that. 'Where?'

'The woods.'

'Who found it?'

I stared her down.

'Fine,' she said, folding her arms. 'Don't tell me.'

I wouldn't. 'Where did you find this one?'

'Under here,' she said, going toward the coffee table.

I slapped away her hand before she could shove the table.

'Well, um . . . anyway,' she said, rubbing her hand, 'it was right under this corner.'

'Did you move the table?'

'Just a little.'

Argh.

'It was before you said,' she reminded me.

I was looking at Jacque's body. Part of me wanted to find something to cover him with and the other wanted to check for rigor mortis and blowflies.

I resisted both, taking Molly's elbow. 'Come on,' I said, 'let's wait outside.'

I sat on a stump as we waited for Pavlik's team to show up, trying to think, even as Molly paced restlessly. 'Don't wander, Molly. It's a crime scene.'

'The whole woods?'

'The sheriff will decide how much of the whole woods. For now, just stay near where we've already walked.'

'Fine.'

Fine. And to my relief, I could hear sirens.

I'd given Pavlik directions – go to Christ Christian and head upstream – and he was the first one to arrive. He was on foot and when he caught sight of us, he waved back to a deputy to bring up the rest of the team.

'You OK?' he asked as he reached me. Molly was nowhere in sight.

'Honestly? Too OK,' I said, getting up from my stump. 'This is a man I've known for years, who stayed in our house and slept in my son's bed, and here I am scanning his corpse for clues as to how long it's been there. It's wrong.'

'Don't tell the forensics people that,' he said and then gave me a quick squeeze. 'But I know what you mean. I'm going to go in. Stay here?'

'Can I go with you?'

'You've already been in there, I assume.' He was glancing around. 'Didn't you say Molly Durand was with you?'

'Yes, and she's driving me crazy. She touched a cell phone she found in there and God knows what else.'

'What were you doing at the time?' he asked, pulling on gloves.

'Me? I was touching the body, making sure he was dead.'

'Of course,' Pavlik said, opening the door to poke his head in. 'And you're satisfied?'

'Body cold, corneas clouded, and I think I saw a maggot. So yes. I'm not sure about rigor. I didn't touch him that much.'

'He's been missing since Saturday morning, and today is Monday. That's forty-eight hours if he died on Saturday. Rigor would have come and gone.'

Pavlik was crouching next to Jacque. 'Gunshot wound to the left temple, close range, as I'm sure you noticed.'

'Suicide?'

'Maybe.' Pavlik straightened. 'A close-in shot to the temple could also be a hit.'

'You think it was a professional—'

'I don't think,' Pavlik said. 'I wait for the pathologist to tell me.'

Yes, yes, yes. 'There's a gun.' I pointed to the pistol that, blessedly, neither Molly nor I had touched. 'Looks an awful lot like the one that killed Egbert, doesn't it?'

'A tree branch killed Egbert,' Pavlik said. 'But yes. This looks like another ghost gun, probably from the same plans or kit.'

Brrr. 'Assembled at home?'

'From parts bought online or printed with a 3D printer,' Pavlik said. 'They're unregistered and have no serial number, of course.'

'Untraceable,' I said. 'You think this was made by the same person?'

'I told you: no thinking,' Pavlik said, turning with a trace of a grin. 'Forensics will tell us.'

I frowned. 'But what does that mean, then? The same person who shot Jacque shot Egbert? Or one of them shot the other?'

'Jacque couldn't have shot Egbert and then himself,' Pavlik said, surveying the room. 'It's pretty clear Jacque died first.'

He did a double take and walked over to the wall with the two chairs. 'This is a 3D printer,' he said, pointing at the contraption on the table.

'Really?' I said, coming over. The printer had a flat base with what I'd mistaken as a drill or saw suspended over it. I could see now that it was a printer head. 'Somebody is using this place.'

'Not just somebody.' Pavlik had moved toward the kitchen. 'We already have a fairly sophisticated gang operating in town, stealing the HVAC units and catalytic converters. Maybe that's not all they're into.'

'Making and selling guns? Is that what you're thinking?'

'Oh, yeah.' Molly's voice said from the doorway. 'I've seen them on TV. It's like DIY. Crazy.'

'Stay there and link your fingers in front of you,' Pavlik ordered.

'Am I under arrest?' she said, hands held overhead, eyes wide.

'You don't have to raise your hands,' I told her. 'Just fold them in front of you to keep from accidentally touching something. It's what I should have told you to do.'

'Before I accidentally touched something,' she said, lowering her hands. 'Yes. Did you tell the sheriff about the phone?'

'Where is it?' Pavlik asked.

'There,' I said, pointing to the counter. 'Molly found it just under that corner of the coffee table and picked it up.'

'Before Maggy told me not to,' Molly said.

I shrugged. 'It's not like you haven't seen crime programs. I would have thought you'd know the drill.'

'I was excited,' Molly said defensively. 'Or maybe not so much excited as horrified.'

Sure she was.

'Adrenaline,' Pavlik told her and then called, 'Anthony?'

'Yes, sir.' Sheriff's Deputy Kelly Anthony appeared at the door.

'Please take Ms Durand outside and take her statement. Then have somebody drive her home.'

'Sir. Shall I send crime scene in?'

'Please,' he said.

As Kelly Anthony saw a reluctant Molly out, the white-garbed crime scene technicians filed in.

'You're not kicking me out?' I asked.

'Not yet,' Pavlik said. 'This is the Durands' place, you said?'

'Yes. Unused by them for years, which is probably why nobody mentioned it.'

'It's not unused anymore.' Pavlik had his gloves on.

'Just so you know, Molly was nosing around in the kitchen, too,' I said. 'It was like I needed eyes in the back of my head.'

'While you were examining the body.' Pavlik opened a cupboard. 'Whoever this is, they have been using it for a while.' He hitched himself up to see the top shelf.

'Copper?' I was trying to see myself despite our considerable height difference.

'Tools.' Pavlik wasn't about to move anything without it being photographed and catalogued, so I'd just have to take his word for it. 'A cutter, for scoring and cutting pipe.'

'Anything else?'

Pavlik opened another cabinet door. 'Looks like supplies for the printer.'

An array of spools of what looked like colored wire were stacked up, along with clear bins of . . . what? I didn't know. But then, I'd never used a 3D printer to make guns or anything else.

'We'll leave these to my forensic people,' Pavlik said, waving a technician toward the cabinet.

A flash from the woman photographing Jacque's body lighted the space. 'Maybe Jacque stumbled upon the thieves here.'

'It looks like somebody has been sleeping here.' Pavlik had stuck his head around a corner and now stepped in.

I followed. 'The cushions from the couch.' The room was empty, except for two plaid cushions that had been aligned for a bed. An old-fashioned crocheted afghan laid in what looked like a hastily discarded heap nearby. 'Why wouldn't they just sleep on the couch?'

Pavlik tipped his head toward the door where we could see the coroner bent over Jacque's body. 'Would you?'

A shiver crawled up my spine. 'They could have moved him.'

'The autopsy should tell us if the body was moved.'

'Sheriff?' The coroner was beckoning from the doorway.

Jacque's body was rolled on to one side now, and the coroner pointed to something at the right side of his forehead just into the hairline.

'What?' I whispered when Pavlik came back.

'He thinks there was a blow to his head pre-mortem,' Pavlik said. 'We'll know more—'

'From the autopsy,' I completed for him. 'But if so, that means it's similar to Egbert's death. Murder posed to look like suicide.'

'Not really posed,' Pavlik countered. 'The gun was nearby, but not in his hand. Jacque could have been stunned by the blow. While he was down, the killer shot him, dropped the gun and took off.'

'I don't suppose we'll find fingerprints on the gun?'

'I doubt it. Kind of silly to go to all the trouble to use a ghost gun and then leave fingerprints.'

'I suppose.'

'But what was Jacque doing here in the first place?' Pavlik asked. 'I don't see him messed up in whatever was going on.'

'I don't either,' I said honestly. 'But I also don't see him waking up during the night and suddenly remembering the Durands had a cabin he could use since Amy kicked him out.'

'And walking here in the middle of the night?' Pavlik shook his head.

'Though that could explain the head wound,' I pointed out. 'Maybe he just hit his head on a tree branch in the dark.'

'Maybe.' Pavlik sounded unconvinced. 'But whatever brought him here, I don't think he planned to stay. He didn't bring his things.'

'What things?' I asked.

'He had a duffle in the car that Amy had packed and thrown at him,' Pavlik said. 'He went out to the car to get it after you went to bed.'

'Poor Amy,' I said. 'Are you going to break the news? I told Sarah to keep her at the shop if she came back.'

'From where?'

'She was going to talk to Becky. See if she knew where Egbert found Jacque's phone.'

'She doesn't,' he said. 'We asked.'

'But you're the police,' I said. 'And Becky is Becky. Besides, I thought it would give Amy something to do. At the time, it seemed odd that Egbert would have found Jacque's phone in the woods.'

'Though now it's entirely possible,' Pavlik said. 'Especially if Egbert was involved in this copper ring.'

'Copper ring,' I said. 'I like that.'

Pavlik rolled his eyes. 'I hate when the media coins a phrase. Now I've done it myself.'

'Even worse,' I said. 'It doesn't begin to cover the other things they may be involved in, like the ghost guns.'

'True.' We were still in what had been used as a bedroom, and Pavlik stepped to the doorway. 'They're examining the printer now. I'm not sure how sophisticated this one is, but it probably has some sort of log of jobs. They certainly had enough filament to keep busy.'

'Is that the colored wires? Filament?'

'The filament is the material that the printer prints with,' Pavlik explained, without making me feel the least bit stupid. Yet.

'Like the ink in a conventional printer,' I said, needing to make the correlation with something in my own world. 'Are the filaments plastic?'

'Thermoplastic or polymers,' Pavlik confirmed. 'So they can be melted and extruded – or squirted – into the shapes. Some of the filaments combine metal or wood powder with the polymers to replicate those materials.'

'Interesting,' I said, frowning. 'Have you found anything that might link Egbert to all this?'

'Besides the money? Not yet, but we'll check for prints and we have his computer. They're going over search histories as we speak.'

Like 'how to make a ghost gun.' 'The printer,' I said. 'They'd need electricity. Do we know if it's—'

The lights in the room flickered on and we turned to see the same technician who had been at Egbert's crime scene standing by a wall switch. 'Power works,' he said with a grin.

'Power and probably water,' I said, chewing the inside of my cheek. 'Even if somebody wasn't using the place, the Durands would need to keep the utilities on, if for no other reason than to keep the pipes from freezing in the winter.'

'True,' Pavlik said. 'They might notice an uptick in usage if it went on long enough. We'll check.'

'No Wi-Fi here, though,' I said, holding up my phone.

'Pity the poor thieves had to use data,' Pavlik said. 'I did mention there's a cell tower nearby.'

'You did. Is that relevant beyond locating Jacque?' Which we now had done, sadly.

'It is because of that.' He nodded toward the phone Molly had found. It was being bagged.

'You'll be able to trace where that phone has been,' I said. 'And who it has called?'

'One of whom,' Pavlik said, going to take the evidence bag

from the technician, 'I'm betting is Jacque Oui. His phone showed a call at four thirty-nine a.m. on Saturday morning from an unknown caller.'

'You think he came here to meet somebody,' I said.

'Or was lured.'

Brrr. 'There are a lot of questions, aren't there? But the biggest one . . .'

Pavlik was busy trying to get into the phone, punching buttons through the plastic bag. 'Sorry. You want an audience for this?'

'Please.'

He looked up. 'Proceed. The biggest question?'

'If Jacque is dead here . . .'

'Who died in the fire with Paulette?' Pavlik was back at work on the phone.

TWENTY

Way to steal my thunder, but Pavlik could be excused. The question was obviously . . . obvious.

And unanswered for now. So, who was missing? We knew Denis Durand left for Chicago on Friday night, but he had been in touch over the weekend, most importantly with Molly on Saturday after the fire.

Helen believed Denis was cheating on her. Was he? I liked the man, but then I liked Ted, and he had cheated, too. On me, no less.

But apart from Denis, we had no other candidates for corpses. Jamie Bright certainly had been out and about this weekend, so it wasn't him either. Or Pavlik. Or Ted.

I was out of men.

'How do you do this on a regular basis?' I whispered to Pavlik as we walked up the sidewalk to Uncommon Grounds' front porch.

'Happily, we don't have that many murders in Brookhills,' Pavlik said. 'And for accidental deaths—'

'You have people for that.' I was squinting up at the windows, trying to see if Amy was inside.

'Well, yes,' he said. 'A deputy will most often notify the family in that case.'

I had my foot on the bottom step when the door opened hesitantly.

'Maggy?' Amy's face already was streaked with tears.

Sarah appeared behind her, a little panicky. 'I didn't say . . . but she . . .'

'You're here to tell me that Jacque is dead.' Amy descended the steps to me and put her hand to my chest. 'Aren't you?'

I covered her hand with mine and nodded.

As Amy's knees buckled, Pavlik managed to scoop her up before she fell. He carried her up the steps and into the shop, glancing around for somewhere to put her down.

Ours was more table-and-chair café than overstuffed sofa coffeehouse, but we did have one reading corner we'd recently notched out and furnished with a coffee table and flowered chair retired from Sarah's parlor. 'There.' I pointed.

Pavlik set Amy gently on the chair.

'I'll get her some water,' Sarah said abruptly and disappeared.

I followed her into the kitchen. 'What on earth did you say to her?'

My partner turned with a glass in her hand. 'Nothing, I swear. Only that you'd called and asked that she wait until you got back.'

'And from that she got "Jacque is dead"?'

Sarah bit her lip. 'It might have been the way I said it.'

'Like . . .'

'Nice?' she tried. 'Concerned even?'

'Oh, Sarah.' Fine time to turn over a new leaf.

'It was after you called to say you were on your way to tell her.' She turned to fill the glass from the filtered water. 'Kind of got to me.'

'I know,' I said.

'Anyway, I don't know why you're so ticked. I'm the one who has had to deal with this huge' – she made a motion with the glass apparently meant to illustrate 'huge' and managed to spill half its contents on the floor – 'range of feelings over the last half-hour. You didn't even have to break it to her when you got here.'

'I was just along for support,' I said, pulling paper towels off a roll by the sink to drop on the floor. 'Pavlik would have been the one to tell her officially.'

'Which presumably is what he's doing now.' She handed me the half-empty glass. 'Would you take this to her?'

'You don't want to come out?' I was astonished. Sarah liked to stay in the know.

'I . . . No. I'll just take some time in the office. This is a little more emotion than I can handle.' There was a bead of sweat on her forehead.

I handed her the glass. 'Take this in the office and drink it. I'll get another for Amy.'

'I just . . .'

'It's OK,' I said, turning to get another glass and fill it. 'You don't have to explain to me.'

'Thanks.'

When I turned back with the water, she was still standing there. 'You'll fill me in later?'

'Of course I will.' I smiled. 'And thanks.'

'Yup.'

When I returned to the dining room, Amy was crying quietly into one of our unbleached eco-friendly Uncommon Grounds napkins. I grabbed a couple more and joined Pavlik, who was sitting on the coffee table across from her.

'Here,' I said, giving her the water and taking the soaked napkin. 'Drink this.'

'I may throw it up.'

'Fair point.' I took the glass back and handed her a dry napkin.

She gave a little strangled laugh. 'I always wonder about that on TV, you know? There's bad news, so somebody goes to get a glass of water like that's going to help.'

It helped Sarah get out of the room. 'Or make a cup of tea,' I told Amy. 'But the one I always loved as a kid were the old movies where a woman goes into labor, and they send one person for towels and another to boil water.'

'Whatever for?' Amy had raised her head.

'I think partly just to give the father something to do,' I said. 'But also, back then, they couldn't get hot water from the tap, so—'

'That really was the olden days,' she said.

'It was,' I admitted. 'These movies date back to my grand-parents' time. I was young enough when I saw them that I worried they were going to boil the baby.'

A stifled laugh. 'Oh, Maggy. That's horrible.'

'I know,' I said, crossing to sit next to her on the arm of the big chair. 'But you laughed.'

'I did.' She rested her head against me and looked at Pavlik. 'Does she ever let you watch a new movie?'

'Never,' he told her.

I think Pavlik would have winked at me if he was a winking sort of guy. But he did smile.

I felt Amy draw in a breath and let it out with a shudder. 'You know the hell of it? I think I've known all along that Jacque was dead, but I just had to keep thinking, keep detecting with you, keep asking questions, keep being mad about Paulette.' She turned her face up toward me. 'Is that why you do it?'

'The detecting, you mean? No, I'm just a meddler.'

This shudder was a laugh.

'But I do know,' I continued, 'that it's easier to be angry than it is to be sad.'

'At least you can control anger,' Amy said. 'It's proactive. Sadness just kind of . . . engulfs you.'

'Sarah would say that's very wise,' I said, rubbing her shoulder. 'Which reminds me, you should call Helen.'

'I will.' Amy sat up and dabbed at her eyes. 'But right now I need to process it myself. With no one to tell me how.'

'If you want nobody to do anything,' Sarah said, popping back out with her purse, 'I'm your gal. Why don't you stay at my house tonight? We can go over there now.'

'Great idea,' I said, lifting my chin in unspoken question to Sarah. She nodded that she was all right now.

I climbed off the chair so Amy could get up.

'Do you need me to do anything?' she asked Pavlik. 'Identify the body?'

'Both Maggy and I did that,' Pavlik said. 'So it's not necessary, unless you want to see him.'

'I'd like to think about that, if it's all right.' Then, to me, as Pavlik went to open the door for her and Sarah, 'Is it . . . was he very bad?'

'One gunshot wound in the left temple and a bruise on his forehead,' I said. 'But he has . . .'

'Say it.'

I ducked my head. 'He has probably been dead since early Saturday morning.'

'I see.' She started toward the door.

'Amy?'

She glanced back over her shoulder.

'You do realize why you've felt all along that Jacque was dead, don't you?'

She turned now and spread her hands wide. 'Hopeless pessimist?'

'You knew that death was the only thing that would have kept him from coming back to you.'

'I kicked him out.'

I could barely hear the words.

'You had a pretty good reason.' I shook my head. 'But you two have had plenty of ups and downs and gotten through them all. He knew you loved him.'

'I did,' she said and started to turn away. 'But if he knew that, why did he kill himself?'

'We don't know that he did,' I said. 'I'm sure Pavlik told you about the blow to his forehead. It probably wasn't the cause of death, but he could have been hit and then shot at close range while he was still stunned or even unconscious.'

Amy was thinking. 'You said the gunshot was to the left temple? Jacque's left.' She touched her hand to her own temple.

'Yes.'

'But then, don't you see?' she asked, facing me. 'He must have shot himself.'

'Why would you say that?' I was puzzled.

'Because it fits,' Amy said. 'Jacque was left-handed.'

TWENTY-ONE

'I think she wants to believe Jacque killed himself,' I said to Pavlik. 'If it were you instead of Jacque, which would I prefer? That you were murdered? Or that you had killed yourself?'

We were still at the shop, which was technically open except for the 'closed' sign I put on the door.

I collapsed into the flowered chair. 'I'm thinking murder.'

Pavlik's eyebrows went up. 'Taking the personal aspect out of it—'

'It's just that murder says you didn't want to leave me,' I continued.

'Murder also says I suffered a brutal, violent death at the hands of another.' Pavlik came to stand in front of me and shrugged. 'But whichever you think is more romantic is fine by me.'

'Well, that's true, I suppose,' I said, pulling him down on to the chair with me. 'Guess I was being selfish.'

'Guess?' Pavlik kissed the top of my head. 'Did *you* know Jacque was left-handed?'

'Not actively, really,' I said. 'I mean, when Amy said it, I could picture him lopping a head off a fish.'

'He held the cleaver in his left hand?'

'Absolutely,' I said. 'While he opined that he didn't know why he was selling me a nice piece of fish when I undoubtedly was going to ruin it.'

'That seems harsh,' Pavlik said. 'You're paying for the fish – you had every right to ruin it.'

Not exactly a stalwart defense of my cooking skills, but fair enough.

There was a knock at the door, and Molly Durand stuck her head in. 'Oh, good. You're still here.'

'We're just leaving,' I said, prying myself out from under Pavlik. 'Or I will be once I close.'

'You go ahead,' Molly said. 'I really wanted to speak to the sheriff anyway.'

I was damned if I was going to let Mini-Me talk to Pavlik without Me-Me. Pavlik was still in the big chair, so I pulled a chair away from one of the tables and waved Molly into it. I settled myself on the edge of the coffee table.

'Did Maggy tell you what I said about Egbert?' Molly asked Pavlik, not bothering to sit down.

'The seven-thousand-dollar sneakers?' Pavlik asked. 'She told me that on the phone just before you found Jacque.'

'That's not the only thing.' Now she did sit down. She leaned forward eagerly. 'I also saw him talking to some random guy. I was trying to think when that was and realized it was after my dentist appointment on Friday afternoon.' She cocked her head at me. 'Dr Thorsen. Is he some relative of yours?'

'Ex.'

'Ohhh . . .' Molly snuck a glance at Pavlik.

'No drama there,' I told her. 'You said this guy you saw with Egbert was sketchy, as I recall, but sketchy how?'

Molly seemed disappointed. 'Oh, you know. Kind of hunched over, wearing a hoodie with the hood up when he was way too old to be doing that.'

'How old is too old?' Pavlik asked.

'Like twenty-five,' Molly answered. 'It was hard to tell, but this guy seemed a lot older than that.'

'Did you notice his sneakers?'

They both looked at me.

'Were they expensive like Egbert's? They would stand out, and if Egbert was working with this guy, he would have money, too.'

'Good point,' Molly said, thinking. 'I don't remember them being anything special, but maybe he's smarter than Egbert and doesn't flaunt his ill-gotten gains.'

Score one for Mini-Me.

'Did you see this man's face?' Pavlik asked.

'Just for a second.' She frowned. 'I was trying to figure out if I knew him, and he caught me staring. Gave me this really dirty look, like he was seeing right through me.'

'And did you know him?' It was amazing how much the girl suddenly remembered about the encounter.

'No,' she said unequivocally.

Pavlik was studying her face. 'You're sure?'

When she hesitated, I touched her shoulder. 'He's not going to know.'

She shivered. 'But he might have been a drug dealer or something.'

Maybe. But I was starting to think arsonist. Unless she had made the man up, of course. 'Did you hear what he and Egbert were talking about?'

'Uh-uh. I was too far away, but it seemed like Egbert was giving him directions. He pointed toward Schultz's.'

I glanced at Pavlik.

He cleared his throat. 'Molly, would you be willing to come in and sit down with our sketch artist?'

'That would be so cool,' Molly said, and then seemed to realize she was supposed to be a serious witness, not a true-crime groupie. 'I mean, I can make the time if you think it will help.'

'It would, thank you.'

'You know,' she said, and I could tell she was writing movie scenes in her head, 'I think Egbert was into something. Something big. Did he ever show you his metal detector? He said it cost like ten thousand dollars.'

'It did look nice,' I said, turning to Pavlik. 'Had a touch-screen and everything.'

'I remember,' he said with a whiff of a smile. 'Did you ever see Egbert hanging around your parents' cabin, Molly?'

'No, but I'm like never there.' She frowned. 'Why was Mr Oui there anyway?'

'We don't know,' Pavlik said. 'Is it possible your parents lent the cabin to him?'

'Oh, no.' Molly's nose wrinkled. 'You saw it. The place is a wreck. It would be like an insult.'

Unless you had no place to sleep. Or hide.

Pavlik's phone buzzed, and he got up and moved away from us to answer it.

Molly leaned toward me, putting her hand on my arm. 'He is so handsome, I can't stand it.'

'Me neither,' I told her. 'Does your dad know Jacque is dead?'

'I texted him to call me,' Molly said. 'I didn't want to leave it in a text message.'

'Good girl,' I said. 'He stayed in Chicago last night?'

'Yeah, and Helen wasn't happy about it.' She shook her head. 'I think she's afraid he's cheating on her.'

'Why is that?'

'No clue,' she said, rolling her eyes. 'She was ticked when he left to drive to Chicago after dinner Friday night, but she's the one who made him come home in the first place. It would have been a lot easier for him to just leave from work. It's like you can't win with Helen.'

'It's Helen again?' I raised my eyebrows at her.

She grinned. 'I call her that occasionally just to make her mad. It's fun.'

I bet it was. Dinner that night must have been a barrel of laughs. Then Denis drove to Chicago and . . . 'What did you and your mom do on Friday night?'

Molly's eyes got wide. 'Are you asking if we have alibis? That is so cool.'

'No, I—'

'Yes, you are. Well, we don't. I mean, I guess *I* do, because I went over to Lindsey's. But Helen is totally without.'

'Without what?' Pavlik had returned to the conversation.

'Alibis for the fire.' She glanced at me. 'And probably Mr Oui's murder, too, right? He would—'

'If I can interrupt,' Pavlik said. 'I need to go back to the office. But I was wondering if either of you recognizes this number.'

He held up a slip of paper with a local telephone number.

'No,' I said, studying it.

'Uh-uh,' Molly said. 'Is that the burner I found at the cabin?'

'Nope,' Pavlik said, tucking the note in his pocket.

'I'll walk you out,' I told him.

'What should I do?' Molly asked, getting up herself.

'Make yourself useful and start vacuuming,' I called back. 'Or go home.'

Pavlik grinned at me as we descended the porch steps. 'Is Mini-Me starting to annoy Mega—'

'Watch it.'

'Magnificent-You.' Pavlik kissed me on the nose.

'Nice recovery,' I said. 'Molly doesn't so much annoy me as take things thirty-five different directions all at the same time for drama's sake.'

'So, the answer is yes.'

'Yes.' We stopped at the squad car. 'That number *is* the burner phone, isn't it?'

'It is, but I wasn't going to confirm that to her. Her imagination is active enough. Still, I thought I should run it past her since it was found in the family cabin.'

'Is it the number that called Jacque's mobile?'

'Yes,' Pavlik said, leaving me on the sidewalk to go around to the driver's side.

'Amy might recognize it,' I told him as he got in.

'Would you ask her?' Pavlik asked, rolling down the passenger-side window so I could hear. 'I'm sure you're heading over to Sarah's after closing anyway.'

'I am.'

'You need me to give you the number again?' He pulled the slip out of his pocket.

'I memorized it,' I said.

'That's amazing and a little disturbing,' he said.

'Like me.' I blew him a kiss.

TWENTY-TWO

As befitted a former real estate mogul, Sarah resided in an exceedingly nice part of Brookhills dubbed, naturally, Brookhills Estates. It was one of the neighborhoods being targeted by the thieves, although Sarah hadn't had any trouble.

Her house was a Victorian – a so-called painted lady, dressed in delicate shades of cream and rose. Elegant and graceful, it was everything Sarah was not. And she loved it.

'Amy's here in the parlor,' Sarah said, leading me into a room painted a clear shade of yellow and furnished in floral patterns.

'Isn't that the same fabric as the one you donated to the shop?' I asked, pointing to the chair where our barista was seated.

Sarah settled on to the couch. 'Good eye.'

I wasn't sure if she was being sarcastic. 'But why give a chair away and replace it with the same one?'

'Because it's not the same one,' Sarah said. 'This is a wing chair.'

'Oh.'

'Wings.' Amy patted the upholstered protrusions framing her head.

'Of course.' I took the other chair – a non-wing, but seemingly identical otherwise – on the other side of the fireplace. 'Much better.'

Amy snuck a grin at me.

'The two identical non-winged chairs seemed too matchy-matchy,' Sarah said defensively.

'This is better,' I said. 'Eclectic.'

'You make fun,' Sarah said. 'But what do you know? You have no eye for design at all.'

'I am not making fun,' I protested. 'In fact, I'm trying very hard not to make fun.'

Amy gave a snort, showing that, at the very least, Sarah and I were a diversion if not outright entertainment.

'Sorry, Sarah,' Amy said, putting a hand over her mouth. 'It's just that your house is such a contrast to your personal style.'

Which was nil. Even before the Uncommon Grounds jeans and T-shirts, Sarah's wardrobe had consisted entirely of baggy beige trousers and long jackets, the pockets of which concealed her cigarettes. Thankfully she had given those up. The cigarettes. The trousers and jackets sometimes made a re-emergence.

'When I was an agent,' Sarah said now, chin in the air, 'I endeavored to highlight the home I was showing, not draw attention to myself.'

'Kind of like a dog show,' I mused.

'Like what?' Amy asked.

'A dog show. You know how the handlers always dress so dowdy? I think it's because they want to show off the dogs.'

'And not fall off their stilettos flat on to their pearl neck-laces,' Sarah said.

'I don't know what I would do without you two.' Amy's smile had gone a little tearful, and she leaned forward as if to hug my partner. 'Truly.'

'Good,' Sarah said and slid out of range.

Amy smiled. 'You've had all the human interaction you can handle, huh?'

'Absolutely,' Sarah said and turned to me. 'What's new?'

This was not, of course, a casual question. Sarah wanted to know about the discovery of Jacque's body, not to mention what, if anything, had happened after she and Amy left the shop.

I glanced at Amy, thinking I'd already been explicit enough with her. 'I don't know how much of this you want to hear.'

'Everything,' she said.

'OK. First, Pavlik wants to know if this number is familiar to you.' I recited it.

Amy shook her head. 'No. Why?'

'Jacque's cell phone—'

'Oh!' Amy was waving her hand like a child in class.

'I didn't get a chance to tell you. Becky said she didn't see Egbert find anything – especially a cell phone – at Schultz's the morning of the fire. She did say, though, that Egbert had a plastic bag of old mobiles in his room.'

'She noses around his room?' Sarah asked. 'Did the man have no privacy?'

Amy smiled. 'I know, right? She said she went in to put away his clean underwear. But what's interesting is that she asked him about the phones and some things she saw on his computer—'

'She went into his computer, too?' Sarah, again.

I asked the more pertinent question. 'What things?'

'Guns,' she said, lifting an eyebrow. 'Like blueprints of guns.'

'Ghost guns,' I said. 'That's what was used to shoot both Jacque and Egbert, himself.'

'Geez,' Sarah said, getting up to turn on the gas fireplace. 'What was the guy into?'

'You really want a fire?' I asked. 'It's June.'

Sarah rubbed her arms as she sat down. 'You didn't feel a chill?'

Egbert walking over his own grave. 'Pavlik's people have his computer now, so I'm sure they'll find the searches, even if he tried to cover them up after Becky's snooping. I don't suppose she saw anything else odd in the room?' Catalytic converters, HVAC units, 3D printers?

'Not that she said. And after she questioned him – this was like a month ago – he started locking his room.'

'And she couldn't pick the lock?' Sarah asked. 'Becky must be slipping.'

'What kind of odd things do you mean, Maggy?'

'It's possible Egbert was involved in this rash of robberies, including the one at Christ Christian. Pavlik says there's good money in selling the metal they harvest from the HVAC units and catalytic converters, and Egbert has been flashing some pretty expensive stuff. Becky told me he bought her a Jimmy Choo roller bag for her retirement. I didn't think much about it then—'

'Other than he's trying to get rid of her,' Sarah inserted.

'Except that Molly says his sneakers cost seven thousand dollars.'

'The red ones?' Sarah asked. 'I guess a kid would know. I just thought they were ugly.'

'I thought they were a rebellion against his mother,' Amy said.

'Maybe they were,' I said. 'Maybe the guns, the copper, the catalytic converters and whatever else he was into were all an effort to escape Becky.'

'Well, he certainly did that,' Sarah said, and I could swear another cold wave swept through.

'Did Egbert kill Jacque?' Amy asked after a second.

'It's possible. We can't know for sure until after the autopsy, but Jacque probably died on Saturday morning. Egbert died on Sunday.'

'We also know that Jacque died at the cabin and that Egbert was in possession of Jacque's cell phone when he, Egbert, died,' Amy reasoned. 'Doesn't that put them both at the cabin?'

I waggled my head. 'Maybe. But all we really know is that Jacque's body was found there, along with the gun we assume shot him. We don't know that it actually happened there. Or that he didn't lose his phone somewhere else in the woods before that.'

'Regardless' – Amy seemed to be losing patience – 'their paths must have crossed somewhere.'

I'd give her that. 'The cabin is interesting, though. There's evidence it was used by these thieves.' I was weighing how much to tell them.

'Stealing HVAC units and catalytic converters is one thing,' Sarah said. 'But DIY guns are a whole other level.'

'I know,' I said.

'You think they're selling them?' Sarah asked. 'Or using them for their own purposes?'

'Like killing Jacque and Egbert?' Amy said. 'And why kill Egbert, anyway? From what you're saying, Maggy, he was one of their own.'

'I don't know. But it seems they were making some real money, so maybe that was leading to friction?' I shrugged.

'What about Jacque?' Amy asked, kicking off her shoes to

tuck her feet under her on the chair. 'He certainly wasn't involved in any of it.'

'Probably not,' I said. 'But—'

'Probably not?' Amy exploded. 'He was a respected member of the community, not some crazy mama's boy roaming the woods.'

'Somebody set the shop on fire,' I reminded her.

'And you're so sure it was Jacque?' Amy's voice had risen an octave.

She did say anger was easier. Or was it me who said it? 'Jacque did have insurance?'

'On the shop? Of course he did.'

'How much?' Sarah asked.

'I don't know,' Amy said. 'He mentioned he renewed the policy just last month, but I don't know any of the details.'

'It likely would be for replacement value,' Sarah said, rubbing her chin. 'And maybe loss of business. It could add up.'

'Now what's your theory?' Amy asked. 'Jacque torched his store and his ex-wife and then shot himself at the cabin in a fit of remorse? Then who is the second body?'

'I don't know,' I said. 'But somebody called Jacque from that number I asked you about at four thirty-nine a.m. on Saturday morning and said something that got him out of bed and into the woods.'

'What time did the fire start?' Sarah asked.

'I'm not sure.' I turned to Amy. 'We said we heard the trucks about ten after five.'

'Yes, so presumably it took some time to spread and for someone to call it in.'

'And the fire response to get there,' I said. 'So, if somebody called Jacque at four thirty-nine, they could have been at the store getting permission to light the fire or telling him that they already had.'

'You're so wrong, Maggy.'

'You don't know that, Amy,' Sarah said soberly. 'People do desperate things in the moment and then regret them.'

'Jacque had no idea Paulette would be staying there that night. I don't buy that he was trying to get rid of her.' Amy was tracing the flowers on the arm of the chair with her finger with such force I thought she might push through right to the batting. 'He's not a murderer.'

'So maybe he tried to call it off,' I offered.

'But then in the early hours,' Sarah said, 'he gets this call saying it's done. What would he do? Refuse to pay? Confess to the whole thing?'

'Either of those things would give the arsonist a reason to kill him,' I said.

'Have you two given any thought to the possibility that Jacque was the victim in this?' Amy demanded. 'Maybe the call was not from somebody he hired to set the fire, but from somebody threatening to set it.'

'You mean, sell me the shop or else?' I asked, thinking about it. 'Jamie Bright—'

'Jamie Bright is your favorite fall-guy,' Sarah said. 'I find it hard to believe that a successful businessman would—'

'Yet you'll believe it of Jacque,' Amy interrupted indignantly.

'Jacque wasn't that successful,' Sarah said irritably. 'By your own admission, he—'

'Then there's Paulette,' I interjected before fisticuffs could break out. 'Maybe she was the blackmailer. You know, give me half or else?'

'Or else I'll burn down the shop with me in it?' Amy was doubtful.

I shrugged. 'For all we know, she was one of those "if you don't do what I want, I'm going to kill myself" types.'

'Suicidal, you mean.'

'Manipulative,' Sarah corrected her. 'But where does the second body come in?'

Amy looked skeptical. 'And who have you cast in the role of arsonist if it's not Paulette? Egbert?'

I bit my lip. 'Maybe. Molly swears she saw Egbert directing a guy to Schultz's on Friday. He could be the mysterious man in the flat.'

'Who was it?' Amy asked.

'She didn't know,' I said. 'She's giving a description to a sketch artist.'

'Well, we know it wasn't a friend,' Sarah said. 'Egbert didn't have friends.'

'Or so we believed. There apparently are a lot of things we don't know about Egbert,' I said. 'Molly also thought he might be into cryptocurrency.'

'Not a crime,' Amy reminded us.

'But confusing,' I said. 'Very confusing.'

'For old people,' Amy said. 'But if he was trading in cryptocurrency, it might explain why nobody, even his mother, knew he had any money to speak of.'

'And yet he bought stuff,' I said. 'Expensive stuff.'

'But back to Egbert and this guy on Friday,' Sarah said. 'You said they were outside Schultz's—'

'Outside the 501 Building,' I corrected. 'Egbert seemed to be directing this guy to Schultz's next door.'

'Which is what I said.'

'Not precisely.'

'Whatever,' Amy said. 'Are you suggesting that Egbert was sending this guy over to set the fire?'

'Not just at that very moment,' I said. 'But if this man was looking for Schultz's, the question is why?'

'He needed a loaf of bread?' Sarah suggested.

Obviously a subscriber to 'the simplest answer is the correct one' school of thought. 'Possible, I guess.'

'Not the smoking gun you were looking for?' Sarah asked with a smirk.

'But why would Egbert want to burn down Schultz's?' Amy asked. 'I mean, unless he was being paid a lot of money by somebody.'

'Revenge for Jacque firing his mother and condemning him to life with Becky twenty-four/seven?' Sarah tried.

It was certainly cause, but: 'If we're right about Egbert's various side businesses, he could have left anytime.'

'Just because he had money doesn't mean he wasn't still a neurotic mommy's boy,' Sarah pointed out.

'It's too bad we can't ask Helen,' Amy said. 'See if our psychological profile of Egbert fits.'

'I was thinking the same thing,' I said. 'We should ask – all she can do is cite patient confidentiality. But maybe she'll entertain some hypothetical questions, at least.'

'I have an appointment with her at ten tomorrow.' Amy stood up to stretch. 'You're welcome to come along, Maggy.'

'How about me?' Sarah asked, getting up as well.

'Somebody has to watch the store,' Amy said, kissing her on the cheek. 'Thank you.'

Sarah's face reddened. 'Oh, stop.'

'No, really,' Amy said. 'Thanks, both of you. I honestly don't know what I'd do if I didn't have you right now.'

'Well, you do have us.' I hugged Amy and then picked up my purse.

'For better or worse,' I heard Sarah mutter as the door closed behind me. 'God help you.'

TWENTY-THREE

I was having a well-deserved glass of wine when I heard Pavlik's Harley rumble up the driveway.

'Pinot?' I asked, raising my glass as he came through the door.

'Nah, not right now.' He dropped on to the couch next to me, barely missing Mocha who was curled up. Frank was serving as my footrest in front of the couch.

'Oops. Sorry, baby,' Pavlik said as Mocha jumped down.

'Sure, *her* you call baby.' I kissed him.

'You want me to call you baby?' He flashed a grin. 'Or maybe "babe."'

'Ugh, I think not.' I squiggled my toes in Frank's fur as I laid my head against Pavlik's shoulder. 'Amy didn't recognize the phone number from the burner phone.'

'Of course not,' Pavlik said. 'That would have been too easy.'

'Anything new, forensically speaking, on any of our many bodies?'

'The body count is four and the answer is no. But since it's finally Monday, Anthony was able to track down Paulette Badeaux's dentist in Paris. He's sending over X-rays for comparison.'

'Though we're fairly sure it's her anyway, from the passport, right?'

'I prefer the identification be conclusive.'

That was why I loved him.

'I did have an interesting visitor to the office late this afternoon,' Pavlik continued.

'Who was that?'

'Molly Durand.'

'She came in to describe hoodie guy to the sketch artist? That was quick.'

'I had Anthony pick her up for that and for fingerprinting. Yours, I have on file.'

'Of course you do,' I said. 'But Molly Durand picked up in a squad car. She must have been in Mini-Me heaven.'

'She was,' Pavlik said. 'But maybe a little scared, too.'

'Of the hoodie man?' I asked. 'How did the drawing come out?'

Pavlik hitched himself up to slide his phone out of his pocket. Then he punched up a photo.

'Huh,' I said, squinting at it. 'Looks kind of like Ichabod Crane.'

'I agree. More cartoon character than real person.' Pavlik took the phone back.

'He's certainly not anybody I recognize from around here,' I said. 'So, what was the interesting part?'

'Interesting?'

'You referred to Molly as "an interesting visitor." Did you mean her describing Ichabod or providing her fingerprints?'

'The fingerprints that she left all over my crime scene, you mean?'

'That would be them,' I said regretfully. 'She's kind of hard to control.'

'She's an interesting kid, as I said. After fingerprinting, she demanded a DNA test.'

'A DNA test?' I repeated, sitting up.

'Yes,' Pavlik said. 'Molly Durand volunteered her DNA for comparison with that of the man's body in Schultz's.'

I frowned. 'Denis is out of town, but Molly can't possibly think the body is his. She spoke to him on Saturday after the fire.'

'She lied to you, to everyone,' Pavlik said. 'Nobody has heard from Denis Durand since he left the house after dinner on Friday night. We've already spoken to Helen, and she confirms that her contact with him has been through Molly.'

'Who was lying.' I'd briefly considered Denis as a possible fire victim and discarded the idea, precisely because Molly had talked to him. I felt betrayed. And more than a little cheated big reveal-wise. 'But why would Molly lie? Especially to me?'

'She was covering for her father,' Pavlik said. 'Apparently these business trips are a regular thing for him.'

'She did say that Helen thinks Denis is cheating. And Helen told me that herself.'

'Helen may be right. And, if so, Molly is actively aiding and abetting.'

'I know that Helen is her stepmother,' I said. 'But she and Denis have been together since Molly was four. Helen is the only mother Molly has ever known.'

'Whatever the relationship, Molly has been lying to Helen and now is doing an end-around her by providing her own DNA for matching.'

'Can she do that?' I asked. 'I mean, does she need parental consent?'

'Molly has just turned eighteen,' Pavlik said. 'If she wants to know if the deceased male is her father, she has a right.'

'But what would Denis be doing at—' I could have slapped myself. 'Denis and Paulette knew each other from Paris.'

'Yes.'

'But if Denis knew Paulette was coming to Brookhills, if he snuck away that night to see her, this opens a whole new world of possibilities. We know Helen is a jealous woman. Maybe she followed him there and started the fire in a fit of pique.' Admittedly it would have to be a whole truckload of pique.

'We'll wait for the DNA before we pursue that particular one. Helen Durand is well aware of her rights.'

As evidenced by her advising Amy not to provide Jacque's personal items for DNA testing. 'You'd think she was an attorney, not a psychologist,' I said. 'But I know she doesn't have an alibi. Denis was gone – obviously – and Molly went to a friend's house.'

'Until late, but not all night,' Pavlik said. 'The fire was started early morning.'

'You might want to check that.' I, too, had a teenager, so I knew this stuff. 'Molly probably got home and went straight to her room. She wouldn't have seen Helen.'

'Unless Helen waited up,' Pavlik said. 'That's what I plan to do with Tracey.'

'Tracey lives most of the time with Susan,' I pointed out. 'And what makes you think she's not already going out at night?'

'She's fifteen.'

'Like I said.'

Pavlik looked uncertain, and I had a feeling he would be calling Susan in the morning.

'Anyway,' I said, 'you can check Helen's alibi if the body *is* Denis.' I stopped. 'That kind of boggles the mind, doesn't it?'

'In what way?'

I ticked it off on my fingers. 'Paulette, Egbert, Jacque and now maybe Denis.' I waggled my fingers. 'Which one of these things doesn't belong?'

We'd given Amy Tuesday off for obvious reasons, so I was alone at the coffee house until Sarah came in at nine and started her workday by filching a muffin from the bakery case. She sat down at the table I'd been wiping. 'Did you hear they caught the thieves?'

'No.' But it explained why Pavlik had been called out in the wee hours. 'We were slammed this morning, so I didn't get any news. What happened?'

'Kids. They were trying to steal air-conditioning units from Brookhills Manor this time.'

'Kids?' I sat across from her. 'Does this blow my Egbert theory?'

'Hell, no,' Sarah said. 'From what you've said you found at the cabin, kids couldn't have hatched this all on their own.'

That depended on the kids, I thought, but I could imagine Egbert in his bedroom on his computer plotting capers for his young cronies. 'Well, I have news, too.'

I filled her in on Molly's visit to Pavlik and our subsequent conversation. 'What do you think?' I asked after I swore her to secrecy.

Sarah got back up to get a napkin from the condiment cart. 'It sounds like Molly is very protective of Denis.'

'It does, doesn't it? And very dismissive of Helen.'

'The evil stepmother,' Sarah said. 'I can see where there would be friction. Helen seems to run the show in that house.'

'Except she doesn't really. Is that lemon poppy seed?'

'Uh-uh, almond,' Sarah said, wiping a poppy seed off her mouth and on to the table. 'How can you not know that? You accepted the bakery order this morning.'

'Because,' I said, getting up to get a muffin of my own, 'each day I order almond poppy seed and the next morning they deliver lemon.' I sat down with my prize. 'Almond poppy seed is much underrated. And amazingly difficult to find.'

'I'll take your word for it,' Sarah said dryly.

'If you don't want yours, I'll eat two,' I offered.

Sarah positioned her forearm protectively between me and her plate. 'Anyway, you were saying Helen is not as in charge as she appears?'

'Exactly,' I said, taking a bite. 'She's obviously insecure about Denis – where he is, what he's doing.'

'Not that she would admit it.'

'So maybe this one time she follows him. Or she intercepts a text message or email. From there, things become beautifully straightforward.'

'Straightforward, if you believe that Helen would set a building on fire to kill her husband and the woman she thinks is his mistress.'

'You don't?' I asked. 'Remember that Denis knew Paulette from Paris. They could have had a relationship back then that Helen found out about.'

'But Paulette was married to Jacque, and Denis to Molly's mother. It was Denis's brother that Paulette was doing drugs with.'

'According to Denis,' I said.

'And Jacque.'

I pushed back from the table and folded my arms. 'Presumably Denis wouldn't tell Jacque if he was fooling around with his wife.'

'Doesn't make for long-term friendships,' Sarah admitted. 'What about Jacque? And Egbert? How do they fit in here?'

'I've been thinking about that,' I said. 'Egbert is the odd man out in this, but he was Helen's patient and into some questionable things. Maybe Helen manipulated him into torching the place.'

Sarah seemed doubtful. 'And Jacque was killed because . . .?'

'He stumbled on Egbert at the cabin.'

'And Egbert died because . . .?'

'Wrong place, wrong time?'

'Which was where? When?'

'I . . . damn.'

'Not so straightforward now, is it?'

'It's getting there,' I said, reaching past her arm to steal the rest of the muffin. 'Anyway, I'm going to Amy's appointment with Helen to see if we can get her to spill on Egbert. Do you think I should also nose around about Denis?'

'No, but you will.'

'Well, I can at least ask if he's back.'

'Yes, you can.'

I put the muffin down. 'Why are you being so negative?'

'I just think you're on the wrong track. What about Jamie Bright? What about his offer to buy out Amy?'

'Jamie made an offer to Amy?' I repeated. 'What are you talking about?'

'Oh,' she said, reclaiming her muffin, 'I didn't tell you that.'

'Tell me what?'

'Amy told me last night that she ran into Jamie Bright on her way back from Becky's. He asked her if, as an officer of Schultz's, she would be willing to consider an offer from him.'

'What offer?'

'A very low one,' Sarah said, shaking her head. 'I've lost all respect for the man.'

'But wait,' I said. 'Amy is an officer of Jacque's company?'

'Apparently. She said Jacque mentioned something a while back and that she signed some papers, but she didn't pay much attention.'

'That doesn't sound like Amy.'

'I know. Love screws with your mind.'

'But why does Jamie want a burned-out store all of a sudden?'

'Because he can get it for practically nothing. It'll cost him less to bulldoze it now and put up a new building than it would have to bring Schultz's up to Bright's standards.'

'The fire did half the work,' I said slowly.

'Exactly.' She popped the last piece of muffin in her mouth. 'Convenient, isn't it?'

'It is. For me, though, the sticking point has always been the origin of the fire. If this was business, why start the fire upstairs?'

'I don't know.' She brushed a couple of errant crumbs into her hand and released them on to the empty plate. 'Maybe there's some equipment downstairs that he hoped to salvage.'

'In your scenario, Jamie doesn't know there's anybody upstairs. The deaths are an accident.'

'Correct. Though I don't see Jamie doing his own dirty work, do you?'

'Egbert comes to mind, of course, or the man Molly saw Egbert talking to.' I tick-tocked my head. 'If Molly wasn't lying about that, too.'

'This is the guy in the hoodie she described for the police artist?'

'Who looks disturbingly like Ichabod Crane. Yes.' I stood up. 'But if this was all about Schultz's, why kill Egbert?'

'Egbert was the torch and knew too much. Or he hired the torch – this Ichabod.'

'Then why not kill the torch, too?'

Sarah pursed her lips. 'Well, we do have a spare body if Denis suddenly shows up alive.'

Again, it required the person who set the fire to die in the fire. I glanced up at the clock and went to snag my purse from the other side of the counter. 'I have to go.'

Sarah followed me to the door. 'There's one other thing that points to Jamie.'

'What's that?' I called over my shoulder as I clip-clopped down the porch steps.

'He approached Amy yesterday morning.'

'And that's significant because?' I stopped on the sidewalk.

'Because yesterday morning, nobody except you, Molly and the sheriff knew that Jacque was dead. You told me on the phone, just before Amy walked through the door.'

'So why approach Amy about selling Schultz's if Jacque was still alive?'

'Unless, of course, Jamie knew Jacque was dead—'
'Because he killed him.'

I saw Sarah's point, but I also saw all sorts of holes in her theory. First of all, Jacque had been missing for forty-eight hours by the time Jamie approached Amy, and a male body had been found above Jacque's burned-out store. Wasn't much of a leap to assume it was Jacque.

Second, Jamie struck me as somebody who planned for any contingency. His first approach had been to Jacque, who turned him down. Then Paulette shows up out of the blue – or not – claiming she is entitled to half of everything Jacque owned, including Schultz's, and is willing to deal. Then when Paulette dies, Jamie approaches Amy, who he happens to know Jacque added to the company management – it's public information if the corporation is registered with the state.

'Coincidence, my ass,' I said aloud, drawing a glance from a curly-haired man descending the stairs from Helen Durand's office.

Coming from a psychologist's office himself, though, he just gave me a sympathetic smile.

'Talking to yourself?' Helen asked from the doorway.

'More like thinking aloud,' I said, mounting the steps. 'Is that more socially acceptable?'

'Some days I don't think there's such a thing as socially *un*acceptable,' she said, stepping aside so I could enter. 'Amy is already here.'

'I hope it's all right that I came?' I asked, following her past a receptionist and into her office.

'If it's all right with Amy, it's certainly all right with me,' Helen said, nodding to her patient.

Amy was sitting in a chair, and there was a notebook on the couch, leading me to assume that's where Helen sat. I took the chair opposite Amy. 'Morning, Amy.'

'Morning, Maggy,' she said. 'I was just telling Helen—'

'Excuse me,' the receptionist poked her head in the door.

'Not now, Moira,' Helen said. 'I'm with a patient . . . or two.' She smiled.

'I – um . . .' The woman wasn't leaving. 'It's Molly,' she whispered.

'You can just tell Molly I'll call her back.' She smiled at us. 'That girl can be very persuasive.'

'You can't call her back.'

'Of course I can. She—'

'She's been arrested,' Moira hissed.

TWENTY-FOUR

Molly Durand hadn't, it turned out, been arrested. But she had been brought in for questioning.

'Apparently, one of her friends was involved in the robbery at Brookhills Manor last night,' I told Helen, after ringing off from Pavlik. We were riding in Helen's Audi – Helen driving, me in the passenger seat and Amy in the back – on our way to the Brookhills County Sheriff's Office.

'Oh my God, Maggy,' Helen said, patting my arm. 'I'm so glad you just happened to be in the office.'

I just happened to be there to pump Helen for information on Egbert. And, hopefully, Denis. It was just pure luck I'd also get to do the same regarding this newest development.

'You're telling me it was kids?' Amy was leaning forward between the seats. 'This gang of slick thieves getting away with air-conditioning units and catalytic converters all over town are high school students?'

'Class project?' I suggested and received a look of disapproval from Helen. The woman was no fun. 'Pavlik didn't give me names, obviously.'

'I'm sure they're underage,' Amy said.

'At seventeen, you can be tried as an adult,' Helen told her, looking straight ahead. 'And Molly is already eighteen, regardless.'

'But Maggy, you said Molly wasn't arrested, right? Has anybody been charged?'

'I don't know,' I said. 'All I do know is that one of the seniors living at Brookhills Manor had a security camera facing out of their first-floor window toward the back parking lot for some reason.'

'Probably birds,' Helen said, not turning. 'Old people like to watch birds.'

I'd take her word for that. 'Anyway, the camera is

motion-activated, and it caught a female and two males loading an HVAC unit into a truck.'

'I'm surprised the manor doesn't have its own security cameras,' Amy said.

'They do at the entrances and the main parking lots,' I said, as we pulled into the county facility's parking lot. 'But this was around the back where the mechanical equipment was located and the manor employees park.'

'Because employees' cars don't matter,' Helen muttered as she pulled into a space.

I undid my seatbelt as Helen turned off the ignition. By the time I looked up, she was already halfway to the front door.

As Amy and I scurried after her, I asked, 'How are you?'

'Still standing,' she said. 'Still moving forward.'

'If a little faster than I'd like,' I said, slightly out of breath.

As Helen went to push the intercom button next to the entrance, the door swung open and Molly appeared.

'Molly.' Helen pulled the girl toward her. 'Are you all right?'

'No,' Molly said sarcastically, extricating herself. 'First they beat me and then they water-boarded me. Hi, Maggy.'

I guess I held a special non-sarcastic place in the girl's heart. I was angry with her for lying, but I also wanted information. 'What's going on?'

She shrugged. 'So you know my friend Lindsey?'

'I never liked that girl,' Helen said. 'Or that Angel person who's always calling, either.'

Molly ignored her. 'Well, somebody stole some equipment over at the old folks' home last night, and they think it was Lindsey and a couple of the guys in our class.'

'You didn't have anything to do with it, did you?' her mother demanded.

'Do I *look* stupid?'

Her mother glared.

'Yeah, I know you think I am,' Molly said now. 'But no, I was with Lindsey earlier, but this was really late. The sheriff just wanted to know what we'd been doing earlier.'

'What had you been doing?' Her mother again.

Molly gave her a shrug. 'Just hanging out.'

'Which is what you say every time I ask,' Helen said. 'I'm your mother. I—'

'I'm eighteen. I can do what I want,' Molly said sullenly.

'Not as long as you live under our roof, you—'

'Excuse me?' Deputy Kelly Anthony had pushed open the door. 'Are you Mrs Durand?'

'Yes.' Helen's hands were playing at her throat as though she was worrying a string of pearls.

'The sheriff would like to see Molly again and asked that you come as well.'

Helen glanced at me. 'Would you come with us, Maggy?'

I saw Kelly's eyes do a half-roll and right themselves.

'I'm not a lawyer or anything,' I whispered to Helen. 'I can recommend one, though, if—'

'No, no,' she said. 'It's just that you know the sheriff and you know us. I'd feel better if you came with us.'

'If it's an official interrogation,' I said, 'I don't think anybody but your lawyer—'

'It's not,' Kelly interrupted. 'I'll have to clear it with the sheriff, though.' She chin-gestured to Amy. 'You might as well come, too.'

We followed Kelly through the halls to the sheriff's outer office where she tapped on the heavy wooden door and went in, signaling for us to wait.

A few moments later, Kelly stuck out her head and beckoned me in. 'Maggy?'

'I don't have to be here,' I told Pavlik as Kelly slipped out of his office. 'Helen just asked me for some reason.'

'She asked you because you sleep with the sheriff,' Pavlik said drily, getting up from his desk. 'But if she wants you to be here, that's fine with me.'

'Amy's here, too,' I said.

Pavlik hesitated. 'Let me tell you this first, then. We have preliminary results from Jacque's autopsy. It confirms that he died on Saturday, probably sometime between eight and noon.'

'That means he could have started the fire,' I said.

'Yes, as could whoever it was that called him.'

That bit of business taken care of, Pavlik went to the door.

'Mrs Durand, Molly – please come in. I'm fine with Maggy and Amy being here, if you don't mind them hearing what I have to tell you.'

'Am I being arrested?' Molly asked, entering the room.

Pavlik waved them to a small conference table where the five of us could sit comfortably. 'No, this is on another matter.'

Pavlik waited for us all to sit – Helen to one side of Molly, me on the other, Amy next to me. The sheriff remained standing. He had a folder in his hand.

'Mrs Durand,' he said. 'I don't know if you're aware, but Molly provided us with a DNA sample.'

'No, I absolutely wasn't.' Helen was tight-lipped.

'And thanks a lot for telling her,' Molly muttered.

I elbowed her. 'Shh.'

'Molly is an adult and therefore didn't need your permission,' Pavlik said. 'She was also fingerprinted.'

'Elimination prints because she touched things in the cabin,' I explained. 'When we found Jacque's body.'

Molly nudged me. 'Shh.'

Fine.

'Anyway,' Pavlik continued, undaunted. 'Given the situation—'

The situation being four bodies and counting, I presumed.

'—we expedited the DNA—'

Molly interrupted this time. 'I just wanted to make sure the body in the fire wasn't Dad.'

'But you've talked to your dad since the fire,' Helen said, and then her face changed. 'You told me on Sunday that he had to stay over another day or two.'

'When was the last time you talked to Denis yourself?' I asked her curiously. It seemed odd to be communicating through their daughter.

'He and Molly like to text each other,' she said. 'I—'

'She thinks he's fooling around,' Molly told us. 'Not that she really wants to know.'

'That's not true.' Helen drew herself up to full height in the chair.

'Is, too,' Molly said. 'You have a nice life, and if you found out Dad was cheating, you'd have to do something about it. Else what would your clients think?'

Molly turned to Amy and me. 'She's all about women taking control of their lives, not letting men walk all over them. But when it comes to herself?' She shrugged.

'Are you saying that you believe your perfect father *is* having an affair?' Helen asked her.

'Why wouldn't he?' Molly snapped. 'He's married to you.'

Silence descended on the room.

I turned to Pavlik. 'You were saying about the DNA?'

Pavlik's expression said he had found this peek into the world of the Durands enlightening.

'Yes,' he said, turning to Molly. 'I'm sorry to tell you, Molly, that the tests confirm that it was your father who died in the fire.'

Helen looked as if she was going to throw up. 'You're telling me that Denis died above that grocery store? But what was he doing there? He left after dinner to go to Chicago.'

'We don't know that,' Pavlik said. 'There was no record of a Denis Durand checking into the Hilton in Chicago, which is where you said he routinely stayed.'

'Where Denis said that he stayed,' Helen corrected numbly.

'There's no sign of his mobile,' Pavlik said. 'It would be helpful if you can provide us with his phone records.'

'Don't you have those?' Despite being whiter than the proverbial sheet, Molly was still asking questions. 'I mean from the phone company?'

'It takes time to get a warrant. If you have access to them online, Mrs Durand—'

'Yes, of course,' she said, businesslike suddenly. 'I'll send them over.'

Molly's face was scrunched up, trying not to cry. Despite contributing the DNA, I didn't think she had seriously considered the possibility that her father was dead.

'But I don't understand,' she said now. 'Why would he have been inside that flat?'

'There was a woman there, wasn't there?' Helen practically spat out the words.

'You bitch,' Molly said, turning on her. 'My father—'

Pavlik held up a hand. 'We did two tests, and both showed parental matches to Molly's DNA.'

'Yes, yes, we understand,' Helen said wearily. 'You're absolutely sure it's Denis.'

But I was used to Pavlik and the way he parsed his words. 'Two tests and two parental matches?'

'Exactly.'

Helen was leaning forward now. 'But . . . on two bodies?'

Molly frowned. 'I don't understand.'

'The woman who died in the fire, Molly,' Pavlik said, 'was your mother.'

TWENTY-FIVE

'So Paulette is Molly's mother,' Sarah said. 'Well, all hell must have broken loose after that.'

'Actually, it went totally quiet,' I said.

'Like all the air had been sucked out of the room and everybody in it,' Amy agreed. 'Which was good. I didn't think I could take Molly and Helen snarling at each other much longer.'

'I'm sorry,' I said to her. 'You have Jacque's death to deal with. You certainly didn't need to witness all that.' Whatever it was.

'Then what happened?' Sarah asked curiously.

'Helen just stood, said "thank you very much for the information" and drove home,' Amy said.

'Barely slowed down to drop us off here at the shop,' I added.

'What about Molly?' Sarah asked, leaning against the counter. 'She's so close to her dad.'

'I think she was shell-shocked.' Amy took a bottle of water out of the refrigerator. 'She was next to me in the back seat and didn't say a word. Just punched away at her phone.'

'She'll have gone viral by now if she posted any of this,' Sarah said. 'But how shocked can she be? She volunteered her DNA because she was afraid the body was her father.'

'I'm not so sure she thought it through,' I said. 'Bursting into Pavlik's office to offer her DNA – it was like she was in a movie.'

'And then it became real,' Amy said. 'Poor kid.'

'OK,' Sarah said, holding up her hands. 'Tell me if I've got this right. Denis Durand had dinner with Molly and Helen on Friday night, tells them he's driving down to Chicago for a weekend conference and, instead, went to be with Paulette?'

'She was the mother of his child,' Amy said.

'All this stuff about Molly's mother dying in childbirth,' Sarah said. 'That was lies, too?'

'Apparently so,' I said. 'But the inconvertible truth seems to be that Denis and Paulette had a child together eighteen years ago. For whatever reason, Paulette let Denis raise her himself.'

'She was an addict,' Amy said. 'She wouldn't want a baby.'

'Do you think Jacque knew?' I asked her.

'About Denis and Paulette?' Amy shook her head. 'He couldn't have looked Denis in the face if he'd known. Jacque wasn't the forgiving type.'

'But what about Denis's wife?' Sarah asked. 'Wouldn't Jacque have known she didn't exist?'

'Not necessarily,' Amy said. 'Once Paulette left Jacque – obviously, before she was pregnant or at least before she showed – Denis would have given Jacque some space. Probably miles of it.'

'True,' I said. 'If Denis acquires this phantom wife who dies giving birth to Molly, who is going to question it?'

'So Denis moves to Brookhills,' Sarah continued the narration, 'where he finds love again with Helen and eventually reconnects with Jacque.'

'Denis was hiding some pretty hefty secrets,' Amy said. 'It couldn't have been easy to live with it.'

'Then to escalate our little soap opera,' Sarah said, 'Paulette arrives in town. She claims she has cleaned herself up and wants to see Denis and Molly.'

'Denis can't tell Helen because she'll assume they're fooling around.'

'Which they may have been,' Sarah said. 'It sounds like the guy is a real hound if his daughter is lying for him.'

'Agreed,' I said. 'Anyway, Denis says he's going to Chicago – and maybe even plans to – but takes the opportunity to see Paulette.' I stopped. 'Where is his car?'

'Good question,' Sarah said. 'Has anybody checked Schultz's lot for an abandoned car?'

I made a note on my phone. 'I'll mention it to Pavlik.'

'Who started the fire?' Amy had gotten quiet.

'Neither Helen nor Molly has an alibi,' I said. 'Helen says she was at home, and Molly was out with her friend Lindsey.'

'Robbing Christ Christian?' Sarah suggested.

'Pavlik says there's nothing yet to tie Molly to the robberies.' I frowned. 'You know, if she *was* part of this gang, it would explain her wandering around touching things in the cabin. She knew we'd find evidence of the group operating out of there and wanted to have a reason for her fingerprints showing up.'

'Wow, that's downright cold,' Sarah said. 'With Jacque's body lying there, she—' She stopped herself. 'Sorry, Amy.'

'It's OK,' Amy said. 'But, again, who started the fire?'

'Helen gets my vote,' I said. 'She was obviously as jealous as hell and suppressing it. She finally blew.'

Sarah nodded. 'Maybe she found out somehow that Paulette was Molly's mother. If Denis and Paulette got back together, Helen could wave goodbye to her semi-happy family, including Molly.'

'Who seemingly hates her,' Amy said.

'I suppose that might be normal mother-and-daughter stuff at that age,' I posited. 'I didn't have a girl, so I don't know.'

'I remember hating my mother intermittently,' Sarah admitted.

Amy was looking at us, amazed. 'You two are missing something.'

'What?'

'Paulette was Jacque's wife. I hate to say it, but if anybody had a reason to kill Denis and Paulette, it was Jacque.'

'She's right, you know,' I said to Sarah.

Amy was out front serving our early-evening commuters as they returned from their offices by train. Sarah had suggested that it would be best for her to stay busy, and Amy fell for it. We were sitting in the office, me at the desk, Sarah in the side chair.

She snorted. 'You mean that Jacque had a motive for killing his best friend who apparently did the dirty with his wife eighteen years ago? Yeah, I'd say so.'

'Plus, there's the added incentive of the insurance policy on the store. Oh, and being rid of the cheating wife who had abandoned him, then had the nerve to resurface with designs on his money. It's all absolutely logical and has been logical from the very beginning. The only problem with the theory—'

'Was that we thought he died in the fire. Or at least I thought that, even though I kind of soft-pedaled it because of Amy.'

'That was soft-pedaling?' I asked.

'I tossed in the occasional touch of unvarnished truth,' Sarah admitted. 'But I agree that Jacque dying in the fire didn't make sense unless he was suicidal, and it was a murder-suicide.'

'In which case, why not set the fire and go off and kill himself somewhere else—'

'Like the cabin. But you don't believe he shot himself there either.'

'It's the blow to the forehead,' I said, picking up a pen to tap it on the desk. 'How did he get it?'

'Like you said, he walked into a tree branch on his way to the cabin from your house in the dark.' She took the pen away from me. 'What's your alternative theory?'

'Egbert. The timing works now that we know Jacque died between eight and noon on Saturday morning.' I pulled in closer with my chair. 'Let's say Jacque made a deal with Egbert to burn down the shop.'

'With Paulette in it?'

I thought about that. 'Yes. Or even Paulette *and* Denis. For all we know, Jacque called Denis to tell him Paulette was at the flat, knowing he'd go see her.'

'But who told Jacque about the affair in the first place after all these years?' Sarah asked.

'I'm betting it was Paulette. Jacque was showing her up to the flat when I left.'

'So they go upstairs and have a heart-to-heart,' Sarah said. 'Paulette is already trying to make Jacque's life miserable by questioning the divorce. Why not pour salt in the wound?'

'By telling him about the affair with Denis. About Molly. Maybe she even told him that Denis was coming over that night.' I could only imagine how angry Jacque would be.

'What then?' Sarah seemed dubious. 'On the spot Jacque hires Egbert to torch the place and commit two murders?'

'I think Egbert thought it was simple arson. The plan might

already have been in motion, since we know this hoodie guy and Egbert met that same day.'

'You think Jacque was already going to burn down the shop and took the opportunity to kill two – or three – birds with one stone?' Sarah's mouth twisted into a grim yet appreciative grin. 'It's kind of genius.'

'So let's walk through the rest,' I said. 'Egbert – or one of his minions – pours the accelerant through the mail slot, tosses in a match and takes off. At four thirty-nine a.m., he makes the call to Jacque, saying that the deed is done, and he'll meet him at the cabin to be paid.' I had a thought. 'Maybe that's what the fourteen hundred dollars in Egbert's backpack was – payment.'

Sarah cocked her head. 'Seems pretty cheap.'

'It does, doesn't it?' I said, chewing on my lip. 'But maybe it was a second payment. Besides, setting the fire was five minutes' work.'

'I don't think criminals are paid by the hour.'

'I know that,' I said. 'But my point is that the job would have appeared easy-peasy until Egbert arrives at the shop with Becky and realizes that two people were killed in the fire.'

'But your theory is that Egbert met Jacque at the cabin earlier to collect the money. After the phone call but before he and Becky went to the store.'

'True,' I said. 'But later, when he realizes that Jacque neglected to tell him there was somebody in the upper flat, he goes back to the cabin demanding more money both for the deed and for his silence.'

'As he should. Jacque has made him a murderer.' Sarah was clicking the retractable pen now. 'If we're right about Egbert, he's a criminal, but it's been robbery and property crimes.'

'Maybe expanding to illegal firearms,' I reminded her. 'But you're right, Egbert is not a murderer.'

'Until he is.'

'Exactly. He confronts Jacque and they fight. Jacque falls, hitting himself on something like the coffee table and lies there stunned.'

'Now Egbert is in a panic,' Sarah continued the narrative and the clicking. 'It's his word against Jacque's.'

'He grabs a gun—'

'Which they were conveniently making right there in the cabin.'

'And shoots Jacque in the head.' Sarah rubbed her chin. 'But who killed Egbert?'

I took advantage of the cessation of clicking to grab the pen and pointed it at her. 'Ichabod, of course.'

'The headless horseman in the hoodie.'

'Ichabod Crane was not the horseman—' I caught myself. 'We suspect that Egbert headed this gang of kids who were doing the robberies. I don't see one of them necessarily moving on to arson. But maybe Egbert brought in somebody else, somebody older, and, as Molly put it, sketchy.'

'Ichabod,' Sarah said. 'Do you think that what Molly says she saw – and I stress *says* – was Egbert giving directions to the guy he hired to torch the place? Right out there on the street?'

I shrugged. 'Not details, of course. Just pointing out the store. Who would pay attention to somebody giving directions to a stranger?'

'Molly, apparently,' Sarah said. 'But even setting Ichabod aside, I guess that any of Egbert's merry little gang could have gotten ticked at him for involving them in arson and double murder.'

'One of the kids they arrested, you mean? The only one I know is Molly's friend Lindsey, who I met briefly. She seemed like your normal teenager.'

'So definitely capable of murder,' Sarah said.

I ignored her. 'I'll run this by Pavlik tonight. It's possible their investigation is heading in this direction anyway. Can Amy stay with you again?'

The person in question stuck her head in the office. 'Maggy, can you come out?'

'Sure,' I said, feeling guilty. 'Sorry for deserting you.'

'No biggie,' Amy said. 'It's just that Molly is out here to see you.'

'I'll come out and give you a hand, Amy,' Sarah said, unusually generous. 'Why don't you send Molly in here?'

I was fairly certain my partner would be listening from around the corner, hoping the girl would spill more dirt to me.

'Hi, Maggy.' Molly appeared in the doorway with a bag slung over her shoulder.

'How are you doing, Molly?' I asked her, waving for her to sit.

'I'm OK,' she said, not taking the proffered seat. 'I just wanted to say thank you for everything.'

'You're leaving?' I asked, pointing to the bag. 'To where?'

'Just a little road trip with a friend from school.'

That's likely what Thelma – or Louise – said. 'Is that such a good idea, Molly? What about your mo— Helen?'

'It's Helen I'm getting away from. And what a mess I made.' She chin-gestured the direction of Schultz's.

'What do you mean? It wasn't you who—'

'Set the fire and killed my father?' she asked, eyes wide. 'God, no. I'd kill myself if I'd done that.'

'Don't say that,' I said. 'It's not something to be flippant about.'

'I'm sorry,' she said, finally sitting down. 'I just meant that I thought I was so cool, offering my DNA and all, like it was a game. Then—'

'You find out that not only your father is dead, but your real mother, too.' I waited a beat, but she didn't answer. 'What made you decide to give Pavlik your DNA for matching?'

'Finding Denis's phone in the cabin.'

'Denis's phone,' I repeated, weighing each word. 'The burner phone in the cabin belonged to Denis?'

'Yes.'

'But I don't understand. That's the phone that called Jacque early Friday morning. You said you didn't recognize it.'

'I lied.'

'Again?'

'Yeah.' She sighed. 'He used that phone to keep in touch with me when he was away.'

'Why not call you from his regular one?'

'Helen would get all bent out of shape if he called me and not her. She was always on him. Where was he? When would he be back? It smothered him.'

'And the affairs?'

Molly shrugged. 'Maybe one or two. But nothing like she accused him of.' She stood up. 'Anyway, I need to get going.'

I got up to follow her to the front of the shop which was now deserted since the six-thirty train hadn't arrived yet. I could hear Amy and Sarah talking from behind the service counter. 'This friend you're picking up – it isn't Lindsey, is it?'

'No, Angel,' Molly said. 'I don't think Lindsey is free to leave.'

'And you're certain that you are? Have you asked the sheriff?'

'Oh, yeah,' she said. 'I gave him my new mobile number.'

I wasn't sure I believed her. 'You have a new phone? Can I have the number, too?'

She recited it and I punched the digits in and let it ring on hers before setting my own phone on the counter. 'How long are you going to be away?'

She shrugged. 'Maybe a week or so. Who knows?'

Going to open the door for her, I saw the battered Volvo parked on the street two spaces away from my Ford Escape. 'Drive carefully. No texting.'

'Yes, Mom.' She gave me a hug. 'I wish you were my mom.'

'Me, too.' To my surprise, I was a little misty-eyed as Mini-Me walked to her Volvo and started it. She waved and did a U-turn to head east on Brookhill Road.

I dug in my apron pocket for my car keys and followed.

TWENTY-SIX

Two things were bothering me as I drove east on Brookhill Road, careful to stay back so Molly didn't spot me. I was aided in that by the fact that she had never seen my Ford Escape. Nor would she find it particularly memorable if she had.

No, the first thing bothering me was the burner phone. Molly knew when she picked it up near Jacque's body that it belonged to Denis, and, therefore, he should have been the prime suspect in Jacque's death. Of course, she instinctively protected Denis, as she had done for years. Not only didn't she own up to what she knew, but she made sure she messed up any prints on the mobile.

But there was a problem. We now knew that Molly's father died in the fire, meaning around five a.m. on Saturday. But according to the autopsy, Jacque didn't die until after eight.

Molly's father didn't kill Jacque Oui. Which opened a new and bizarre possibility that I found hard to even contemplate.

Oh, and the second thing that bothered me?

Jake Pavlik never would have told a witness and possible suspect in a string of robberies that it was just fine to take a road trip.

Molly Durand was lying, yet again.

Damn. The Volvo had slowed to turn left, and I slammed on my brakes to avoid rear-ending the very vehicle I was trying to follow. I swerved around the Volvo unnoticed and then pulled a U-turn in time to catch Molly's Volvo pull into a spot in the now-deserted Schultz's parking lot.

Funny place to pick up a friend, I said to myself.

I parked my car on the street and waited until Molly got out of hers and approached the building. There was a conventional door next to the glass sliders, and that's where she disappeared. But how did she get in? Did she have a key or was the door broken or left open for her?

And why was she here in the first place?

Revisiting where your mother and father died a horrible death seemed a little creepy. As was her reaction when we found Jacque's body in the cabin.

Ghoulish, I'd thought then.

I skirted the parking lot on foot, lest Molly see me pass by the big sliders, and crept to the door she had entered. Patting my pocket for my phone, I tried the knob quietly. Unlocked.

Stepping cautiously into the store, I saw that the interior was much as it was when I was here with Pavlik. There were more ceiling tiles down and more holes fallen through, probably the result of sitting water from fighting the fire. The smell of mildew was strong as I walked through the store. It would turn to mold soon, compounding the damage if something wasn't done. Not that there was anybody to do it.

So many dead. And now, finally, I thought I knew why.

I heard a creak, or maybe it was just a shifting of weight above my head.

'Hello?' I moved toward the massive hole in the ceiling at the back of the store. The ladder that had been on the ground the last time I was here was braced in place for access to the upper floor. 'Molly?' I called up. 'Are you up there? I don't think it's safe.'

Her face appeared next to the top rungs of the ladder. 'Maggy? What are you doing here?'

'Same as you,' I said. 'Nosing around. I saw your car in the parking lot.'

'I wanted to see where my father died before I left.'

But not her birth mother, though she hadn't known Paulette. 'How did you get in?'

'The door was unlocked,' she said. 'Do you want to come up? We haven't had a chance to look until now.' She was playing Mini-Me again, appealing to my curiosity. 'Better come quick before it gets too dark.'

'I don't think it's a good idea,' I said.

'Ouch,' she said, pulling back.

'Are you OK?'

Her tip-tilted nose appeared again, and she seemed to force a smile. 'I just caught myself on a nail here. It's just a scratch.'

'You'll need a tetanus shot,' I told her, taking a couple of rungs of the ladder so I could see better. 'Is it bleeding?'

'A little. It just kind of poked in and out, though, so it's probably fine.'

'A puncture wound is how you get tetanus,' I told her. 'Come down and I'll take you to the walk-in clinic.'

'Fine,' she said. 'But I want to take a quick look before we leave. We won't have another chance, you know. They'll knock this place down.'

And for good reason. But I carefully climbed another couple of rungs up, glancing down at the floor below to make sure the ladder was braced. When I looked up again, Molly was gone. 'Molly?'

A few rungs higher, I could see into the burned-out space. It was getting toward dusk, and the only light slanted through the holes the firefighters had made in the roof.

I could make out Molly standing with her back to me, head bowed. 'That's where the bedroom is,' she said, pointing toward a burned-out doorway. 'Or was. That's where he died.'

'I know,' I said quietly.

'Of course.' She turned and nodded toward a space just to the right of where I was. 'And that's where she died – my mother.' Her voice broke.

I climbed the rest of the way up, but stayed close to the ladder, sitting my butt on a beam so as not to accidentally step through an area weakened by the water and fire.

'Molly,' I said gently, 'did you know she was your mother? Before Pavlik told you.'

'Yes.'

'Denis told you?'

A single nod. 'Friday night on the way home to dinner. He said her name was Paulette and that she wanted to meet me. One big dysfunctional extended family.' She laughed.

'Well, that sounds . . . nice.'

'She was an addict when she had me, you know.'

'I do.' A second or two went by. 'Molly, did you set this fire?'

'No.'

'I know you went out with Lindsey that night, after your family dinner. Did you and your friends—'

'Now you're asking if we were out stealing air-conditioning units?' She laughed. 'That's what Helen thinks, too.'

'I know that's not true, at least that night.'

'No.' She stuck her chin in the air. 'I followed him that night.'

'You followed Denis.'

'I thought he was coming to be with her, with Paulette.'

'You thought Denis and Paulette were getting back together,' I said. 'Did that make you mad?'

'No, not really,' she said, shaking her head. 'Even a crack whore couldn't be as bad as Helen.' She flashed a white smile in the fading light.

'Then why did you do it?'

She outright laughed now. 'You do think I set the fire.'

'I did think it possible,' I said. 'You've been so evasive and misleading. Scheming, even. But now—'

'Now what?'

'Now I think Denis set the fire.'

'Denis set the fire?' Molly demanded. 'But it was my father who died in it.'

'Exactly,' I said quietly.

Molly kept swinging. 'You thought the same thing with Jacque and you were wrong.'

'Absolutely,' I said. 'There were plenty of reasons for Jacque to start the fire, but not for him to die in it. When it became apparent he hadn't, I came up with ways he could have been responsible for the fire and then murdered. Hooded arsonists, double-crossed partners, even suicide if we could get around the head wound somehow. But something that you said at the shop made me realize it was a much simpler puzzle than I'd imagined. It was just that a piece was missing.' I shook my head as I got to my feet.

'Why?' Molly asked. 'What did I say?'

'That it was Denis's burner phone in the cabin.'

Her eyes flicked sideways. 'I didn't mean to get him in trouble. It's just you asked why I gave the sheriff my DNA, and that was it. Finding his phone scared me.'

'Finding Denis's phone.'

She stared at me. 'Yes.'

'You're very smart, Molly, and you know it. Why did you stop by to say goodbye?'

'I thought it would buy me some time,' she said. 'Helen is going to realize I'm missing and go ballistic.'

'But there I would be, saying "Oh, no – Molly's just on a road trip with Angel. She'll be back."' I grimaced. 'I'm not as snowed by you as you think I am.'

'Ooh, speaking of snow,' Molly said, 'did you hear what they found in the bathroom?'

I'd been edging closer, careful to step along the beam that I'd first settled on, so I didn't fall through. 'The cocaine? Yes. I thought Paulette had reverted to her old ways. Or maybe she never quit. But it wasn't her coke, was it? It was his.'

'Denis never touched drugs,' the girl said, backing away. 'Even when he was young.'

'But I'm not talking about Denis, Molly. I'm talking about your father.'

'Denis.'

'No, Gabriel.'

TWENTY-SEVEN

'**M**y little brother.' Denis emerged from the bathroom. 'I really did think he was dead.'

'Until you walked into the flat on Friday night,' I guessed. 'You were expecting Molly's biological mother. But her biological father, too? That must have been a real blow.'

'Only because Gabriel managed to destroy everything he touched. I didn't want him anywhere near Molly.' He put his arm around the girl.

'You could tolerate Paulette showing up and supplanting Helen in Molly's mind, but Gabriel? No, you've been pretending to be Molly's father for so long, I think you started to believe it.'

'I am her father,' he said tautly, right hand in his pocket. Molly laid her head on his shoulder.

'How did you get away with taking Molly in the first place?' I asked. 'Was Gabriel too stoned to realize he was a father? Or did he just not care, like Paulette?'

'They were always stoned,' Denis said. 'Even with Paulette pregnant, the two of them would disappear for days, smoking crack and doing God knows what. Then one day they didn't come back.'

'But you obviously found them,' I said, pointing at Molly. 'Or at least you found Paulette.'

'Paulette called me after she had Molly, and I met her at some squalid youth hostel. She said Gabriel was dead and she needed money. She was only too glad to give me Molly in exchange.'

'Why didn't she call Jacque?' I asked. 'Couldn't she have passed Molly off as his?'

'Jacque wouldn't have sex without a condom, if they were having sex at all by the end. He knew Paulette was an addict and wanted nothing more than to be rid of her. He'd never

have taken her back and certainly wouldn't have believed
Molly was his.'

'And two years after she disappeared, he started divorce
proceedings.'

'So I understand.' Denis shrugged. 'But Jacque and I had
lost touch with each other by then. He didn't want to know
where Paulette was. But for me, Paulette was with Gabriel
and Gabriel was still my brother. I tried to do what I could.
It was only after I moved here that Jacque and I became friends
again.'

'So when you met Paulette and took Molly, Jacque wouldn't
have even known,' I said. 'And I assume there was no first
wife who died in childbirth?'

He shook his head.

'What about birth documents?' I asked. 'You must have
needed something to get Molly into the US.'

'Molly was registered as Molly Durand with Paulette
Badeaux and Gabriel Durand as her parents. My name is Denis
Gabriel Durand. Gabriel's was Gabriel Denis Durand.' He
smiled. 'My parents didn't have much imagination, and those
were the only two names they could agree on.'

'So they used them twice,' Molly said, turning to smile at
Denis. 'That's kind of fun.'

'You should step away from him, Molly,' I said.

'Why?' she asked. 'It's not like he stole me. He saved me
from a horrible life with a crack whore as my mother.'

'Who cleaned herself up to die horribly in this fire, along
with your father.' Who, admittedly, was still an addict.

She shook her head. 'We don't know Paulette was clean. It
could have been an act. And besides, they weren't my parents.'

'Egg and sperm donors,' Denis confirmed.

'Paulette told you Gabriel was dead.' I wanted to keep them
engaged until I could figure out what Denis's plan was. 'Did
she believe that?'

'She had no idea where he was. She just wanted money.'

'But obviously they reconnected.'

'She said she ran into him recently.' He shrugged. 'Maybe
Molly is right about Paulette still being an addict, because I
can't imagine Gabriel associating with anybody besides his

dealer. Apparently, they were reminiscing, and Paulette told him about Molly. And how well Jacque and I had done in America.'

'How would she know about that?'

'Jamie Bright had just contacted her about Jacque, and Brookhills rang a bell. She had a vague recollection that a mutual friend mentioned I'd moved there.'

'You didn't stay in touch with Paulette?'

'Hell, no,' he said. 'But I'm sure she was delighted to find both Jacque and I were in Brookhills. It was Bright who dug up Jacque's marriage in the first place, and Bright who flew Paulette here from Paris. Gabriel, sensing an opportunity to score a payday or run a scam of some type, followed.'

'When did you know they were coming?' I asked.

'Paulette called me at the office on Thursday. As for Gabriel, like I said, I didn't know he was alive until I walked into Jacque's flat on Friday night.'

'It must have been quite the reunion. You hadn't seen your brother for more than eighteen years.'

A regretful smile. 'He was amazingly unchanged – a little older, a little thinner, but still a user in every sense of the word. He and Paulette were planning to take half of everything Jacque owned.'

'But they wanted something of yours, too,' I said. 'Something more valuable, I think.'

He pulled Molly closer. 'They offered to keep quiet about Molly, to walk away and stay away if I paid them fifty thousand dollars.'

I raised my eyebrows. 'Molly wasn't worth fifty thousand?'

'That would be just the start. He would be hanging around, my druggie brother, embarrassing me and tapping me for funds whenever he needed something.' He shook his head. 'He'd do the same to Jacque if he could. Gabriel was a liar. He was always a liar.'

Like father, like daughter.

'You should have just told me, Dad,' Molly said. 'You had to know I wouldn't love you any less.'

'There were also legal issues,' I told her. 'Denis left the

country with you. Paulette and Gabriel could have claimed that he kidnapped you.'

'But I'm eighteen now. They couldn't just take me back.' She glanced at Denis. 'Could they?'

'I didn't think so, sweetie, but how could I be certain? Or know that I wouldn't be extradited to France? Everything I built here would be in jeopardy, don't you see?'

Actually, it was getting too dark to see much of anything. 'When you left the house after dinner that night, you came here.'

'I'd given Paulette the number for my burner phone. She texted me after Jacque left the flat and asked me to come by. Said she had a surprise for me.'

'That didn't worry you?'

'It did,' he acknowledged. 'But not knowing what she wanted worried me more.'

'Did the three of you argue?'

'No,' he said. 'I can be very charming when I want to be.'

I was having trouble remembering that right now. He was giving me the creeps.

'I hugged them both – even acted overjoyed to see my brother again.' He laughed. 'I think I even called him Lazarus rising from the dead. Although I didn't have to keep that up for long.'

'Because you killed him?'

Denis seemed affronted. 'Because he was doing lines and passed out in the bedroom.'

Oh. 'What about you, Molly. What did you know about this?'

'I told you. I followed Denis that night. I thought he and Paulette were . . . you know.'

'I wouldn't have done that,' Denis said.

She got on tiptoe to kiss his cheek. 'I know that now.'

Sweet. But then he'd burned people to death. 'Did you know Molly was outside?' I glanced at her. 'I assume in the alley?'

She nodded. 'Behind the stack of pallets.'

'Of course not,' Denis said. 'I would never have involved her.'

'Where did you get the gasoline?'

'By the truck,' he said.

I'd keep asking as long as he kept answering. 'How did you light it?'

I barely made out the flash of teeth in a smile. 'Smoking was yet another bad habit Paulette hadn't given up. I grabbed her cigarette lighter from the coffee table.'

Which meant premeditation. Denis had left the flat planning to set it on fire. 'And you saw all this?' I asked Molly.

She nodded, and even in the dim light, I could see she was pale. 'I saw him go up the stairs with the can of gasoline and then a flash as the fire started.'

'You didn't call anybody?' I asked.

'No, I couldn't. He's my dad.' She took a deep breath before she continued. 'I ran. But the next day when they said a man was killed along with the woman—'

'She assumed it was me,' Denis said, pulling her tighter. 'That I'd gone back inside and died in the fire.'

'Can you blame me?' Molly asked. 'You weren't answering my calls on either cell phone.'

'I destroyed my regular phone so I couldn't be tracked,' he said. 'And the burner I turned off because I knew they'd realize the call to Jacque had been made from it.'

'Why did you leave it in the cabin?' I asked.

'I didn't mean to,' he said. 'When you came in—'

'Wait,' I said, holding up a hand they likely couldn't see. 'You were in the cabin when Molly and I found Jacque's body?'

'In the bedroom. I went out of the window.'

'Did you see Denis there?' I asked Molly.

'No.' And then, apparently, a re-evaluation. 'Well, actually yes. When I saw the phone, I thought he might be there. But I couldn't understand how.'

'And while you were waiting for the police,' Denis said, 'I managed to flag Molly down.'

Which explained why the girl was wandering around outside and I'd had to rein her in until Pavlik got there. 'The entire story you told me at the coffee shop just now – that you recognized the phone as your father's and that's why you wanted to have your DNA tested? Was that another lie?'

'That was on me,' Denis said. 'I told her to provide the sample before Helen could give the police anything to match.'

Smart. 'Because your DNA from anything Helen provided to them wouldn't be a one hundred percent match to the corpse. It would indicate that your supposedly dead brother died in the fire, which would be a disaster. If Molly offered up a sample, though, it would show a parent/child relationship, proving that Molly's father had died in the fire. Everyone would assume that was you.'

'Denis,' Molly said.

'Denis,' I repeated. 'When you told me about the burner phone, you said it was Denis's.'

'What of it?' Denis asked. 'Molly knows my first name.'

'Of course she does,' I told him. 'But Molly always called you her father or dad when she talked about you. It was in contrast to how she spoke of Helen, using her first name sometimes to irritate her or show disrespect. Molly never disrespected you, Denis. But if only to keep things straight in her own mind, she started thinking of you as Denis and the man who died in the fire as her father.'

'That's not true,' Molly stamped her foot, and I could hear a ceiling tile below break loose and fall.

'I'm your father,' Denis said, ruffling her hair. 'Right, Molly?'

'With Molly's DNA proving that her "father"' – I did air quotes, though nobody probably could have seen them – 'was dead, it left Denis free to run. Which is what I assume you're doing now.'

'We're both leaving,' Molly said. 'Together.'

'Obviously you've been in touch since the cabin yesterday,' I said. 'How? Denis didn't have a phone.'

'Bought a new one from a vending machine at the gas station.' He shrugged. 'Easy.'

Duh. 'Is your car here, then?' Might as well tie up my loose ends.

'No, I left it in the depot lot right under your very nose.'

It made perfect sense. Nobody would notice a car left overnight at a train station. 'You used the gas station phone to text Molly then.'

'Using the name Angel, so she would know it was me.'

'Angel,' I repeated. 'Helen thinks she's one of Molly's friends. And Angel is the person who you're going on the road trip with, right, Molly?'

'Dad always uses Angel when he texts me from his burner phone.'

'Because your middle name is Gabriel, like the archangel,' I said to Denis. This was a weird father/daughter relationship. Or uncle/niece, which didn't make it any less weird.

'Exactly,' he said.

'I can see why you killed Paulette and your brother.' No, I couldn't. 'But why kill Jacque?'

'Jacque.' I could hear both affection and disappointment in his voice. 'I called him from the alley outside the shop. I knew what Paulette and Gabriel were up to – what they would do to my life here and to Jacque's, too. I was so, so angry. I had the gas can in my hand and the lighter in my pocket.' A pause and then, in a low voice, 'I called Jacque.'

'You wanted him to talk you down?'

'I'm not sure what I wanted.' I saw the silhouette of his hand go up to his forehead. 'When he answered, he was very short. Whispered that he was at your house and couldn't talk.'

'You woke him at four thirty in the morning,' I pointed out. 'Jacque couldn't have known you were asking permission to burn down his store with two people in it.'

'I know.' He said it softly, barely audible. 'He said he would meet me at the cabin later.'

'When was "later"?'

'That's what I asked him, and he said eight. I told him that was too late and hung up.'

'And started the fire.'

'Yes.'

I waited a beat. 'Jacque must have had second thoughts. He was gone when I left at five.'

'I didn't know that.' He swallowed. 'He was a good friend, better than I deserved.'

'Did you go to the cabin?'

'Yes. I didn't know where else to go, really.'

'You should have driven to Chicago,' Molly said, 'and checked into your hotel. No one would have suspected.'

My little Machiavellian.

'When did you get to the cabin?' I asked.

'It was before eight. I was planning to get cleaned up, but Jacque was already there. He smelled gasoline on me and saw the state I was in and demanded to know what had happened. You know the way he can be.' His words were coming faster and faster, but now his sigh seemed to shake his whole body. 'So I told him.'

'What was his reaction?'

'He went crazy.' I could hear indignation in Denis's voice. 'I could understand it as far as Paulette and Gabriel were concerned, but then he started talking about his store and how important it was to him and Amy. As if this ridiculous grocery store that didn't even bear his name was *their* child. I couldn't bear it.'

'You hit him.'

'No, no – I just pushed him. But he caught himself on the coffee table, and when he regained his balance, he had a gun in his hand. It was surreal. I managed to get the thing away from him, but he fell and hit his head on that table.'

'Was he unconscious?'

'More stunned,' Denis said. 'He rolled over and the way he looked at me . . . the look in his eyes. I knew he would never keep quiet. I wouldn't be rid of him any more than I would of Paulette and Gabriel.'

'Where did the gun come from?'

'The gun that Jacque pulled on me?' he asked, apparently to underline the fact that his victim had started it. 'It was on the coffee table – three identical ones that almost looked like toys. Jacques seemed to assume they were mine.'

'They were in your cabin,' I said. 'And if Jacque had been poking around that cabin since dawn, he would have seen evidence that they had been assembled there.'

'The guns?' Denis was incredulous. 'Not by me. I wasn't even sure it was real until I put it to his forehead and pulled the trigger. And then it was too late.'

Oh my God. Did he expect me to feel sorry for him because

his third murder was an accident? 'Can you blame Jacque for being afraid of you? Not only because of the guns, but because you smelled of gasoline and had just confessed to committing arson and double murder.'

'He was the one who picked up the gun,' Denis said again. 'I was only protecting myself.'

'Jacque probably didn't even know the thing was loaded or, like you, that it was a real gun,' I said. 'He was in fear of his life. And he was right to be, because you took advantage of his being down and shot him in the head.'

'But I had to, don't you see?'

'You hoped it would look like a suicide,' I said, 'and you knew him well enough to pull it off. Anybody else might have shot Jacque in the right temple. But after a lifetime of friendship, you knew he was left-handed. It was only the blow to the forehead that raised any doubt that it was a suicide.'

'I thought they'd assume he hit his head when he fell,' Denis said. 'After he shot himself.'

Molly was shaking her head. 'But he was on his back when we found him. You should have turned the body over.'

'Oh.' Denis sounded sheepish that he hadn't thought of it.

'"Oh" – is that all you have to say?' I asked. 'Molly is giving you helpful tips on how you could have more efficiently murdered your friend.'

'I'm just saying . . .' Molly said and wisely left it at that.

I cleared my throat. 'You slept in the room next to Jacque's body?'

'Just that one night. Then I . . . I moved here on Sunday and slept in Jacque's office.'

'How did you get into—' I interrupted myself. 'You must have taken the store keys from his pocket.'

Which weren't on the same ring as the Peugeot keys that I still had in my purse.

'Yes.'

'But what about Egbert?'

'What about him?' Molly asked.

I kept my attention on Denis. 'How did he get Jacque's phone?'

'He came here Saturday after I . . . after Jacque died.' His voice was a near-whisper now in the low light. 'He had a key.'

Now I did address Molly. 'Because Molly had given him a key, so she and her friends could use it. Right, Molly?'

I heard rather than saw her shift uncomfortably. 'It was mostly just to keep stuff they stole until Egbert could sell it.'

'When you say "they," you mean "we," don't you?'

'Sometimes,' she said. Then to Denis: 'I didn't do anything really bad. I just didn't rat on the rest of them.'

'What about the guns?' I asked.

'The guns, Molly?' Denis's tone was disapproving, even though he seemed to be the last person in a position to cast stones. 'Really?'

'Ghost guns,' she explained. 'They were mostly plastic and they did seem like toys, until you put real ammunition in them.'

'Which is why they were loaded,' I said. 'You all must have been there checking out how they worked.'

'Egbert wanted to make them to sell.' I could barely make out that she was holding up her hands. 'I didn't want anything to do with them.'

Quite the piece of work, Becky's son, Egbert. Criminal mastermind leading a gang of teenagers.

'What happened, Denis?' I asked. 'Did Egbert walk in on you and see Jacque's bod—' I stopped, thinking. 'Wait, that doesn't work. Egbert was killed farther south, near Brookhill Manor. And that was the next day – Sunday.'

'Yes, but Saturday I heard the door unlock and hid in the bedroom. Egbert came in bold as can be.'

'Did you recognize him?'

'He was one of Helen's patients,' he said. 'And not the most tightly screwed one. When he saw the body, he took a picture of it. I thought he'd call the police then, but he didn't. He went through Jacque's pockets and took his phone, but I'd already taken the keys. He took a gun from the table, too, and Paulette's lighter, which I had set down.'

Trophies? 'I can see why he took the phone. The sheriff could trace it to the cabin and Egbert wouldn't want that. Dumping the thing somewhere else would give him time to clear the place out if he had to. But what about the rest of the stuff? It's bizarre.'

'Blackmail,' Molly said. 'He said he started blackmailing people because Becky would come home with all sorts of gossip from the store. The really juicy stuff Egbert would use to get money. He got very good at it.' She hesitated, then, 'He knew why Paulette and Gabriel were in town. That they were my mother and father.'

'But Becky couldn't have known that. She—' The missing piece. 'Gabriel was Ichabod.'

Silence.

Oh, right. 'The sketchy man in the hoodie talking to Egbert on the street,' I explained. 'Your description to the police artist made him look like Ichabod Crane in . . . well, never mind. But am I right? That man was your father?'

'Yes,' Molly said. 'Which explains why I thought there was something familiar about him and why he looked so hard back at me. He was a little like Denis, but a sick, evil version of Denis.'

Who was sick and evil enough for me, thank you. 'But why did Gabriel tell Egbert anything?'

'He asked for directions to Schultz's, and Egbert could tell he was a user. Egbert offered to sell him some coke; in return, Gabriel invited Egbert to do a line with him.'

'Which is when Gabriel spilled the truth about why he was in town,' I said. 'Egbert approached you with what he knew?'

'Saturday night. He wanted me to tell Denis that they had to meet the next day. That Denis should bring the money.'

'Did he say anything about Jacque's body at the cabin?' I asked.

'No, but as far as Egbert knew it didn't have any connection with me or Denis.' She shrugged. 'I'm sure it was a problem, though, with all Egbert's stuff there.'

A problem that Egbert hadn't had a chance to clean up, thanks to Molly.

'You didn't tell me about any meeting with Egbert, Molly,' Denis said.

'Of course not,' she said. 'It was Sunday, and we didn't find Jacque's body until the next day. I didn't know you were alive.'

'Oh, sweetie,' Denis said. 'I'm so sorry for everything I've put you through.'

Touching. 'How much money?'

'Five thousand,' she said. 'But I could only get fourteen hundred, so I took that.'

The cash in Egbert's bag.

'I told Egbert that we'd meet him the next day at noon with the money.'

'Sunday.' At High Noon – nice touch.

'Yes, I said that,' she said a little impatiently. 'I met him by the creek behind Brookhills Manor and told him Denis was on his way. I knew Egbert liked me. He was even feeling sorry for me and saying how Denis had lied to me and stuff. I had a backpack on, and when I took it off, I dropped it, knowing he would pick it up. When he did, I hit him with a tree branch I'd hidden in the bushes.'

That's where politeness would get you, apparently. But then, Egbert was a blackmailer, a thief, a drugs and arms dealer – and, now, a lech. 'He was also shot.'

'That's because when I went through Egbert's backpack and saw the gun, I realized I could stage it to look like suicide. I made a campfire with the branch I'd hit Egbert with and some other wood. Then I shot Egbert and started the fire.'

'Let me guess,' I said. 'With Paulette's lighter, which you'd also found in the backpack.'

'Yes.'

'You even knew the little trick with his glasses. You recovered them from wherever they flew when you hit him and set them in his cap.'

'A suicide always takes off their glasses,' Molly said.

'Yeah, well, I asked the sheriff about that, and he wasn't so sure. He thought it was something I'd picked up from TV. And he was probably right. I should have guessed you did the same.'

'Still,' she said, 'it looked good, didn't it? Then I went straight to Schultz's and chatted up the deputy in the alley where you saw me.'

'Nice alibi,' I admitted. 'So now what? You two slip away, and the final scene of the movie is the two of you ordering Mai Tais on the beach?'

'That's the plan,' Denis said.

I heard a click. 'You have a gun, don't you?'

'Yes,' he said. 'Sorry.'

'Don't be sorry,' Molly said. 'Maggy deduced it.'

'That doesn't mean I want to be shot by it,' I said. 'But, yes, Denis said there had been three guns on the table. Egbert had taken one and the second was on the floor next to Jacque when we came in. Since there were no guns on the table when Molly and I entered, you must have taken the third one, Denis.'

'Shoot her,' Molly's voice trilled.

'Molly, I . . . I . . .'

'Yes. Shoot me, Denis.' I was already feeling my way back along the beam that I'd followed toward the bedroom. 'Make your daughter proud. You thought the worst thing that could happen was for her to be brought up by drug addicts. But look what you've turned her into.'

'Shoot her!' Molly screamed again as I reached the ladder and started down.

'I can't see in the dark.' Denis's voice was getting closer. 'Molly, don't push past—'

A shot rang out overhead.

I ducked as a body sailed past my head and landed with a thud at the bottom of the ladder. It was followed by the dull clunk of a plastic gun.

TWENTY-EIGHT

'You should have called me *before* you went in,' Pavlik said. 'And not through the main switchboard.'

We were standing outside the glass sliders of Schultz's, and I was being read the riot act, not only because I'd telephoned Pavlik *after* the main action was over, but because I'd done so from a phone he didn't recognize – Denis's gas station burner. Though I did call 911 first. 'I—'

'You went into a burned-out building – a crime scene, no less. With two killers, as it turned out.'

'I know,' I said ruefully. 'But to be fair, I didn't know Molly was a killer. And I couldn't be absolutely certain that Denis was alive, much less *in* the store.'

He raised a hand in that 'What?' kind of way. 'Why else would Molly have gone there?'

'Snooping, of course. She was leaving town and—' I stopped, not even convincing myself. 'That's what she wanted me to believe, but of course I didn't.'

'No, you thought she was going to pick up her murderous stepfather and go on the run.'

'I'm not sure Denis qualifies as a stepfather,' I said. 'Uncle, of course, but—'

Pavlik looked murderous himself.

'I left my phone in the shop,' I explained. 'Molly gave me her phone number and I stored it and set the phone down. When I went to follow her, I forgot it and didn't realize until I was already inside.'

It was a lie. A white lie, not the whopping Moby Dick-size lies that Molly told. I'd checked my pockets for my phone as Molly went into Schultz's. I didn't find it, but I went in anyway.

'I'm well aware that could be me.' I nodded to the blanket-wrapped body being strapped to the gurney inside the store. 'I'm just sorry anybody had to die.'

Pavlik relented and wrapped an arm around me. 'To be fair,

as you would say, four people had already died. And if not for the tussle over whether to shoot you and one of them falling through the ceiling, you would be dead.'

'And worse, not here to tell the tale, which is a good one,' I said. 'My body would have laid here until somebody stumbled on it.'

'Not likely, since *you*'d be dead.'

True. Sarah called me the corpse-stumbler, a title I perversely cherished.

'And Molly,' I continued grimly, 'would have left on her supposed road trip, with nobody thinking twice about it.'

'I'm not sure about that,' Pavlik said. 'Murders aside, we would have found out she was involved in the robberies and assumed she'd taken off to avoid prosecution.'

'But not with Denis, of course. He was dead, as far as everybody was concerned. And without him as the link, I'm not sure you'd ever have connected Molly to my death.'

'You don't think much of my cognitive capabilities, do you? My team's forensic expertise?'

'Of course I do,' I said, patting him on the cheek. 'I'm sure you would have gotten there eventually.'

'Thanks.'

'Maggy!' Sarah and Amy were breathless when they reached us.

'We just heard,' Amy said. 'Are you OK?'

'Yes, I—'

'Who's that?' Sarah pointed at the gurney, which was now being wheeled carefully through the sliding doors.

'It—'

'Denis Durand?' Amy said in disbelief. She was staring at the man in handcuffs behind the cart. He was sobbing. 'But he's dead.'

'Then who is—?' Sarah gestured again to the gurney being loaded into the ambulance. She turned back to me. 'Molly?'

I nodded.

'Denis killed his daughter?' Amy asked, disbelieving.

'Not exactly,' I said. 'Molly fell through the ceiling trying to get Denis to shoot me. And she's not really Denis's—'

'If you'll excuse me,' Pavlik said, setting me aside. 'I'm

not sure I have time to hear you explain it all over again.' He kissed me on the forehead. 'I'll be home late tonight.'

'I'll wait up,' I said and turned to my friends. 'This is going to take a while. Want to talk over coffee or wine?'

'Wine,' they chorused.

'Then it's my house.' I hooked elbows with them.

'I've been thinking about Jacque,' Amy said after a second, her head bowed. 'That text message he sent the morning he died, saying he was sorry and not to think badly of him. I've imagined those words meant all sorts of things—'

'That he burned down the store, committed double murder,' Sarah enumerated. 'Maybe suicide.'

'I had him down for bigamy at one point.'

Amy managed to give us both the side-eye. 'Yes, well, whatever I thought in my darkest hours, I feel this odd sense of peace now. Like I know what he meant. We were having a rough patch due to the store and Paulette. Jacque felt responsible, but it had nothing to do with him and me. We were good.'

'And he loved you,' Sarah said. 'Hence the whole "my love" thing.'

'But it was more than that.' I was thinking of Denis's recounting of Jacque's last minutes. 'Jacque saw his future with you. That's why he didn't want to sell Schultz's. Not because he was stubborn or proud, but because it was for the two of you.'

Amy stopped short. 'How could you possibly know that?'

'I just do,' I said. 'I'll tell you more, but first home and—'

'Wine,' Amy said. 'And maybe pizza.'

'Well, I was going to say I had to let the dogs out, but yes to all of the above.' I sighed. 'I'm starting to think we should have opened a winery instead of a coffee house.'

Sarah grinned. 'It's never too late.'

A staccato horn sounded, and we stepped aside to let the ambulance creep past us. No siren. No hurry.

'Until it is,' I said.